R.S.V.P.

The note was in a scraggly hand, clearly the work of someone who wrote down very few things and those mostly for his own use.

"Dear Doctor Woodword," it began, misspelling his name and getting him irritated right from the start. "I am Captain Morgudan Sapenza, once of the proud ship *Amandal*, now, as you know, half sunk in the great lake, but still master of her crew and systems. I am sorry to have had to do this, but after all this time we have become desperate and feel we have nothing to lose. This is a backward planet, but we have some comforts of civilization below, and we have many modern tools of our trade. We must talk, but your own ships and company can easily do me great harm and then where am I? So you will have to come to where the messenger here will lead you. It is not far and you have my word that no harm will come to you now will you be touched. You may bring a fully armed bodyguard to insure this. I will wait for you with a way for us to speak. If you do not come, I will leave at least one of our guests from your company there by two hours before sundown today, or rather I will leave the body and you shall see how this person died. The next time if will be two. Then four an hour after that. And so on. I am sorry, but it is the only way I know of to insist that you come. Until then, I remain, very sincerely, Captain Morgudan Sapenza."

BAEN BOOKS by JACK L. CHALKER

Tales of the Three Kings:
Balshazzar's Serpent
Melchior's Fire

The Changewinds
The Demons at Rainbow Bridge
The Run to Chaos Keep
Ninety Trillion Fausts
The Identity Matrix
Downtiming the Nightside

BALSHAZZAR'S SERPENT

JACK L. CHALKER

BALSHAZZAR'S SERPENT

This is a work of fiction. All the characters and events portrayed in this book are fictional, and any resemblance to real people or incidents is purely coincidental.

A Baen Books Original

Baen Publishing Enterprises
P.O. Box 1403
Riverdale, NY 10471
www.baen.com

ISBN: 0-671-31999-X

Cover art by Bob Eggleton

First paperback printing, July 2001

Library of Congress Cataloging-In-Publication Number 00-031145

Distributed by Simon & Schuster
1230 Avenue of the Americas
New York, NY 10020

Production by Windhaven Press, Auburn, NH
Printed in the United States of America

For James White
from the Sole Survivor

PROLOGUE:
THE LEGEND OF
THE THREE KINGS

Rationalists predicted that religion would be the first thing to fall when humanity finally went to the stars and found no gods, no heaven or hell, that could not be explained in physics and the other sciences. Scientists never had been all that good at predicting or understanding human culture and sociology; they never even noticed that, when they finally went out there, every deity and supernatural belief system known at the time went right with them.

Humanity was late to the stars, considering how young in its life it had begun the quest, but, like all things it had done, once it decided to go and had the means, it went like wildfire.

The discovery of the wormgate system and the way in which it could stabilize and link wormholes that folded space and took you many times faster than light by the simple method of stepping around it made space travel efficient and affordable.

First out were the unmanned, super-hardened ships that could withstand the forces within a naturally occurring wormhole and exploit and force it open, go through, and establish a temporary stabilizing gate on the other side. Then came the follow-ups, mostly robotics with some human supervision, who would convert that makeshift gate into a permanent and optimized one. Then a small maintenance station both for the gate and ships that might come after was built and stocked, so that parts and labor were available as needed.

Natural wormholes created weaknesses within several parsecs, allowing other holes to form. Most were quite small and many were highly unstable, but the little probes punched through and were successful, at least most of the time.

Next came the government types, of course, in quasi-military equipped highly reinforced ships, looking for alien lifeforms and new worlds to exploit.

And they found them! Not exactly alien civilizations, but certainly alien lifeforms in incredible abundance in a universe that seemed filled with potentially human habitable planets. Much of the alien life was basic and primitive, the equivalent of Earth's insects and animal and plant life, strange as it might be to the humans who went out there. Still, while nothing was a precise match to Earth forms, and much was surprising and even revolutionary to science, nothing really broke the rules.

Nothing also seemed to have evolved intelligence, let alone civilization, beyond the most rudimentary;

evolution was borne out, but the requirement for a fast-thinking brain seemed to be a low priority in nature's schemes. Interest in the program waned, as humanity's fickle public always tended to do when things went along without real surprises, and the scientists and corporations who depended upon it sought other methods of funding the still expanding program. Ultimately, they came up with the idea of selling off some of the best planets to interest groups back on Earth and on the few planets that had been developed to bleed off excess Earth population. It seemed an outrageous and unworkable idea. How many groups would even *want* their own planet, anyway? After all, even if they were livable, the only reason to sell them at all would be because science and government had decided that the worlds had nothing profitable to offer. And who could afford it? Certainly all of the worlds in question could be used in a self-supporting mode, assuming importing and developing Earth plants and animals that could thrive there and using the mineral resources for building, but all this would offer would be a return to a more primitive life with little to bargain with.

The answer was, just about *every* group and leader with a dream or a vision or a political theory wanted a world. Every established religious group, and religious dissident group, and every cult open and secret that had survived history or had emerged from it wanted their own world. And they all seemed to have amazing abilities to raise sufficient funds to get one, too.

Soon there were hundreds, spread all over the near galaxy, connected by a network of self-powered and self-maintained wormgates that, mapped, looked like some drunken spider's webbing. But the one thing they weren't, not really, was independent.

The Earth System Combine wanted a single level of control, a single military force, and control of the economy of the entire expanding system if only to pay for its own expenses and expansion. To do this over such a vast distance and with so many quasi-independent "colonies," direct political and military control would be expensive and impractical. Instead, the economic system was divided so that none of the worlds established out there were in more than the most basic sense self-sufficient. Oh, most could certainly maintain a subsistence living, perhaps much better than that, but for the latest technology, the cutting edge of what was possible, they were made cleverly interdependent, with no single world having more than a tiny part of the whole and often specializing in certain things. Any worlds that matured and chafed at interstellar rules and regulations, or balked at their share of the "user and facilitation fees" paid to the Combine, were welcome to drop out. It was then that they discovered how dependent they really were, and what it was like to be on your own in a cleverly constructed system that even controlled access to its own parts. If you weren't a member, the costs and fees were huge, and prohibitive to a degree.

Some tried it anyway, but no terraforming was *that* far along or *that* absolute, and none of the worlds were true Earthly paradises. The worlds settled by ones who stayed out and cut all ties were often revisited out of curiosity decades later by Combine ships only to be revealed as worlds where no human survivors could be found.

The skills that had originally made humans dominate their home planet were now dead; nobody knew them anymore. The machines did it, but who programmed and maintained the machines? And what happened if no more machines came?

And each rebel thus became an example, all without firing a shot. The Combine grew fat, and lazy, and rich, and complacent.

Nobody knew what had caused it, nor who. The best guess was one more grab for power by yet another faction back home who ran into a ruling clique who decided that if they couldn't have the power and control nobody else would. A miscalculation, a failure of intelligence or perhaps a misjudgment of will. Perhaps it was an unforeseen enemy in their midst or from somewhere else in the vast starfields. It didn't matter.

Whatever it was, what happened was that, one day, with no notice and no particular alarms, almost a third of the wormgate system, the part that led back towards Earth System and the headquarters of the Combine, simply stopped. Nothing more emerged from the gates, even though traffic was ordinarily brisk, and, perhaps as ominously, nothing that went into the gates after that one point ever was seen or heard from again.

Messenger probes went in and never came out. There was some indication that they may not have arrived *anywhere*.

It was the Great Silence.

Two thirds of the system, and part of the military and commercial fleets, remained working and intact, but it was from the developing to the least developed points. There was no longer any direction, and the finely tuned interdependency which included the third now gone could not exist any longer. Worlds did not fall into savagery or worse, at least not most of them, but they were far more on their own than before, and

the ones who now ran what was left of the show were
the ones with operating spaceships.

The trouble was, that was a commodity that was
strictly originated from the Combine and near Earth
systems; there weren't any spaceship factories in the
remaining two thirds, nor the automated systems to
create them and power them safely. There was maintenance, yes, but that was it, and going through artificially enlarged and artificially maintained wormholes
left little tolerance for error.

The military tended to become a force unto
itself, claiming all jurisdiction over interstellar space
and the gates, financing itself by taxing the commercial ships that still ran. The commercial ships
became the prizes, trying to continue their runs,
keep their ships safe and maintained, and avoid
both the military and potential pirates and privateers at the same time.

Things were breaking down and fast. Only the most
profitable worlds and markets were of interest; most
of the other worlds were forgotten, neglected, or just
ignored.

It was another century before the Supreme Cardinal of Vaticanus, a world maintained and developed
as a religious retreat by the Roman Catholic Church
before the Great Silence, became one of the first to
try and put some order back into the system. Without contact with the Pope or even knowing for certain if there still *was* one but maintaining out of faith
that there *had* to be, the board of cardinals who'd
run the retreat and seminary world had run things
as they hoped God wished, awaiting a relinking with
Earth. It hadn't come, and now they were finally using
some of their wealth, some of their connections on
the more developed colonies, and their backup of the

vast Vatican library system to send out a few dedicated priests to try and find the lost worlds.

It was probably because his name really *was* Ishmael.

The small probe ship came out of the void with the keys to Heaven, Hell, and perhaps someplace in between; it brought with it evidence of fabulous riches and perhaps more, but what it didn't bring back was a road map to the stars.

Along with the spiritual part of humanity, the legends, both good and bad, had also survived, particularly amongst the few who still knew of or could follow the patterns of the scouts to the stars. Fear, doubt, and death were out there, it was true, but perhaps not only that. Somewhere out there, in stories and songs and legends from forgotten origins, were the Three Kings.

Every civilization had at least one; every faith as well. It might be the Kingdom of Prester John, or the fabled El Dorado, or, on a more ethereal plain, it might be called Paradise, Heaven, or a state of Nirvana. On a more secular level, it was the big one, the find of a lifetime, the jackpot, the ultimate strike. Nobody really knew what it looked like, but everyone had their own vision, their own dream, and their own deep down conviction that, sooner or later, they would find it.

The major difference between all of those and the Three Kings was that almost everyone was convinced that the Three Kings existed, and there was in fact physical evidence of it. The trouble was, its location was as mysterious and mystical as any of the others.

Ishmael Hand was one of the breed of loners the church called Prophets and everybody else called scouts. Half human, half machine, merged into a cybernetic ship that was almost an organism in and of itself, able to build, or perhaps *grow* would be a better word, the probes and contact devices it required, these volunteers to go forever into the eternal void in search of the unknown had a million motives. Hand was a mystic, and not alone in that category of scout; he had turned himself into the ultimate pilgrim, searching among the stars, praying, meditating when in between, looking for something that may be out there, may actually be within his own mind, or might not exist at all. To those who sent them out, the motive didn't matter, so long as the supply of volunteers continued.

It was initially done entirely by machines; smart machines, machines that were every bit the observer and evaluator, but those machines proved lacking in several ways. They had never been living beings, born and raised in organic environments, feeling what organic sentient beings feel, understanding in non-academic ways what organic sentient beings really wanted or needed. They could only send back samples and reports; they could never send back impressions that others might understand and interpret. They could quantify, but they could not dream.

Sentient beings like the human Ishmael Hand, however, also had their limits, not just physical but mental and emotional as well, and they didn't live long enough for some of these distances, nor did they have the precision and detail that cybernetic equipment could bring to a job. The marriage of creature and machine was, after much trial and error, found to be the perfect vehicle.

Within, of course, limits.

For if they were not a little bit mad when they

left, they certainly were after decades of roaming the vastness of the universe, yet their machine sides were precise and detailed. As time went on, it often became difficult to interpret all the data properly. . . .

Once an uncharted system was sighted, scouted, and thoroughly investigated, the procedure was simple. The ships themselves were almost organic; they could take in debris, dust, rock, whatever was out there and convert it to what they needed, just as their external scoops turned some of it into the interstellar fuels that ran them. From this material they grew small probes according to designs within their complex memory banks, and sent them everywhere in the system. Every type of analysis was performed, every part of everything evaluated. The most dead of worlds could contain something of great or unique value.

Premiums, of course, were first and foremost lost colonies; then solid planets within the life zone that could be the source of new life or, if not of anything particularly interesting, turned with minimal cost or effort into new colonies. Beyond that, they looked for things they had never seen before, beautiful and unique creations, *knowledge*.

There was a lot of life in the galaxy; that was well known. The trouble was, only a miniscule portion of it had any brains at all, and of the handful of races bumped into by expanding humanity none had been anything but primitive.

Ishmael Hand had recognized what he'd stumbled on almost immediately. Long before the Great Silence there were half-whispered tales of them, but never, until now, solid physical evidence of their existence. Three planets in the life zone that had not gone bad over the eons was just about unheard of; even two

was almost never seen. That was why, Hand specu-
lated, nobody had really found the Three Kings since
the ancient and messed-up machine-only scouts had
first reported them.

Not three planets, not exactly. One *enormous*
planet, a world at the outer limits of even gas giants,
and three moons, very different, yet each with thick
oxygen-rich atmospheres and water.

The largest one, bigger than the Earth, wasn't the
sort of place you wanted to visit. As big as it was,
it contained vast active volcanic fields, and in some
places the land was forever changing, floating and
twisting where lava fractured it.

And yet there was water, even two huge oceans,
making almost a dance of solidity and water and then
fire and flux, then water and solid land again and then
another fiery area. Much of it was concealed in
clouds, but now and then there were breaks and those
breaks, considering the size of the place, showed the
bizarre and fractured landscape below. It was hot on
its surface, even in the "cool" solid regions, but perhaps not *too* hot. There was vegetation, in a riot of
colors, wherever it could cling and not be burnt off
or knocked off by internal forces. It wasn't a nice
place to live and work, but it was fascinating if only
because nobody, not Ishmael Hand nor the vastly
larger and more complex thinking machines of the
home empire he'd abandoned, could figure out how
the heck a planet that dynamic and contradictory
could possibly exist. Although the Three Kings name
was ancient, it remained for the scout to make sense
of it, and he called this huge planet Melchior.

And then there were the other large moons, among
countless rather standard small ones. One of the larger
ones was warm but not a raging madhouse like the

huge planet below that held it captive; almost twenty-five thousand kilometers at its equator, a small planet in captivity, it was a wonderland of islands large and small in a continuous sea, more than forty percent land yet with no major gaps so that any part of the water could be called an ocean, nor land masses so huge that they might be considered continents. It was a world of lakes and islands, teeming with plants and perhaps small animals, wild, primitive, and beautiful. This moon Hand called Balshazzar.

The third moon also had an atmosphere, but it was farther out, cold, full of bizarre and twisted rocks and spires, great sand desertlike regions of red and gold and purple, yet somehow it retained, without large bodies of surface water, nor the thick vegetation that would normally go with such an atmosphere, a significant amount of water vapor in the air that rose in the night from the ground in thick mists and vanished in the light, and which, somehow, kept an atmosphere containing oxygen, nitrogen, and many other elements needed for life. The atmosphere was thinner than humans liked it, but they could exist there, as they'd learned to exist atop three and four kilometer mountain ranges on their mother Earth and elsewhere. This third moon Hand christened Kaspar.

"None of the figures make a lot of sense, I admit," the scout's report continued, "but it will make some careers to determine how these ecosystems work. God is having fun with us here, challenging us. I do not have the means to start solving these riddles, but I feel certain that you have ones who have more than that."

The worlds, in their own ways, also lived up to their ancient reputation judging from the samples sent back.

Here was a small sack of apparently natural gems, gems as large as hens' eggs and colored translucent emerald or ruby or sapphire with centers of some different substance that, when viewed from different angles, seemed to almost form pictures or shapes—familiar ones, unique to each viewer, subjective and ever-changing devices of fascination. Once glimpsed, machines could make synthetic copies that were almost but not quite like the real thing, of course, but the real thing was unique in nature and thus precious.

There was sand in exotic colors, mixed within containers but nonetheless unmixed, as if the colors refused to blend with each other and the individual grains appeared to prefer only their own company. The properties were electromagnetic in nature but would take a long time to yield up their secrets, particularly how such things could have come about in nature.

Plant samples at once familiar and yet so alien that they appeared to be able to convert virtually any kind of energy into food, including, if one was not careful, any living things that touched them. Rooted plants that nonetheless responded to sounds and actions and would attempt to bend away from probes or shears and whose own energy fields could distort instruments and short out standard analyzers.

But most fascinating of all were the Artifacts.

They were always afterwards called the Artifacts, with a capital "A," because there was nothing like them and no way to explain them. Ishmael Hand found no signs of any sentient lifeforms on any of the three worlds, nor ruins nor any signs that anyone had ever been there before, but he, too, understood what was implied by the Artifacts.

They were not spectacular, yet they were the greatest of all finds. One was a simple cylinder, perfectly machined, with tolerances so small, with dimensions so perfect, that one had to go down almost to the atomic level to find a flaw. And it was machined out of an absolutely one hundred percent pure block of titanium.

It also looked very much as if it had been manufactured in a lab within the past few hours, yet the tag with it indicated that it was lying half buried in the surface. It was only at the atomic and subatomic level that it was discovered that the entire thing was coated, to the thickness of only a dozen atoms, in a hard coating that was close enough to one used in human manufacturing that it was inconceivable to think of it as natural.

The second was a gear, perhaps a half a meter around, with one hundred and eighty-two fine and perfect teeth. It, too, was machined just like the cylinder, to absolute perfection, and it, too, had the synthetic protective coating.

The third and final Artifact was a one-meter coil, made out of a totally synthetic and absolutely clear polymerlike substance and created to the same perfect tolerances as the other two. The coil had nineteen turns and its ends were smooth, not broken. The substance was unlike any that had ever been seen before, yet made of stuff that contemporary labs would have no trouble duplicating. In fact, it was easily as good as what was being used but cheaper and easier to make.

"There must be a lot of this junk around," Ishmael Hand's report noted. "Consider that my probes were able to discover these three pieces with ease, although none are all that large. Don't try and put them together, though. I doubt if they're from the same device. In fact, I'm near *positive* that they aren't. You see, the coil came from Balshazzar, the gear from Melchior, and the cylinder was sticking out of the purple desert sands on Kaspar."

After all this time, Ishmael Hand could only have faith that anyone was even listening. He had been sent out from a holy world, a retreat and a monastic place to find what God had in mind for him. One of its orders had trained many of the scouts like Ishmael Hand in the mental disciplines required of such a life, and had carefully picked and then prepared them for the long, lonely Communion. Once the Great Silence came about, they had but a few dozen such ships fully outfitted and not many more candidates than that. They sent half back in the direction of the Arm and Old Earth in hopes of reestablishing contact; the others, like Hand, were sent forward to find the colonies and remap what might well be out there. Thus it was that Hand had discovered what had already *been* discovered, but which had also been lost. His broadband, uncoded broadcasts back to every region where there might be listeners was public property. He was not out there for riches or material rewards.

There was enough interest and excitement among any with spaceships in the rediscovery of the Three Kings now to attract the best and the worst of spacefaring humanity. There was only one problem. While the reporting probe contained the samples and the report and vast amounts of data, nowhere inside could they find the star maps or location data nor the beacon system that would allow them to get there in a hurry.

This was the fourteenth solar system Ishmael Hand had reported on in the long years since he'd launched himself into the unknown, but it was the first and only one where the location data was lacking. It wasn't like Hand to have any such lapses, and he certainly gave no indication in his report that he didn't expect a horde of expeditions to be heading out to the Three Kings straightaway. Nor did any of the data suggest damage or instability in Hand's ship and cybernetic parts. Not even His Holiness in Exile and his monastic group understood what might have caused problems with Hand at this key moment.

And yet nowhere, absolutely nowhere, in *any* of that data, did it show where the heck the Three Kings were, and at no point was there enough of a star sky given that would allow the position to be deduced.

Hand, as usual for him, wound up with a long string of prayers and chants from the Bible and other holy books, but then he stopped in the middle and added, "You know, if I wasn't sure this was the Three Kings I'd have never named them that. I *still* considered naming them something else, but there's much to be said for tradition. Nonetheless, beware! The three perfect names I would otherwise have bestowed on these little beauties are Paradisio, Purgatorio, and Inferno. But which was which would only have confused you secular scientists anyway. God be with you when you arrive on these, though, for nobody else will be, and your lack of faith might well be the death of you! *Amen!*"

And that was the end of the report.

The Three Kings had gone from legend to reality, but were now more maddeningly desired and more maddeningly out of reach than ever.

But they had been discovered not once, but twice, even if centuries apart. By hook, by crook, by luck, faith, or perhaps destiny, somebody would discover them again.

Or solve the mystery of Ishmael Hand.

Those in space now divided neatly into two types of people. There were the profane—the pirates and raiders who made a living from a bit more knowledge of the colonial worlds' positions and assets than most others—and the holy. Not just the Ishmael Hands and the Catholic priests and nuns who followed him and his kind, but the others as well, the evangelists and teachers of every conceivable faith who could put together a ship and who were as determined as Ishmael Hand to return the truth of God to the lost colonies.

Many of them dreamed as well of finding the Three Kings of Ishmael Hand.

I:
ON FAITH & MOUNTAINS

Faith moved *The Mountain*; it had long ago come to
Muhammad, and received a chilly reception, but now
it was heading for friendlier but less exotic worlds
farther in towards the galactic melding.

And, indeed, as always, faith moved *The Mountain*,
faith expressed in the sums large and small that had
paid for its construction, its outfitting, and its traveling expenses.

There were a number of such ships, large and
small, moving throughout the known galaxy, repre-
senting every conceivable faith and some inconceivable ones as well, and while this one was more
conventional than not, its faithful aboard were not
considered exactly mainstream Christians. Then, again,
since the Silence and the long years that followed it,

the same could be said of many faiths on the former colonial worlds.

It had been predicted that when humanity finally went out and colonized the stars that this would collapse the parochial religions of Earth, save, perhaps, for some of the cosmic types like Hinduism and the introspective like classical Buddhism, but it hadn't happened. Indeed, cut off for long periods and by vast distances from the rest of human culture, it was the religions of humanity that kept them together, kept them sane for the most part, and provided the same sort of social framework as the settlers of the American west or the Siberian and Alaskan east had spread with such faithfulness. But long distances did not bring with them a sufficient number of conventional clergy, nor did the doctrine and study of conventional faiths remain locked in stone. With distance came distortion, and error. And, after the Great Silence severed contact with the mother churches and seminaries, save only the Roman Catholic one, came the greatest evangelical boom since the days of Earthbound colonialism, mostly due to the actions of men and women to whom God spoke after destroying the old civilization that had strayed from the True Path, whatever that Path was, not due to trained and ordained clerics.

Most were also commercial types, or they hitched a ride on commercial vessels. Spaceships were few and far between and precious. But a few had their own ships, or partially converted freighters to their floating colonies, and the ones without prohibitions against blowing the hell out of pirates, privateers, and outfoxing the occasional military patrol did quite well.

The Mountain was one of the truly *grand* ones, a tent show with a tent so great that it would have been like some early preacher's visions of Heaven. Nobody knew how anyone save Vaticanus could have afforded to put together such a craft, let alone maintain it. That alone made it a matter of great curiosity, wonder, and awe, and even some suspicion among the planetary governments.

Traveling between the stars and in and out of star gates the ship didn't look so grand; like most, it was a great power plant scooping up and converting the debris of ancient solar system formation and the cosmic dust of the void into the power to get to the gates and make the jumps. Once inside such a gate the ordinary rules of space-time did not seem to apply; depending on the speed and angle with which your ship entered, you would travel for minutes, hours, days, or even weeks or months, and come out, well, somewhere else, at another gate, impossibly far from where you'd begun, yet often, by the strict chronometers of the gates and maintenance stations around them, before you had left where you'd come from. Nobody had ever met themselves in real space, but there were often temporal surprises for the freighters and military craft that loosely connected the worlds of humanity out there. It was an eerie kind of secondhand time travel that committed spacefaring folk to themselves and themselves alone.

That was why *The Mountain* also had living quarters for almost a thousand men, women, and children. Whole families were there; they met, married, and procreated in the main forward area of the vast two-point-five kilometer rotating cylinder. *That* was the *Mount Sinai*. A smaller ship actually was contained inside the nose, and was launched only when *The Mountain* was safely docked in stable orbit around an inhabited planet. This was called, when separated,

Mount Olivet. Joined, they were always just *The Mountain*. The pattern and layout were similar enough to that of a freighter that it was clear that the big ship had been adapted from one, but it looked nothing like a standard freighter now.

Mount Olivet was small by comparison to *Mount Sinai*, it was true, and was designed to land on worlds even if they had no spaceport. In truth, it was an impressive, oblong-shaped craft of creamy white material over a thousand meters long and six hundred meters wide, and it descended on a flat base that was itself a hundred or more meters high. It was powered by a magnetic field drive and was designed for a totally self-contained landing. Indeed, its shape and size made it unwelcome at conventional spaceports, which was just fine with the crew that would take it down to surface after surface. They required a huge flat area not far from some population center yet far enough so that such a landing was practical and the ship, after that, would be accessible.

Finding that type of space, and a crowd that didn't also come well armed and ready to tar and feather at the minimum was a job in and of itself.

As soon as *The Mountain* cleared the automated wormgate, the first order of business was to pull up and scan the entire region. Many of the wormgates were in poor shape and the ship's technicians often spent days or even weeks inside the automated station making at least basic repairs and checks to insure that they could comfortably stay a bit yet get out quickly if need be. In-system probes looked for the reason why the gate was there. It always meant a colony, of course, but so many of them were discovered failed and dead, so many had not been viable once the Great Silence had cut them off, or, worse,

had become vulnerable to those who roamed the
space lanes now with no regard for life but only an
appetite for plunder. Others had descended so far into
barbarism that they were ignorant of their own origins. Some were hostile, often for good reason, to all
outsiders and needed to be coaxed into acceptance
of *The Mountain* and its mission, or, sometimes,
written off when no compromise was negotiable.

Nobody knew the reception they would get, but
there was no question that the second planet in the
eight-planet system was Earth Type A, inhabited, and
retained at least some technological information.

They were being scanned from monitors mounted
on the gate as well as from scanners in fixed orbits
farther in-system, and those scans were being beamed
to the second planet.

This was not necessarily happy news. It implied
that high-tech defensive systems were probably also
deployed and still operable, and that this would take
a bit of diplomacy before proceeding.

There was no purpose in delay, though. They were
potential targets even where they were, although it
was unlikely that there would be any actions that
might blow up the gate as well. That was a true last
resort and would close the door for good on any hope
of friends finding them.

Still, right now the planetary defense system knew
more about them than they did about it or the planet
and people it guarded, and that had to be rectified.

"Reconciliation ship *Mountain* to unknown planetary
civilization," the captain called via an all-frequency
radio link. "We are pleased to have found you, but we
have no idea who you are. You are on none of our
charts. We come in faith and friendship as an arm of
our Lord Jesus Christ. We have sophisticated databases

and robotic synthesizing and repair systems, and we
have agricultural seed, culturable DNA for domestic
cloning of farm animals, and much more." Many places
would run from an evangelical group, particularly one
with a ship this grand, but it was a lot harder to turn
down the more material benefits they also brought and
bargained for access to the hearts and minds of people.

There was no immediate reply. The captain waited
a minute or two, then repeated his call almost word
for word.

Still silence returned.

He shrugged and turned to see the Doctor entering
the bridge. Everybody snapped to, even though they
were used to the big bear of a man who looked and
sounded much like a biblical patriarch but with the
patience of a divine right monarch convinced of his
infallibility.

Doctor Karl Woodward, Ph.D., was just short of
two meters tall, and built so broadly and solidly that
he filled a space. He wasn't fat; in fact, he was in
excellent shape for a man his age and delighted in
challenging younger members of *The Mountain*'s family in all sorts of heavy exercise. He had flowing
white hair that tumbled over his shoulders, and a
full beard that gave his face a kinder look than
perhaps the body's build projected, and his rough,
ruddy complexion beneath all the hair was cut only
by sharp but very cold deep blue eyes. When he
spoke, it was always the voice of the prophet, the
voice of command, and in a deep, spellbinding
baritone.

He waved his hand idly at the captain. "Keep
going. It may take them a while to decide if they even
want to talk to us."

The captain shrugged and nodded, but noted, "It

may be all automated as well, sir. We've run into that before, particularly if this is a pirate world or old military or maybe just plain paranoid."

"They're *all* paranoid at this level, Captain," the Doctor responded. "But most paranoids don't trust machines to do their vital thinking for them. Haven't yet seen that, doubt I ever will. We *do* have live bodies on that world out there?"

"Definitely, sir. Hard to tell the size from this distance, but the best located of the three continental land masses appears to have a significant although not overwhelming population. Good climate, looks like decent rain patterns. The others are a lot more rugged."

"How many?"

"Computer scan estimates no more than eight to ten thousand, well scattered, no cities, although it looks like everything is centered around a series of tiny towns. Surface roads indicated, mostly unpaved, but development does show a spoke pattern. JoAnn, that's your department."

A young woman with flaming red hair, in a tight fitting red bridge deck suit, looked at her console. "Aye, Captain. Landing site was near a large inland lake, which is fairly common, and somewhat centrally located. It appears they had a basic spaceport, the usual layout, but there's not much sign it's been used in recent memory or could be. The scans are definitely being reported to the complex there, but it's not like it's the capital city we might expect. In fact, I'd say it has only a few hundred inhabitants, no more than the obviously agricultural support towns in the central plain. There may be an administrator of sorts, but I would sincerely doubt if there is even as much as a centralized governmental authority with any real clout. No presidents, Maximum Leaders, or whatever. This is a classic frontier pattern."

"That's not a lot of people for this length of time," the Doctor commented. "Any snakes in their Eden we can see?"

"No, sir. Climate's good and it appears that agriculture is thriving. It may just be that there weren't very many people to begin with, or that many of them left when the Silence descended and never came back. All that's guesswork. Anything more would require we go down there and look."

The Doctor's massive white eyebrows went up. "What do you think, Captain? Should we send somebody down to look? Can we cover them?"

"I think we could cover them to planetfall, sir," the officer responded, "but once they were on the ground they'd be sitting ducks. I'd recommend a robotic probe. Harder to protect, but it would give us information without risking lives."

"I know *that*!" the Doctor snapped irritatedly. "Don't patronize me! *Ever!* I helped design this thing, remember!"

Everybody on the bridge froze. When the Doctor was in one of his moods, which was more often than not, he couldn't be pacified, was on a hair trigger, and often would just replace anybody who pissed him off. Everyone on the bridge was there by the grace of the Doctor; even the captain could wind up supervising latrines if the Doctor so chose. A combination admiral and pope, the Doctor was not very democratic. And even those who'd been around him his whole life could never be sure what was real and what was act, but they had known, seen, and sometimes felt the consequences of guessing wrong.

"How many unmanned probes we got left?" the big, bearded man asked, settling back into his chair.

"Nine, sir. And three of those are mostly being used as spare parts and models for spare parts. That last go-round with the *Joy of Islam* left us spent. Give me a few days with a competent shipyard or munitions factory and I can replace them all, but not with less."

The Doctor tugged a bit on his bearded chin, thinking. "All right, we'll try one. Protect it as best you can and try and recover if at all possible."

"Cover it, sir? You mean defend it if it's shot at?" This was quite unusual practice for an unmanned probe, even if they were in such short supply.

The Doctor got up and stretched, then nodded. "That's right, Captain. Notify me when it's within data collection range. Notify me even faster if someone or something takes a shot at it. And, if anything does, try and neutralize it."

"Neutralize . . . ?" The captain knew what the instructions were but he wanted it spelled out for the record.

"Blow it to Hell, damn it!" the Doctor snapped, then exited the com. He paused a moment, then added, "And let's leave one Q and A channel open, the most likely one to be used, but let's broadcast on the entire rest of the spectrum. Take a vote, then assemble and transmit at near overload on those channels the worst sounding hymns of all time. If nothing else, *that* might get some action!"

The captain sighed. "Well, you heard him. Deborah, Rachel, I'll let you be the music committee. Everybody else on the probe and defensive station. Let's see who's down there!"

❖   ❖   ❖

It took a couple of hours of diagnostics and programming before the probe was ready to go, and then
they knew it would take days to reach the inner planets. The engines on the probes were among the fast-
est small engines ever devised, but distances were still
vast and none of the wormgates was ever placed close
enough in to be warped or disrupted by major planetary gravitational fields or in likely areas of cosmic
debris.

The first trick was to launch the probe in such a
way as to make it clear to any defender that it was
indeed a probe and not a weapon. That was easier
said than done, and relied on some experience and
tried-and-true methods, but that didn't stop the entire
ship from being put on alert when it was launched,
weapons at the ready.

The same defensive system that scanned them
when they arrived also locked onto the probe, but,
as with them, appeared to make no aggressive moves
as a result. As the probe closed in on the largest gas
giant and used its great gravitational force to supple-
ment its jump engines, more scans snapped on, but,
as before, nothing fired at the spherical probe. Either
the system wasn't armed for defense, was incapable
of it, or was willing to allow the potential aggressor
a look at things. There would have been nothing *The
Mountain*'s crew could have done to protect the probe
had it been shot at; with every passing minute the
time delay for a reaction increased. The probe's own
computer was pretty much on its own.

A bit more than three days in, and just a hair more
than halfway to the inner planet, the defensive system
acted. It wasn't a serious defensive blow, more a shot
across the bow of the probe, clearly missing deliberately but with the intent of slowing or halting the thing.

It came from an undetected free-floating platform that was too small and too well shielded to show up on instruments until it revealed itself, but when it did, it showed, too, that there were no lifeforms aboard. This was automatic.

The probe showed some defensive prowess, whirling and twisting while using some energy for its own shields, but instead of slowing it used every ounce of available power to get the hell out of there while taking a more evasive, zigzag style inward course.

The gun platform suddenly flared into life and began a rapid pursuit. Clearly it would not just be a bow shot if it could close, although it remained to be seen if it was capable of doing that.

"Very weak energy signature," the gunnery officer noted back on *The Mountain*. "It's showing its age and its lack of service. I'd say these folks no longer have space travel in any useful sense. Look—you can see how it's losing the race. I'd expect— *Ah!*"

There was a major energy surge from the gun platform, as if it had suddenly shot everything it had at the fleeing probe, but it was certainly not enough. The probe easily swerved even as the beam fired, and didn't look back.

"Reading only trace energy on the platform," one of the artillery crew noted. "That platform's spent."

"Notify the Doctor and send this to whatever console he's closest to," the gunnery officer ordered.

"Done!"

The Doctor was on the intercom within two minutes. "It missed?"

"Yes, sir. No problem. But, of course, if one of them does that this far out, it's sure as shooting that there'll be more and meaner ones closer in."

"Doctor to bridge. Close to the position of the platform. See if you can snag it. I doubt if it'll be in any shape to resist and our shielding should take whatever it might give. Let's see who made it, and when."

"This could be a trap to lure us into just that," the First Officer commanding the bridge at the time warned him. "Do you really want to risk the ship at this juncture?"

"Faith, Number One! We're founded on *faith*! This is *God's* chariot! I gave you an order and I expect it to be carried out, not questioned!" he thundered, then paused a moment before adding, in a much more conversational tone, "Besides, if we're so damned paranoid we'll run from these antiques then we should get out of this business!"

The First Officer nodded, more to himself than to any other authority, thought a quiet and personal prayer, and then said, "Half ahead. Maintain full alert defensive mode, slowly increase speed to two-thirds pulse if clear."

The ship was basically computer controlled, and was used to interpreting the orders of its long-time bridge officers. In fact, the whole of *The Mountain* actually required few human crew members to run efficiently, although it was hardly a luxury liner type of ship. Much of the routine maintenance, such as collecting soiled clothes, cleaning the vast areas of the ship, changing linen, and so on, were done by humans because there were no robots or robotic services of that sort to do them, and, in fact, probably would never be allowed so long as the Doctor was running things. The key systems were automated, even gunnery, although at all such positions, from the bridge to gunnery to engineering, there were humans present to confirm, block, or manually override as might be needed, and these were also experts at checking out and testing their equipment.

Many of the less crucial functions aboard might have been automated but deliberately weren't. The Doctor wanted everyone to have a job that meant something to the whole.

By the time *The Mountain* was in approach range of the one hostile gun platform the probe itself was almost to the warm, blue and white world that was their objective. There had been several attacks, but always tepid ones, and never with great power or with anything other than automated systems behind them, indicating that this whole defense grid was sadly undermaintained and out of whack.

This was doubly reinforced when *The Mountain* reached the platform, placed an energy plasma shield around it, and hauled it in. The poor platform was almost an object of pity aboard ship; it kept trying to defend itself and shoot up the works, but it just didn't have any juice left. Gunnery experts in repair spacesuits actually approached and boarded it, tracing and dismantling its self-destruct mechanism even though instruments said that there was nothing left there to explode.

"Standard Mark XXIX," the chief gunnery officer reported. "It's so pitted that it's clear nobody or nothing's been here to service it for maybe a century or more, and whatever made the big dent shorted out a lot of its power. Logic circuits are still okay, though. Readout says it was placed by Eleventh Mars Corps, UC Navy, one hundred and sixty-one years ago." He whistled. "This is an old trooper, then, if it's never been rebuilt or serviced."

"At least it dates the colony, since it's probable that this and the other defensive units were placed here when the colony was established as part of the network," the Doctor commented.

"So they got set up and it wasn't long before the Silence. That could explain why it's so undeveloped down there. I bet they never even got a lot of their initial shipments. Hell, they probably didn't have anything more than the stuff they initially brought with them, and that would have been really the basics. By this point that could be a *very* primitive agricultural colony down there."

"So you think everything here is automatic, and in as poor shape as that thing?" the Doctor asked.

"Probably, but I wouldn't underestimate one or two of these units of better escaping the ravages and actually functioning. You never can tell."

"Oh, I believe we *can* tell," the Doctor told him. "And in a matter of hours we'll have a look at just what they've managed to maintain down there. Cheer up! If it's like you say, then we may be able to help them out and lift them up. God brought us here for a reason. Consider what would have happened if one of the pirates had found this place first."

He never understood why they didn't think of themselves as the good guys, and it worried him. He was a better teacher than *that*.

The probe's data confirmed their suspicions of a fairly low level technology even though the colony here had been saved to a large extent by the climate, isolation, and the fact that they'd been set up so close to the Silence that nobody'd heard of them or blundered into them before.

The initial centralized city was stock prefab architecture and was composed of large administrative-type buildings and warehouses. There was no indication that it was ever used as a real settlement or capital, only that it was the place where everything was landed. Some cultivated fields surrounding the complex showed that there was continuing activity there, but on a subsistence level.

A technological culture would have had few if any roads; hovercraft and air mags would have made them superfluous. Here there were not only roads, but dirt roads, many deeply rutted, as well as heavily trod paths and trails. The farther from the central core they looked, the less signs of automation or any kind of prefabrication existed.

Development had been more or less radial due to the vast interior plains, the abundant rivers and lakes, and the apparently year-round mild climate. The fields looked quite snappy close in to the landing site, but became more ragged although not less abundant as the distance from the site increased. Houses tended to be the marshmallowlike prefab of the old Combine close in, as did the big buildings at the center, but you didn't have to look far to see little evidence of that sort of technology. By the third "ring" of settlement, most of the houses appeared built of some sort of adobe, quite natural and matching the available materials. There was evidence of some building in wood and stone, but it appeared that they hadn't quite gotten the full hang of that as yet.

What was most eerie was the total lack of any energy pulses or sites or transmissions along the surface. Not only were there no aircraft, there weren't any powered conveyances of any sort to be seen or detected.

"They're either extremely resourceful or they are members of an old order recidivist cult," the chief anthropologist, Ruth Morgan, noted when looking at the finely detailed three-dimensional pictures coming in from the probe.

"You mean like the Old Order Amish or the like?" the Doctor responded. "We've already seen and traced all the known ones from them and similar groups. That doesn't mean they weren't out for a simpler life, but we've seen too many dead worlds where colonists thought they knew how to do things by hand."

"Still, this group is basically growing grains, fruits, and vegetables the old way," she noted. "Those fields are tilled by animal power. There's no electric grid at all. And yet, I'm not at all sure it was intended that way. You see those herds there? They're *crindin*, a big, lumbering creature our records indicate is from an old Silenced colony called Mandolan. They were picked to be brought here and probably used in that way, since they're not known to be edible by humans. They make great oxen if you know how to use a yoke and plow, though. Hard to believe many people did."

The Doctor frowned and looked at the closeup of the big beasts, that in many ways resembled six-legged two-trunked monstrous purple elephants. "Interesting. I'm beginning to grow more and more curious at this colony's past. I think we ought to keep getting data as long as possible but go on in." He punched the intercom. "Captain, high orbit. I don't want us seen from the ground, but I want to be close enough to do our setup work. I don't feel danger here, but I do feel mystery."

The Doctor turned back to the anthropologist. "Any sign of churches or other types of houses of worship?"

She shrugged. "I'm sorry, Doc, but I can't tell. The buildings are so crude we wouldn't expect them to risk a steeple, and there's nothing in the shape of any of the buildings to suggest a cross or similar outfit. No minarets, either, and certainly nothing in the towns to indicate Buddhism or one of its offshoots. My feeling is that it's either pretty secular, possibly Hindu or an offshoot of it, or another faith with little liking for the trappings of organized religion. They may just worship as they please. Until we're down there, we can't know."

"People?"

"You can see some of them there in those freezes from the survey. Reddish brown skin predominates, but that doesn't mean much in that climate. Hair seems to be either coal black or pretty white, mostly bearded. The dress looks functional, probably hand-made, and fairly standard. Women are wearing either a pullover patterned dress or some sort of pants and loose shirt pretty much like the men. Long hair, which indicates few pests, but I don't see much sign of beards from the admittedly limited sample. The inter-esting shots are these, taken in one of the warmer regions near a shallow lake. The lake appears thick with rice, and the lands around look to be some variation of cotton plants. Look there—see the move-ment? Men, women, boys, girls, all out there clearly picking cotton by hand. I bet that in the rice har-vest season they do the same thing in the lake. The trail network connects them to basically a quarter of the other farms, suggesting a trading system. Rice and cotton take certain conditions you don't need for wheat and maize, for example, and I don't see a lot of indications that these cotton pickers process their crop in bulk. I'd say they trade."

"Well, it looks promising," the Doctor noted. "I think we ought to send some folks down there and get a practical lay of the land. Anybody in the mood to go Biblical and take a long, hot walk?"

"We are always ready," Morgan assured him without a second thought, and, while pleased, he accepted that at face value.

II:

ORPHANS OF THE SILENCE

There were an infinite number of ways to approach a new world of which you knew nothing, including the full frontal assault, as it were, where you just landed as yourself and had faith that the locals would be more curious than hostile. In this case, with so little known but such a primitive layout below, it was decided that they'd send down two young but experienced Arms of Gideon looking as innocent and fresh-faced and nonthreatening as possible, one male, one female.

John Robey was twenty-four standard years old, about a hundred and eighty centimeters tall, with a strong but ruggedly handsome face, short-cropped sandy brown hair and brown eyes. His companion was Eve Toloway, twenty-two, about a hundred and sixty centimeters, with a near angelic face, olive complexion, and big green eyes. She and John had worked together now and then, but this would be their first away team experience together, and her first at any time in her life. They were selected by computer and approved by the Doctor as appropriate for this mission.

Both of them had been born and raised within *The Mountain* and knew no other life or ways. Both were sincere, dedicated, and well trained. They both wore white robes with hoods made out of a material that was far more than it seemed, and would help protect them from the potentially harsh and possibly unknown dangers of a planetary climate. Consistent with the Doctor's beliefs in his interstellar religious commune, John would be in charge down there, but that didn't imply inferiority on the part of Eve but rather a chain of command of sorts. In fact, their leader often joked that he thought women were superior to men, which is why the Bible set up things with the weaker sex in charge. Otherwise, he said, only half joking, men would soon be obsolete.

The small scout cars were precious to a ship like *The Mountain*; although incapable of interstellar flight, they could land just about anywhere, take off straight up faster than most people could see, and were silent and secure. Once they'd contained complex self-aware computers as backups; they were designed for such things. Now it was strictly a basic system, though, not because of any paranoia or fear on the part of *The Mountain* or the Doctor, but basically because those things had required first-class specialized maintenance and by the time *The Mountain* had acquired its current scouts the old computers had either become too unreliable to use or had been removed. It didn't really matter because of the way they were now used anyway; *The Mountain* actually flew them remotely from an area between the bridge and gunnery control, and in a pinch the passengers could take over and fly them manually.

They would both be on a leash, but everyone on the big ship and the scout understood that, once down, they were pretty much on their own.

Robey settled into the right-hand chair, Toloway the left. They buckled up, then went through the flight checklist like experienced pilots, and finally the last seals hissed into place and Robey said, "Angel One to Father—ready when you are."

"Very well, Angel One. Stand by. Counting down."

In front of them a digital clock started backing down from sixty seconds. When it reached zero, there was a sudden lurch and a feeling of falling as the solidity of the big ship fell away and they were in space.

Robey looked over at his companion. "You okay?"

She nodded. "I'm excited. I've never been on a real planet except in the simulators before."

"Well, I hope you're prepared for it. It's not what it's cracked up to be. Stand by. Angel One to Father."

"Go ahead."

"Let's go on in, assuming we're not fired on. I think we'll start where they did, and see what's left of the first colony."

"Very well. Agreed. Check and insure that your watches are in synch with the scout and us. You'll be coming in about an hour after sunup, and at that latitude you'll have about eleven hours of daylight from right now. I'll bring you in near the donut-shaped central administrative structure. Planetfall in . . . seventeen minutes."

They could feel the craft twist and turn and adjust, but inside there was only silence and the sudden sight of the planet in their forward screen. It was night below, but the terminator was fast approaching.

"No lights at all below," Robey noted. "I have a feeling that what's left of this colony is entirely around where we're headed. I sure pray that they're better off than they seemed."

"Huh? What do you mean?"

"Well, if they're on the decline and dying out and we can't stabilize things, then it's going to be a real dead world down there. We could never absorb a fraction of a population that big."

She hadn't thought of that, but there was only one way to approach it and stay sane. "God's will," she breathed.

The terrain was a bit more diverse than it had seemed from the pictures aboard the ship; the central continent was quite green, with dense trees, lots of rivers and creeks, and it had a kind of rolling topography, flattening out to a great plain only around the original landing spot.

Every time anybody saw colonial buildings they wondered what in the world people were thinking of when they built them. Although most were quite massive, they looked like giant clay or dough structures extruded from gigantic toothpaste or paint tubes and then built up one pasty layer at a time. In fact, they were the products of pragmatism; it would have been far too expensive to take such buildings with a colony; that bulk and weight was best utilized for carrying seed and core machinery and initial survival supplies and equipment. From the earliest days of space exploration, though, it was recognized that worlds where people could set themselves up were made of the same stuff, basically, as all the worlds they'd come from. Several building machines were developed that actually could grind up and transform rocks and silicates into a substance that could be used to literally form buildings to need. Those machines were a lot easier to bring to a new colony and a lot less bulky than prefabricated dwellings. They also had computerized models preprogrammed in case nobody was really architecturally inclined, and most had used them.

The effect was a sameness of puffy-looking structures from world to world and culture to culture, just like the ones here. The thing was, though, that the stuff *did* wear well; although obviously not in regular use, and probably abandoned if the power was gone, these looked in remarkably good shape.

The scout put down in what would have been the central "square" of the initial colonial headquarters after checking and finding nobody obviously very close to the landing site. That didn't mean that natives weren't around, but they certainly didn't seem to be in evidence.

The buildings all had the typical rough, rounded, unfinished exterior look to them, and as they took much of their color from the materials they'd transformed, this batch was a collection of dull pinks and sickly moss greens.

The hatch hissed, and then swung up and away, and then Robey, followed by his smaller companion, emerged, hoods up over their heads to protect against the unfamiliar hot sun. The hatch automatically closed behind them when they cleared the landing site, and the small scout continued to vibrate, ready to take off at a moment's threat or to protect the two passengers.

It *was* hot, certainly over thirty, perhaps thirty-five, and surprisingly humid for being so far from an ocean. The sky was filled with puffy white clouds, and the air was still, almost leaden, and smelled of decay.

Robey gestured to his companion, and they started walking to opposite sides of the square, then around it, taking a look at anything they could see.

There *were* signs of the original project. Pieces of the initial setup machines lay strewn all over the square, and there were parts of one thing or another here and there. Many of them looked dismantled or cannibalized, but some of them just sat there, as they probably had for a century and a half or more, since the power ran down.

The power wasn't *supposed* to run down for a century or two, though, which only confirmed their first impression. Nothing they saw had been brought here new; most of it was as much the product of junkyard reconstruction as a lot of the technology in *The Mountain*. It was almost as if this place hadn't been cut off by the Great Silence but rather established *after* it occurred.

They crossed back to the center near the scout and compared notes.

"What do you think, Brother John? A pirate den that didn't work out?" she asked him.

He shrugged. "I doubt it, Sister, but this is definitely not anybody's grand design. Refugees, maybe, from other places. That would explain the crindin and some of the insects I've seen here, which are definitely not native to any one planet. Let's take a look inside the main building over there. It *had* to be Administration."

The door had long since vanished, but it was a dark hole inside, and he reached into a pocket in his robe and pulled out a strong directional flashlight. With that, they both entered, stepping over all sorts of rubble.

It didn't take long to know that they were going to learn little from inside the place. What had been useful to others had been carried away, even if it had to have been dug out of the walls and floor. Areas where there would have been computer screens and command consoles looked wrecked as well; even if they couldn't run computers remotely, somebody thought that the interface chairs probably would be comfortable, or that the screens might make good temporary walls.

"There is something to be said for writing things down on hard copy," Eve commented. "There's absolutely nothing here, not even a logo, to indicate who they were."

"That's why we don't let the machines take over back home," he responded, meaning *The Mountain* for "home." "Civilization was already almost totally illiterate when they moved out here. They didn't *have* to read anymore. It was only the abstract scholars like theologians who thought it was important. That's why we know our origins and our history and the various versions and interpretations of the words of God, but these people probably don't even remember that there's another planet someplace, let alone a lot of them."

She sighed and nodded. "Well, Brother, somebody taught them to use domesticated animals and how to build and plow and sow and reap without machines, so they have *some* skills you wouldn't expect."

He grinned. "Let's go see and ask them."

She nodded. "I'm kind of curious to see those big animals close up, too."

Even though they could have flown to the nearest people in the fields or even the next town in short order, there was never any thought of doing it. Instead, they would walk, unaccustomed as they were to the difference in gravitation, over *The Mountain*'s artificial but totally stable one gee, and the natural atmosphere that seemed a bit richer if also smellier than that in the ship. Gravity here was, in fact, a bit lighter, although not dramatically so. It wasn't enough for grand gestures and feats, but it did make things seem a bit easier, a bit less stressful, to do.

They walked through the courtyard between two of the old buildings and out onto the plain beyond. There was a lot more junk lying around all over here, but it was consistent with what they'd seen in the square. They'd come, they'd set up what they could with what they had, and they'd finally, and apparently within a fairly short time, run out of power to keep a modern town center and colonial headquarters going.

"I wonder where their ship is?" she mused.

"Huh? Oh, not here, that's for sure. They were offloaded, the defense system was set up, probably also using units from other places, and then whoever brought them all left. Well, we'll see what these folks know, if, at least, we can get anybody to talk to us. I've never been on a recidivist world before, but the records show that half the time the people tend to run like hell when they see strangers or sometimes try to attack them."

She looked around and mentally gave a prayerful plea to God. "Thanks a lot, Brother," she said sourly.

Having no particular knowledge of the locals, they picked what looked like a decently worn path and started off, oblivious of the direction. If settlement had been radial from this point, one direction was as good as the other.

The road showed signs of wear; it had once been well traveled, an ad hoc paved path perhaps three meters across, but clearly no highway. Wind and rain had battered into it, taking the wear and tear from earlier times and widening and worsening those effects. It was obviously a well-traveled road no longer, but one cracked, pitted, smoothed, and rutted like some exposed rocky outcrop in active weather. The people might still farm the areas near the old landing site, but they didn't go there any more and hadn't for quite some time.

They walked along rather casually, taking in what sights they could and speaking only now and again. Both were aware that they were probably being observed, and they wanted no sense of threat or intimidation to emanate from their manner, nor any sense of fear, either. They did stop after an hour or so at the bank of a small stream and, after taking samples and checking with a pocket analyzer, determined that the water was in fact just that, and they drank. It was warmer than they would have liked, kind of appropriate for hand washing rather than drinking, and it had other oddities, but it quenched thirsts and their analyzer assured them it would cause no ill effects.

"What's that odd aftertaste?" Eve asked him, making a slight face. "Tastes like *plumbing* or something."

John laughed. "That's minerals dissolved in the water. It's perfectly normal and the way things work on real worlds. You've just never had to drink any water that wasn't purified and distilled."

"Water shouldn't have a taste," she insisted.

He shrugged. "I admit to some hesitation, but not

on taste. The trouble with this sort of natural spring water is that you never know where it's been."

She almost spit it out, but managed not to. Either she'd have to stand the stuff or she wasn't ready for this kind of work, and she definitely wanted to be ready for this kind of work. Still, his somewhat teasing comment bothered her because, while said mostly to get her goat, the fact was, it was also the truth. She was in the first stages of realizing what living in a primitive or natural environment really meant.

They were fast walkers and in good shape on a lower than standard gravity world, though, so they made very good time, and within three hours they came to the outskirts of the closest village on the road.

It was the smell that got them first. The stench of human and animal waste, and the effect on it and anything else organic in a hot, wet climate was almost overpowering. The insects, perhaps drawn by this, were also quite heavy and some of them bit, and there were the sounds of animals all around, including, unexpectedly, the barking of dogs.

There weren't any pets as such allowed on *The Mountain*, but there was an entire animal wing, a zoological department as it were, where a number of animals were kept and bred for various purposes and where, just as important, large stores of fertilized animal embryos and a comprehensive DNA record of just about every animal known plus representative stem cells to grow them if need be were kept. Every child born and raised on the big ship had been introduced to the smaller, less threatening animals, small friendly dogs and affection-starved cats in particular, because they were part of the experience the Doctor thought important in growing up so long as they didn't have the run of the ship.

"Don't expect these dogs to be friendly," John warned her. "Just because ours are doesn't mean that they weren't also bred as watchdogs and guardians. Stay away from them if you can while here; you simply can't be certain which are playful and which might be killers."

Still, that might be easier said than done, she realized. While some of the bigger, noisier dogs seemed to be restrained by leashes affixed to poles in the ground, others did wander around. Fortunately, the barkers were mostly tied, while the wanderers barely acknowledged their existence or approached, sniffed around, then went on when they were not fully appreciated.

There were some cats, too, mostly asleep under things and in shady spots. They looked big and fat, which meant that they were well fed at least. On what wasn't so clear, but colonies tended to introduce cats when they had a small varmint population to control.

The houses looked a bit less ramshackle on the ground than they had from the air, but they certainly didn't seem like places either of the spacefarers would have felt comfortable in. The walls appeared to be local adobe-type mud, with thick tan walls and narrow doors of wood that seemed to be covered with some sort of incongruous mesh screening that certainly couldn't have been locally produced. "That's salvaged stuff," Robey commented. "It's weathered quite well. I suspect everybody got some here, but I can't imagine it being common the farther out we go. Some of the pipes doing drainage here look slick and well machined, too, but the patches at the junctions are crude and jury-rigged."

Eve looked around. "I doubt if they do more than sleep in those places," she noted. "No chimneys, roofs are salvaged slates, pitched thatch, or similar. The bigger buildings near the town center would have to be common barns, and I suspect that the area over there with the big covered pit and the stone slab tables and benches is the common kitchen."

She was about to deduce more when several figures emerged from some of the houses and one of the large barnlike structures, carrying sacks over their shoulders or large jars on their heads, all heading towards the "common kitchen." They all looked young and strong, wearing thin gray cotton one-piece dresses and little else, and they were all women and girls. They all had coal-black hair trailing down and reddish-brown skin and there was a definite racial kinship in the features, possibly due to close intermarriage.

Sexual division of labor, Eve noted mentally. She also noted that while some of the youngest girls looked no more than five or six, there were no babies or really small children in evidence and none of the teenagers appeared pregnant.

The young women caught sight of the strangers almost immediately and stopped, staring. They didn't seem scared, more like people who have seen something they had never seen before and had not expected ever to see.

"Try calling to them," Robey whispered to Eve, thinking that maybe woman to woman would be a better introduction.

"Hello!" Eve called to them. "Do any of you speak my language? Or what language do you speak?" The educated of most colonies had a working knowledge of some form of English, which had grown to majority usage way back on Old Earth as an international standard, even though the accents and local variations could be atrocious. Many of the ordinary folk, though, like these, tended to speak a local language or dialect. Eve had some working knowledge of seventeen Earth-derived languages, and John twelve, with only four overlapping, but beyond the primary set of English, Hindi, Spanish, and Mandarin the possibilities were endless. These people looked like what the old records gave as the Hindi speaking people, but you never knew. Certainly when they continued to gape at her she repeated her query in Hindi, but got no farther.

As the standoff continued in the increasingly hot midday sun, there came suddenly the far-off sound of what might have been a trumpet or similar horn, and then another on the other side of the village an equal distance away. They seemed to jolt the young women into some kind of furious action, in which they simply ignored the two strangers and began scurrying around, working hard, stoking up the fire pit, dumping out the food, starting the evident preparation of lunch. They did call, even shout to one another, but at first it sounded like gibberish.

"Mooka gan pickup brunin die!" one called to a small girl, who whirled and ran back off into the barn, giving the dumbfounded strangers a furtive glance as she went near.

"Not exactly filling them with awe and wonder," Eve noted sourly as young women worked feverishly at their tasks.

"Well, they know we're here, and I guess they figure we're not going to attack them and they'll have a whole town to feed pretty soon who'll need to be fed regardless and *they* might get mighty pissed off at the lack of a meal and *they* will still be here tomorrow."

"Did you catch any of the language?"

He shrugged. "I think it's English, or a dialect of it, probably well removed long before these people's ancestors got plopped down here and moving much further since."

"You have any ideas? I certainly don't want the town mad at us because we loused up the lunch routine."

He nodded. "I think we sit over there in the shade, where there's something of a breeze to take the stench away, and we let the anthropologists and computers up top figure out the language if they can. We'll get noticed soon enough when the rest of the town gets here."

She nodded. "That's what I'm afraid of."

John took a small transmission rod from his equipment belt under his robe, put it on maximum and directional, and pointed it at the increasingly busy group of now fifteen or twenty people who were preparing the meal.

After a few minutes, the general channel opened and the receivers implanted in their ears returned data.

"Fairly basic English, not easily traceable as dialect although centuries before, the base was probably Cockney, as were half the English dialects of the world."

"Can you give us a filter?" Robey asked them in a soft voice, not wanting to attract any more attention right now.

"Basic, yes. There's a lot of words and terms that are certainly too localized, so until you can match them to things or actions they'll still come out garbled, but we can get a basic pidgin for this group. You'll have to pick it up yourself for speaking purposes."

"Okay, send, both of us."

All that would do was to use the receiver implants to reformat the language they were hearing into something more understandable. It simply helped figure out the sense of the sounds by making them a bit more familiar, correcting for speed and mispronunciations, and from *that* both the monitoring linguistic computer and their own skills would allow them to learn it well enough for conversation. This had been a part of training and simulation, since this sort of problem was quite common, but neither of them had ever actually had to use it before.

Some results were dramatic.

"Gala, hon, you be foot wash so dance the dough pit," one woman's instruction to a girl of eight or nine came through. Soon it was clear that there was a great deal of dough being prepared in a fixed stone-lined trough, and the way it got kneaded was for Gala and several of her friends, after washing their feet, to simply jump in and start jumping up and down and kneading with their feet.

"'Dance the dough pit.' I kind of like that," Eve commented. "It has a kind of lyrical charm."

"I'm just happy they wash their feet first," Robey responded, less impressed.

Soon the whole stoneworks was chugging along and the heat was building up on an already hot day, while the smoke wafted into the air. There were stone ovens along the sides that clearly were designed to keep different temperatures for baking, large open pots for simmering stews and the like on the sides of the central pit, and all sorts of oils and herbs put on fruits and vegetables that were mixed and heated and turned on the larger grates. It was quite impressive, and worked like clockwork, everybody knowing their part and doing it. When

one of the younger ones would balk or slip, somebody else would be right there to make things right
and then get everything back on track and schedule.

The fact was, the heat and smoke weren't pleasant but when the wind did send them briefly their
way, the two outsiders found the uglier smells of the
village replaced with very good, sweet-smelling and
even exotic-smelling odors.

"Think they will invite us to lunch, Brother John?"
Eve asked him.

"I'm not sure if they'll even *acknowledge* us," he
replied. "I have to admit, I was somewhat prepared
for a hostile appearance, or the awestruck bit, or the
fear of outsiders, but it never once occurred to me
that we'd be almost completely ignored. No curiosity, no worries we'll make off with the family jewels,
nothing."

She gave him a wry smile. "I doubt if they have
anything even they would consider worth stealing
other than maybe themselves and their kids, and that
doesn't look like anything you'd do here. And I think
they're curious, all right. It just isn't their place to
open up to us. Nobody wants to take the responsibility, particularly *that* group. Look at how very
young they all are! Kids!"

"Kids are among the most curious of creatures, or
haven't you noticed?" he responded. "No, I think that
it's a little hard living here. Those 'kids' are an integral
part of the whole and are as essential to survival as
the bigger, older folks. They had to grow up almost
immediately, and they know their place."

About twenty minutes along, the distant trumpets
sounded again, only this time both seemed much
closer. The crews were clearly coming in, and if anything, the frantic pace the girls were setting increased.

Eve frowned and shook her head in puzzlement. "I'm not sure what's what here, but maybe we're missing something."

"Huh? What do you mean?"

"Could *you* make flour, cultivate and protect yeast, and make bread for a hundred? Seriously. I couldn't, not without the computer in my ear telling me just what to do step by step, and even then, I'd need all the ingredients set out before me. These people, to put it bluntly, know too much about how to do it themselves."

He sighed. "I don't know. I've seen this sort of thing in the records before, when automation slowly failed and they had time to learn or be taught how to do it before the power ran out. Still, there's no evidence that they *ever* had much automation here, and it's for certain none of them are looking at cookbooks. Well, if we can get one of them, or the ones who are coming in to eat, to *talk* to us then maybe we can get a few answers."

"I thought when we got down here and met our first people we were supposed to get answers," she noted sourly.

It wasn't long before the rest of the village came in, with dogs leaping about and barking and lots of talking amongst themselves at such a babbling rate that even the filters didn't help.

Sounds of much larger animals also abounded, but if they brought in the elephantine crindin, they didn't bring them anywhere near the communal kitchen and dining area.

One thing that immediately stood out was that there were few old people, or at least few who looked old. Not that there wasn't some gray, but it seemed premature, the results of a hard life rather than a long one.

The men seemed to one to be in excellent condition; there were muscles over tight bodies and nothing in the way of fat. There *were* plenty of scars on their reddish-brown skins, scars which stood out for that contrast, and even some missing digits or limbs here and there, but none of the injuries appeared to be the result of any sort of combat. These were subsistence farmers and herdsmen and they showed the inevitable price of long days of primitive manual labor.

Male dress tended to be a pair of cotton pants in one of a half-dozen faded colors, well worn and ragged. Some wore faded cotton shirts of the same condition, others were bare from the waist up. Most also wore something on their heads as protection from the sun, but it varied wildly, from turban-like cloth wrappings to burnooses to hats with broad starched brims. Many had big, droopy mustaches, some had beards, all had pretty long hair, but in just about every case the hair was neatly trimmed, a point of pride, obviously.

One huge man with arms thicker than John Robey's thighs and a huge drooping mustache seemed to be something of a leader, although there wasn't much sign of orders being given or any sort of direction. He just seemed to be the center of attention, and they tended to listen to what he said and laughed when he smiled and so on. Their training told them that this reaction was less fear than respect; this man was leader because they wanted him to be. What interested the onlookers the most was that he quieted down the group, they bowed their heads, and then they chanted what had to be a meal blessing of some kind even though it was next to impossible to make out. Then they began grabbing for the food and drink and the roar started up again.

At first the crowd, numbering perhaps twenty-five or thirty people, mostly but not entirely men, hadn't even noticed the strangers sitting off to one side, but they were quickly made aware of this by the women doing the cooking and serving as soon as the grace had been said. The others immediately quieted down once again, but not to the prayerful silence of the blessing and took furtive, if rather comical, note of the newcomers while pretending not to. Still, they continued eating, apparently waiting for the big man to make a move.

The big man was munching on a leg of something or other—Eve said a silent prayer that it wasn't dog—but both his big black eyes were intent on them. Finally, with much of the meat inside him and a stiff flagon of whatever they were drinking downed like a champion, he got up and slowly walked over to them as everybody else held their breath while pretending hard not to notice.

"Heyu! Name what village comin' you from? Nevah seen dressin' like you wear. Got you mo' tradin' cloth?"

They got up and faced him, trying to look non-threatening as the training guides always cautioned. Considering that the guy they faced was about the same bulk as the two of them combined, that advice seemed like a sick joke at this point.

Praying that the filter would work, John responded, "Sir, we are from *The Mountain*. We have much to bring to you if you want it."

The big, bushy eyebrows went up. "Mountain? Mountains here flat!" He laughed. "Mountain never heard of in *dis* place."

Robey gave him a returned grin. "Not there," he pointed towards the man, "or *there*," pointing forty-five degrees off, "or *there*, either," pointing in back, "or even there," pointing to the last cardinal direction. "*Our* mountain is *there*." He pointed straight up.

There was a sudden gasp from the villagers, and for the first time the pair of strangers felt fear and hostility. There were whispers of "Found! Us dey found!"

It was clear that these people had some sense of their origins and weren't, at least in some degree, as ignorant of the reality of the cosmos as they might have appeared.

"We are not raiders," John assured them. "We are not here to take anything nor harm anyone in any way. If we were, would we come like *this*? We have seen what the raiders have done in other places. They don't come to talk and make friends. They come in and simply take."

The big man looked none too trusting for that, but he approached them boldly and reached out and fingered the sleeve of Robey's garment. His hand was still greasy from the leg he'd just eaten, but he noted that the grease simply wouldn't stick to the off-white robe. With a blackened fingernail he flicked it off as if it were simply a bug on the robe and not a grease smear. "Make you dese?"

"Our people make them, yes."

"Make on your world?"

"On our spaceship. We have no home world. We are always traveling from world to world."

"You look for home, can't go?"

"No, we live on the ship. We were born there. Our task is not to have a home like your people. The ship is home. We are servants of the living God. We bring His word to whoever God may lead us, and we try and live by example the kind of life His servants should, although it is a hard way."

The village chief stifled a laugh. "Huh! Yes. Must hard be to live with *dat* 'stead of groundlings like us. No smellin' de shit dere, huh?"

"That's not the kind of hard I meant. When everything fell apart, long ago, a man of God was out here and he had a few followers and many who had been brought to God on some of the worlds out here. With their help, God did the impossible and led us to the building of a great ship that would do His will."

"How you know God and not luck? Or maybe Devil Angels?"

"Because of the work we have done, the miracles that continue for us, not the least of which is that our leader is the third man of God now to take this message out and so twice God has lifted up another man to be His Arm."

As the man spoke, the filter kept refining itself. It was as if, as they spoke, the big, rough man with the nearly indecipherable off-English tongue was learning their way of speaking. Only the fact that his lips no longer quite matched what they heard betrayed the technology in the way.

"Nice talk. So you go around in your fancy ship and you find us poor cut-off peasants trying to live from day to day and you preach and then you go back to your fancy ship feeling like you done somethin' holy and you go away."

"Not exactly," Robey replied, although the big man was a bit closer to the mark than comfort allowed. These people looked like something out of ancient history but they weren't to be underestimated. They weren't nearly as ignorant as they appeared, and even if they had been there was always the cardinal rule of all contacts: *"Never, never,* never *confuse ignorance with stupidity."*

"What then?"

"We wish to preach, or, more properly, teach, that is true. We do not believe that all need to come, or *anybody* for that matter, but we will bring God's message. If it is received, we will be joyous, and we will leave learned, ordained people with you to live and die here and nurture the faith as a farmer nurtures his crops. If it is not received, we will shake off the dust and go on, and not return again. We believe that God chose His people before the universe was formed and that only those He wishes to hear will hear. In any event, so long as we are here our resources are at your service. We will joyfully give you any knowledge, whatever technology we can, all sorts of things that perhaps can make life easier. We will repair things, including your ancient defenses that were no match for us and would be even less so for a raider or rogue military ship. In any event, you will be better off when we leave than when we arrived."

The big man thought about it. "So," he said at last with a sigh, "what makes you think God is not already here?"

"We believe he is," Robey replied. "Otherwise we wouldn't be here. We know nothing about you, your origins, your customs, or your own religious beliefs. We will gladly learn yours if you will listen to ours. We have no fears in that regard."

The big man thought a bit more. "We must go back to work now. Not much time for this talk. Priest, you come with me, we will talk while I work. The nun can stay with the village women."

Robey laughed. "I'm not a priest. I am ordained a minister, but we have no priests—or nuns."

"You're not—what is the word? No sex?"

"Celibate? No. That is not a part of our faith."

He grinned. "Then you will *definitely* come with us to the fields! And, after we eat the last meal, *then* we will take this before all the village. I may not buy what you are selling, but we may listen."

And that was fair enough, they thought. Breakthrough at last. Now they'd have a chance to hear the Doctor and see him descend in *Mount Olivet*.

That always wowed the crowd.

III:
FESTIVALS
OPEN & HIDDEN

The women were not used to any strangers, and they shied away from her. Eve knew that she was going to have to do something to break through that wall or it was going to be a pretty lonely wait.

Clearly the puzzle was in why these people were here at all. This wasn't a colony, or, at least, it wasn't initially set up as a conventional colony, nor had it collapsed from an advanced state like so many others. Eve was absolutely certain that this wasn't a bottoming out but the best life these people could manage.

Although many women were out in the fields working with the men, clearly the party left back in the village was part of the cultural division of labor they'd set up. If the sexes were equal in the fields, though, why only women and girls here?

The answer soon became obvious when she followed the women from the cleanup to a large covered area behind the barn. It was a little different than the other structures, with a thick thatched roof and sturdy stone and wooden pillars holding it up, but with only a gauze-type netting around it, possibly more salvage, which allowed air in but kept the inside enclosed and somewhat protected from flying insects and wandering animals. The dogs could probably get in, but, she noted, they were definitely trained not to.

It was a kind of nursery and day-care facility all in one, and for such a small population it was very full indeed. Although many of the new mothers had been field workers and carried at least one baby in a kind of backpack when they'd come in, clearly this treatment was meant for only the youngest, or perhaps certain children. There were many more here, watched over by very obviously pregnant young women, most of whom were far younger than Eve but somehow looked older in the face and particularly the eyes, and clearly they were not first-timers since their swollen breasts were being used for wet-nurse duty on a host of little squealing ones.

The kitchen staff became the day-care types; none of these were obviously pregnant, and some would be unthinkably young for that, and it was they who took the older children, from toddler stage onward, and played with them mostly outside, and tended to their needs. Cotton diapers held with some sort of homemade pins or special ties were for the small infants and for the sleepers and others who might be inside. The toddlers to perhaps four- or five-year-olds who made up the rest of the nursery were stark naked when playing outside, although if one or another started to go they were quickly whisked over to a pit latrine to be conditioned to do the right thing.

Still, two of the younger girls, perhaps no more than ten or eleven, had the unenviable duty of mostly standing around with a homemade broad scoop made from some sort of gourd and an equally homemade whisk broom to clean up accidents. It still stank, but so did the whole place. Eve made a mental note that some kind of odor conditioning should be included in all that training they gave them. These women were born and raised here; they were almost oblivious to the stink. It was certain that you *could* get used to it, be able to tune it out more or less, but to somebody whose experience was in breathing filtered air in a closed environment where cleanliness was next to godliness this took some getting used to.

Eve decided that if anyone was going to speak to her it would probably be one or both of those miserable girls on the kiddie poop-scooper patrol. Kids either tended to shy away from anybody they didn't know or become very open. At least these two weren't going anywhere for a while.

They looked at her when she approached but didn't say anything nor return her smile. "Hello," she said, sounding as friendly as she could. "I'm Eve. I couldn't help noticing you two drawing a less than fun job here."

One of the girls turned and shrugged. "Beats changing and cleaning diapers," she noted pragmatically. "Besides, somebody's got to do it. Otherwise the babies would be steppin' in it and all. *They* don't care."

The other girl nodded seriously. "Can't waste nothin' here. It's our duty, just like we was out in the fields. Put the part back people can't use, and it'll feed the soil and grow stuff people can."

So that wasn't a latrine over there, it was a compost heap of sorts. Feces, from the youngest baby crap to the oldest person in the village, was mixed and returned as fertilizer. Eve found the idea both practical and unappetizing. She made a mental note to eat nothing here that hadn't been thoroughly cooked.

The whole area was filled with lots of nasty looking flying things of varying sizes from gnat through butterfly, but they were neither of those nor anything in between. They served the same purpose as insects, or so it seemed, but they looked very strange and grotesque to Eve, and when they landed on skin or particularly decided to crawl up the sleeve of the robe, they caused itching.

"Do any of these things bite?" she asked nervously.

"Some of 'em, yeah. Mostly give you little pinprick sores or maybe a little rash. They can't do nothin' to people, though. Our blood kills 'em, and they only usually bite if they're protectin' themselves," the first girl told her. "In fact, I'm surprised they're swarmin' here. They usually don't like our smells. Must be somethin' you got on."

Mental note number two: forget bath oils, deodorants, etc., when landing in primitive areas. They won't do much good beyond the first ten minutes anyway, and they might attract bugs.

There was one particularly large black bug that seemed a loner but flitted around as if curious. One came suddenly close to Eve's face and she saw that it was a teardrop-shaped black creature larger than her thumb with countless legs folded up underneath it and wings that moved so fast they seemed nearly invisible but which gave off an almost mechanical hum. What was startling, though, was the head, on the broad top of the teardrop. It looked almost like a face, with two larger than proportional oval eyes with black pupils, a kind of twisted proboscis, and a wide slit of a mouth that seemed to be smiling. She swore that the thing looked right at her with the same studied intensity as she examined it, and then it opened its wide mouth to reveal some nasty, undulating growths that passed for teeth, cocked its head, and sped off.

"We call 'em hummers or sometimes humbugs," the first girl told her, noting the exchange. "They're always curious but they don't do nothin'. Nobody's even sure what half these critters eat, but some of the little ones there, the pinheads, they took to our grain, so we got natural pollinators."

"You seem very knowledgeable about farming," Eve told her.

"It's what we do," the girl replied matter of factly. "Kinda boring but it beats starvin', I guess. It's a little dry here so we grow mostly wheat and maize, with some veggies down by the creek, and we breed some animals and use 'em for different things. The extra we trade with the villages around who grow other stuff, and we get rice and cotton and stuff like that from the wetter parts of the land. It kinda all works out, I guess."

It *was* true that they seemed to have hit on a world that was just right for survival, at least on this level. There seemed no sign of sickness; she hadn't heard so much as a cough. Alien diseases were almost always too alien to pass between interstellar species, and most people had already been genetically protected in decades and centuries past before they were even allowed to go out to the stars.

Still, this was a hard life far from the complex super hospital of *The Mountain* or many of the more modern colonies, and there were cancers from the sun and from things in the environment you might never have thought of, and lots of lesser but still deadly dangers. She still hadn't seen anybody that *really* looked old, just young people who looked far beyond their years.

"Can I ask your names? You know mine but I don't know yours."

The first girl shrugged. "I'm Madi, and she's Ilee."

She nodded. This was *some* progress, anyway. "I am very interested in your life and culture here, but I guess you and your people aren't as curious about me."

"Curious got nothin' to do with it," Madi told her simply. "We don't believe in askin' questions 'bout things that're none of our business."

"We are still learning your ways," Eve responded carefully. "We don't mean to pry, even though we *are* curious. But if we don't learn about you, we won't know what is proper or improper in your eyes. We weren't raised with your ways, so we haven't any idea what the rules are. Can you understand that?"

That kind of threw them. It simply hadn't occurred to them that somebody might *have* to pry just to find out that they shouldn't pry. When you were a provincial ten-year-old faced with such a conundrum and smart enough to know it, there was only one thing you could do: shift the focus.

"Well, we didn't ask you to come," she retorted, as if this was sufficient.

"But we had to come. God guides us to where He wants us to be. We deliver his message to any who want to hear, but nobody has to come hear it. The word is our seed. If it takes and grows, either in a people or even a few individuals, then we rejoice. If it doesn't, but falls on poor soil and dies out, we know that they heard the word and rejected it, and we feel sad, shake the dust from our feet, and go, never to return."

"My daddy said he heard a preacher or priest or whatever once," Ilee noted. "He says the guy never stopped trying to get everybody in the whole universe to believe the same stuff and that he was a real pain and a pest. Your god don't do that?"

Eve smiled. This was something of a breakthrough, even with a ten-year-old. "No. We think God wants some people to hear and others not, but that it's a choice. Many, maybe most people have heard the message over thousands of years and either didn't accept it or didn't really follow what it meant. We are looking for the few who can."

"But you was born to believe that stuff," Ilee pointed out. "You don't know if it wouldn't be just crazy stuff if you was us and we was you, right? *You* never had to choose."

It was a challenge that she was well aware of. "Well, everyone has doubts from time to time if they're right. But if we're right, things have a way of showing it. Many of our people have had real problems after they've seen some of the worst things people can do to each other. We've come on worlds where raiders have pillaged and destroyed and left only horror behind. Thousands, maybe tens of thousands, dead. There are some natural disasters, too. It's real hard to keep faith alive when you see the torn bodies of dead babies." She wondered if, considering the setting and the ages of the two girls, she was being too graphic.

"You seen that?"

"I've seen the pictures of that, and heard of it from the people who are older than me but who went to those places like I'm here now. Some could not go on and left us and settled on other colonies because they could not maintain their faith. We're all challenged by something sooner or later that makes us doubt. That's because there's evil in the universe, and even in each of us, as well as good. Most folks don't really believe in evil; they believe that bad things happen by accident or because people go bad from things in their own growing up and the like. But there *is* evil. Real evil."

Ilee frowned. "So what kinda god lets babies be killed?" she asked skeptically. "What kinda god lets evil go on? I'm not sure I *like* your god."

"Me, neither," Madi added.

"We think we're being tested," Eve told them. "There are big rewards if you pass, but the test is very, very hard and most folks flunk. But it's got to be real tough or it isn't a good test. Going back to farming, let's say God planted all of us, but He only wants to pick the very, very best. If He doesn't let evil go and keep testing us, then how will He ever know? We wouldn't be choosing, we'd be like toys who had to do whatever their owner told them."

The two girls looked out at the field, where some toddlers were giggling as they tried kicking away a crude ball covered in a tough, leathery skin that was almost as big as they were. "Yeah, but *babies . . . ,*" Ilee muttered, thinking of it.

Eve was afraid she'd used the wrong analogy in her conversation, but what could she do? She had to take whatever wedge this closed-mouthed society gave her. She wondered, though, if maybe she should have tried it with some of the older women. After all, these girls were younger than the age most people began any religious instruction on *The Mountain* beyond the very simple ideas of good and bad. Dead babies related to their experience, but it was hard to explain to a ten-year-old why God might allow it.

The more she thought about it, the more depressed she got, too. For all the facile responses and quick retorts on the question of a moral universe, she wondered if she could explain *that* to anybody.

It was tough to explain what you don't understand yourself.

The big man's name was Gregnar, it turned out. He might well have had a last name, but family names were not used, or so it seemed. At least, every single person Robey asked for a family name responded "Smith" with something of a grin. The idea that he was being put on didn't bother him nearly as much as the lurking fear that maybe they really *were* all named Smith.

As he watched them work in the fields, interacting with one another, joking, occasionally cursing, and particularly after he pitched in on some heavy lifting, he began to form a theory about these people and this world.

For one thing, it was amazing what you could learn from a culture's curse words. Not just their origins, but references to God or gods or other such entities, pleas, attitudes, you name it. This group had the full panoply of great cussing; while he heard nothing new, he thought that, in one afternoon, he'd managed to hear every variation he'd ever encountered before. While the Doctor would be disappointed—he was a collector of new ways people could cuss—Robey hoped that the monitor team up above had tender ears. This was an earthy group, to say the least. Still, there were some unique exclamations, like "By the twin Rocks of Eban!" and the like that might prove useful. He hoped the computer aboard ship could find a match for one of them, if they weren't just newer local ones.

Putting the cursing together with the attitudes towards outsiders and the reaction that was so dramatic at lunch—*"Found!"*—these people had to be fugitives, or, rather, the descendants of fugitives. That was why this place was off the old commercial charts and had no other references. The genhole gate, of course, was charted, but it was one of tens of thousands and there wasn't any indication that it wasn't just the latest in an exploratory chain that had not yet been developed.

They had certainly come from more than one world and one culture. The curses and the variety in names coupled with the apparent universal use of a form of English showed that they'd had wide exposure to different cultures and attitudes and that they'd had to settle on a language that was probably not native to any of their ancestors but was practical to know simply because it eliminated that divide when setting up a new colony.

What had they been running from that had thrown them together like this? And what were they still scared of?

The dark skins and generally similar features didn't really mean much; there would be a lot of intermarriage in just the early stages and there was no way to check every village and make sure that there weren't more dramatic differences. Still, it looked like there was one dominant group and it pretty well was absorbing the others.

All of this was deduction; even though they quickly got used to him and even joked about his "getting dirty with the peasants," they volunteered just about nothing. Whatever their immediate ancestors had run from, it was something they didn't want to bring up.

He wasn't in the same physical condition they were, but they seemed impressed that he could hold his own. Preachers weren't supposed to have muscles or work with their hands; the fact that a lot of it was good physical conditioning via daily workouts aboard ship and the lesser gravity of this world he'd still not learned the name of, he decided not to explain.

He walked back with them just before sunset. They were a tired group, but they had done a fair day's work and they were ready to eat and relax. And *now* Gregnar was willing to talk to him about what came next.

"So you want to preach to us, is that it?"

Robey shook his head. "No, not me. Our leader is a great teacher and scholar and he's the one we want you to hear. You and as many others from villages in the region as can be reached. If we plant well, then some like me will remain to teach and train. If not, well, you will not see us again. It is our way."

"But you will spread the news that we exist," the big man pointed out.

Robey wasn't sure if he was being threatened or merely sounded out. "No, we don't work that way. In fact, we're right now repairing and upgrading the defense system from the old days that should have been a real challenge for us but wasn't. Anybody else who comes here will have a *much* harder time. We can't guarantee security—who can but God?—but we can make it as good as we can."

Gregnar seemed interested, and as he invited both John and Eve to eat with them, he became more open and friendly. It didn't take a genius to notice, though, that this openness was strictly one way.

"You have no home but your ship? You have no world that sends you?"

"No. A great many of the faithful built and modified our ship on several different worlds where spaceships could still be built or fixed. It was a freighter, but after the Great Silence broke things down, it was used as the basis for building our community. 'Home' to us is Heaven, when we will be reborn in new bodies in the presence of God. Until then, we bring His truths to those who will hear."

"So how will you do this here?"

"We have many people in the villages around here by this point, so we'll pick a place that everyone can get to and we'll put down and set up. Then we'll move, until we've managed to teach everyone."

"Sounds like it will take you years here."

"If we had to do it by walking and riding distance, probably, but we have ways to show everything to villages over a wide area if they are too far to get to us and back in time. We have been at this a long time. We will not disturb things for long that do not wish to be disturbed."

"So where and when will your great leader put down first?"

"Not far from here," Robey told him. "That is, unless there is an objection from you or others as to where. We had planned on doing it perhaps on the hard flat rocky region about nine kilometers south of here. It is a good location for getting people from many villages in and back, and it will support our ship."

That seemed to really interest him. "Your ship will land near here?"

"Our interplanetary module will, yes. The starship part was never designed to land and will not."

"Inter—?"

"Interplanetary. A part of our larger ship that's a ship in and of itself. It is designed to land on planets and can go between them if need be, but it can not go between stars. It docks with the starship most of the time, and undocks to bring our platform so that people may come. It is impressive to see land, in fact."

"I would like to see that, yes. I don't think there will be any problems on the flats. Just don't come down on or near crops or rivers and creeks or flooded areas. We will need those."

"Don't worry," Robey assured him. "We know what we're doing."

Eve, later, wasn't so sure. As the group cleaned up from dinner and finished off tankard-sized gourds full of dark, heavy beer brewed by the village itself in preparation for going to sleep, she got her companion to one side and switched off filtration. This wouldn't keep a local from overhearing, but it would make it about as hard for them to understand the talk as they'd had initially understanding the villagers.

"So, it's all set," he said, sounding smug and satisfied.

"Yes, but I don't like it. I watched the women today, and I watched that man you were so chummy with and his companions. They're up to something."

"Don't be ridiculous! They're closed-mouthed, yes, but I think that's because they're the grandchildren or great-grandchildren of a convict ship or rebel captives or something of that nature. They're still basically hard-working subsistence farmers."

"That may be, but they're not ignorant. Whatever they've been taught, it's pretty complete considering I saw no schools. They know astronomy, they don't have many superstitions about places or things in space, and they seem pretty knowledgeable about the way things are considering there's no evident reason why they should. Something about this smells."

He shrugged, obviously not bothered as she was. "Well, don't worry about it. It's not our call, anyway. It's the Doctor's to decide, and he's got the staff to really make things go or not go."

"Still, do you mind if I put my reservations on the record?"

Again he shrugged. "Suit yourself. I just don't see it."

She nodded grimly. "Yeah, nobody ever sees the one that gets them, and we're the ones here on the ground."

The Doctor did not explain his reasons for making decisions. He was an often friendly and sometimes gentle man, but he was a total autocrat. He alone, he believed, was answerable to God; his people were answerable to him as God's messenger.

And the Doctor decided to come down.

It was an impressive sight to the crowds who watched the ship descend, and there were *always* crowds since it never could or did sneak onto a planet. These people were poor and hard working but they were not in want; nobody seemed to be hungry, and it was not necessary to have everybody in the fields all the time. Once they saw the descent, or heard of it beforehand, they tended to start moving to where they could at least get a good view of the thing coming down from the stars.

The unconventional and expensive magnetic field drive on the *Mount Olivet* was notable for its near silence; save for a sonic boom or two, there was no sound at all as an object larger than some small farming villages descended, rock stable, over the landing site and then, slowing to a dramatic crawl, it blotted out the sky as it descended finally to the site itself, extending hydraulic cushioning rods like some bizarre robotic centipede just before it landed. With these "legs," more than a hundred of them, and a constant monitoring of level by the ship's computer, *Mount Olivet* was as stable as a real mountain.

Almost immediately the transformation began from ship to meeting site. A thin tentlike covering wrapped around the legs, producing an internal enclosure that was nonetheless open to the ground and nature as required, and then, off a series of moving stairs and belts, men and women in white work clothes supervised a robotic crew of roustabouts in setting up the entire experience. Onlookers could hear great things going on, and see shapes and lights moving all over inside the "tent," but as showmanship demanded they were not permitted yet to see what lay within. To find out all the details there, they'd have to go to one or more of the meetings that would be held so long as the Doctor and, if he and his people could be believed, God told him to be there. It was free, no cost, no obligation, but you had to physically attend either at the landing site or, if too far away, go to one of the great tents that was even then being erected, along with transmission equipment.

The smaller scout ships flitted back and forth between the big ship and the remote locations, ferrying personnel, robot workmen (since it had been determined that these people would not take up pitchforks and torches and try to slay mechanical monsters), and supplies from Bibles to more secular pleasures like large containers of what would be revealed to be something these people could *not* properly make—ice cream.

They had a wide range of basic religious beliefs but the majority in the area seemed to have a vision more Roman Catholic or Anglican in nature, even if crudely formed and modified in the telling without clergy or Bibles. Still, most of them would know what the Doctor was talking about when he spoke, and that was a lot easier than some of their audiences.

There *was* the building sense of occasion about the region, though, which was also what they hoped for. It was a break from the dull, drab routine of life, something different, and while they didn't neglect their duties, the villagers in John and Eve's assigned village as well as other villages in the area tended to start looking forward to the show and adjusting major operations so that, for at least the period when the Doctor was there, they would be able to go see him.

The Doctor's people tried to reinforce this with gifts of treats and trinkets and offers to arrange for larger groups to travel together. They also began distributing basic Bibles in book form, and were somewhat startled at the apparently high literacy rate. They had some problems with the stilted and poetic style of the Bibles, but most of the villagers over ten or twelve could manage to read them, remarkable in a society that appeared on the surface to write nothing down, and whose ancestors had certainly come from a culture where computers could answer everything and even tell or dramatize and thus where literacy was almost certainly rare.

More mystery. There was no sign of paper production

or paper of any sort, so what did they write on and with? And where?

This bothered Eve and several of the newer Arms of Gideon who'd come down for the final prep, but in most cases there was just too much to do to solve minor mysteries that were considered, at best, intellectual curiosities and not things that were important compared to their real mission.

Eve, however, felt that any population that hid much of itself from strangers, even to that degree, was not a group you should turn your back on or take for granted. Not that she was worried that the whole operation was in danger; she had faith both in their ultimate appointment by God and also in her knowledge that they were well equipped to take on the worst technology could offer. Rather, she was worried that whoever was behind these people did not realize that, and that some, perhaps some of her own people, would be harmed or worse if this blew up.

Conferring with the Command Center and also with other Arms of Gideon, however, she found them receptive to her reports if not enthusiastic believers of her suspicions, and they took it in stride. They were pros by this point.

Still, with virtually everyone from *The Mountain* caught up in the excitement of a new set of what the Doctor called "Classes," the only attention being paid to the locals was to insure that they could get to the pavilion, or see it on giant screens, and get fed and have sufficient facilities including vast pit toilets, and all the rest of the mechanics of it.

Eve, brushed off by Festival Security, and with nothing specific to do in the setup, decided instead to keep her eye on Gregnar and some of his buddies.

The first thing to do was to solve the mystery of her count. More than once she'd counted everybody in the village, from the squealing babies in the nursery and on mothers' backs to the field hands and animal handlers, and the number had always come up around a hundred and twenty, give or take a couple. And yet, during the days, there would be times when she'd take the count and there would be up to a dozen people missing. Even allowing for not seeing a few in the fields, it seemed an excessive number to be gone, and the number always seemed to be men. Certain specific men, in fact, including, now and again, Gregnar himself, or two of his best buddies, Alon and Krag, who were pretty much cut from the same cloth both physically and mentally.

Eve could hardly be inconspicuous, but she was beginning to know the area well enough to know where in the fields she could place herself and be likely to see without being seen and to hear without being overheard. The trio of men's pattern varied very little, with all three going out to the most active spot where planting, harvesting, or irrigation was taking place on an intensive scale; then one of them, usually Gregnar, would remain while the other two would begin walking the circle in opposite directions. One time it would be Alon going left and Krag right, the next time the reverse, and every once in a while Gregnar would replace one or the other of them. She followed one once completely around the village, realizing that at some point he probably did notice she was there but not really caring, and it seemed like a routine patrol. The man would examine the areas, looking apparently for breaches in the irrigation canals, checking winches, even checking crops and soil, and then keep going. It took one about an hour to get halfway, or opposite the main day's workplace, and there he generally waited until his compatriot coming the other way would reach the same spot. They'd stand or sit, talk for a bit, then head off again in opposite directions, this time apparently checking on anything the other reported. In another hour, more or less, they'd be back at the main work site and from that point they would both confer with Gregnar, then pitch in as needed until the lunch call.

In the afternoon, they'd do it again.

There had seemed little reason to keep tracking them, except that twice—once just the day *Mount Olivet* landed, the next the day before the start of the Festival and the classes—the two men didn't return in an hour, or even an hour and a half. And yet two, maybe two and a half hours later, each would wander in from the opposite direction as if nothing at all were out of the ordinary.

Where had they gone?

Not into the village. By now there were Arms of Gideon about and they, too, had enough sense of routine that they would have noticed something out of the ordinary, like two of the men coming in when they normally did not.

It had been Alon and Krag this morning breaking their routine; she decided that, if Gregnar decided to replace one of them in the afternoon rounds, she would follow.

She also reported this to Security, who essentially brushed her off. "You're seeing demons in the bushes," the Officer of the Day, a particularly arrogant bastard named Cordish, told her. "Still, if it'll make you happy, go ahead and follow. If you find any trap doors into the Fifth Dimension, let us know."

"Maybe if you'd do a little field work instead of relying on your computers and scans you might actually find out a few things," she retorted. "But you should inform the Doctor that something is not right here and let him evaluate the evidence." That was standard operating procedure and standing orders.

"Do not tell me my job," Cordish snapped. "The Doctor has much to do today preparing for tonight. He doesn't need paranoid fantasies interrupting his mission. If you find something, *then* come back."

If I do find something, and you haven't tipped the Doctor, then you're in for a trip to Hell without leaving the body, she thought, but knew there was no purpose to pressing things. She'd managed to get the message across properly and, not incidentally, to have it both on a security recording and on her own backup just in case things went bad and Cordish decided to shift the blame.

She sought out John Robey, who, like her, had been reduced by the frenzy of activity and organization to mostly helping out, and quickly told him what she'd found.

Robey was skeptical that it meant anything, but willing to take a look. "Probably sneaking off to a still or something," he told her. "But, just in case, I think you're right to be overcautious. We can handle more than *these* people can hand out, but it won't stop some of ours being hurt if we have to. We just don't know enough."

When they reached the work area just after lunch, Robey was a little more interested. "They're certainly up to something, those lugs," he told her. "You could see them whispering this way and that at lunch, and I noticed they didn't drink nearly as much as usual." He reached into a pocket and pulled out a small controller with a set of tiny switches. Activating it, he threw a single small switch, then pointed the device at a spot in the cornfield. His robe, so snowy white, began to darken, then take on the coloration of the field. It was not a uniform color, but rather a very good one with mottled patterns designed to make it very difficult to see him. He then handed the device to Eve, who activated it with her thumbprint and then did the same.

"Wish I'd had one of these when I tracked them before," she muttered.

"We're lucky to have this one. Not exactly standard issue."

"Where'd you get it?"

"It was volunteered by one of the Security staff guarding the goodies out at the ship," he told her.

"Volunteered?"

"Don't ask. Just remember that God helps those who help themselves."

She handed it back to him. "Don't lose that. If we have to explain this color later on, we'll be in more trouble than if this is some alien trap."

Now they only had to wait.

It was a bit past fourteen hundred on their watches when the three local men, who'd been working different areas, knocked off and walked over to confer. Robey pointed his communicator at them and frowned. "That's odd. Interference."

She almost jumped. *"What?* How is that possible?"

"It's not, unless it's either us or something else on our level. You may well have something here."

"Want to contact Security?" She hated the idea of going through them, but this was at least evidence of a kind that Cordish might accept as suspicious.

"Tried. It's there, too."

"I don't understand. If it's all over, why isn't this place suddenly crawling with our people, scans, you name it?"

"I doubt if it's universal. I think it's very low level and probably so limited it might not even get picked up by the ship. That implies that one of those three has something that they can turn on or off."

It was gone as quickly as it appeared, but now the three had stopped their conversation. Gregnar shouted to one of the other farmers that he was going to do a go-round, as he called it, and that Krag would remain.

Robey looked at Eve. "I'll take Gregnar, you take Alon. Check in every few minutes and let me know if anything happens the moment it does. Got that?"

She nodded. "You want to call *Sinai* and get us both traced?"

"Not a bad idea, if they'll go for it. I'll handle that. Better be off, and this time don't be seen! Stay well back. He's off, and so's my man!"

She slipped through the corn, trying to be quiet, and came to a wide area between rows just near the edge of the planting. The corn was high enough to mask her, and there was a stiff enough breeze that she hoped she wouldn't be easily heard. The trick would be to keep Alon in sight while satisfying him that nobody was there.

For several minutes, it was easier than usual. Once out of sight of the other villagers, Alon quickened his pace, more concerned with getting somewhere fast than with looking for any shadows. Still, at least twice he suddenly stopped and whirled around, as if to catch anyone who might be following, and on the second of these he took a good two minutes staring right into the corn rows. She froze, and even held her breath for a while although she was certainly too far behind him for that to be a factor. Had she been in her usual white he would definitely have seen her, just one row in, but if he saw her now he certainly didn't show it.

Quickening his pace, he reached a main irrigation canal, now almost dry because it wasn't being used, and, without much hesitation, he jumped down into it and began walking out from the corn and towards fields planted only with a cloverlike crop used to refresh the soil and prevent erosion.

That made it tough, since it meant she'd have to come out of her hiding place in order to keep following him. Nonetheless, this was nonstandard enough behavior that it was worth following up—and reporting.

"Brother John?" she whispered.

"Go, Sister."

"Alon is in the clear, walking away in a canal."

"Looks like my boy's not where he wants to be yet. Stay well back, be careful, but see where he's going."

By now, Alon was almost a speck on the horizon, only his bobbing head visible. She decided to step out, first looking at the canal and then reporting, "No problem. It's wet at the bottom but mostly mud. His tracks are pretty obvious. I'm going to go at a slow pace here. It can't be all that far—where he's going, I mean. They never are more than an hour and a half late."

"Well, my boy's just turned and gone into a pretty tall wheat field here. This isn't gonna be easy."

"Be careful!"

"Yeah, you, too. If this *isn't* a still they're going for, then there's gonna be one *hell* of a security stink."

And maybe the answer to this puzzle, she added

to herself. Nothing was going to keep her from finding her man, not now.

"Uh oh!"

"What?" she asked, nervous.

"He's doubling back! He's short-cutting directly for you!"

IV:
OPPOSITION
FROM THE UNDERWORLD

Eve still hadn't been able to determine just where Alon had vanished, or how, but she was suddenly conscious that she was on a flat area far from any sort of real cover with someone rushing towards her who would not be happy to see her there. The pale yellow camouflage on her robe was fine if she were in the wheat fields or even hidden by the maize, but it kind of stood out on the broad, hard dirt and rock surface. The only practical cover were some low bushes along the irrigation canal, but they weren't much help since if Gregnar followed Alon's lead he'd run right down through the ditch and would again be certain to see her. Hoping that the big man wouldn't expect anybody to be here and, if he suspected he was being observed, he would think only of being followed, she ran as fast as she could as far away from the canal as possible, and, when she felt time had run out, she simply flattened herself on the ground facing the canal.

It was just in time. Gregnar burst from the cornfield about twenty meters from where she lay flat, but she saw immediately that she needn't have worried. The big man was in a real hurry and didn't even look around, instead jumping right into the irrigation ditch and running along it, his head comically bobbing up and down as he trotted grimly forward until, at probably the same point that Alon had vanished, there was a crackling sound and then no more bouncing head.

John emerged from almost the same spot Gregnar had in the cornfield and stared. From his angle he'd been able to see the big man run straight along the ditch, and apparently vanish.

Eve got up, quickly brushed the dust off, and made straight for her companion. "You thought I was kidding," she commented.

Actually, he'd thought that the rookie out for her first real assignment had simply overreacted, but this—this was something very different.

"Security," he called, mentally opening the comm link.

"OD here. Yes?" It was that damned fool Cordish again.

"Robey here. We have two local men now who have been followed as they went well away from others. I just witnessed one of them go along a canal and suddenly vanish from sight."

"You probably just couldn't see him anymore because of the angle," Cordish snapped. "Don't bother me with this! The Boss is out and roaming around right now and he's brought his bicycle. Worse, he's mumbling about borrowing and riding a crindin. Just what we need. Now, if there's nothing else—"

"I don't mean I lost sight of him," Robey responded. "I mean to report that he went through some sort of force field barrier or gate and dematerialized as far as we could see. Toloway had reported another man doing the same earlier."

"Don't be ridiculous! These people have nowhere near that sort of technology, and, besides, if they did it would have registered here."

Robey had just had about enough of the arrogant bastard. "I am recording this for later inquiry," he told Cordish icily. "I have now reported an anomaly and potential threat to us, the ship, and most particularly to the Doc and our mission. If you choose not to act on it, it is *entirely* on your head and on your responsibility alone. Is that understood, *Brother* Cordish?"

It was a risky thing to do, but Robey felt that his first responsibility was to the whole, not to his superiors. He knew that Cordish's standing orders were to notify the Doc immediately of *any* problems, particularly of a security nature, and to also act to contain the problem until a decision could come down from on high. Cordish now understood that his neck was the one in the noose; if this developed into anything nasty then the Gates of Hell would be preferable to the Doc's wrath. On the other hand, if it was trivial, Robey had just made an enemy who would never forget.

Robey was understandably nervous at the latter possibility, but he resented even more that he'd had to go to this length just to get the incompetent son of a bitch to do his job. If Cordish didn't like taking risks and making decisions, he should never have accepted the job.

"Very well," Cordish sighed at last, sounding none too pleased. "I'm sending a small tech crew with scanners over to your location. Keep out of sight of the locals until they arrive, and if any of the ones you've been following show up, let them leave, hopefully without being aware of you, and remain where you are. We'll get to the bottom of this."

"Yeah, right. Will do," Robey responded. He prayed to himself that this really *would* be nothing, but there was no way in the world that any kind of high-tech system like he'd witnessed should be here, particularly in the hands of these people, and most particularly without being detected.

Neither of the native men reappeared by the time the tech crew showed up, each riding a well-worn but serviceable mag scooter. As with Cordish, they couldn't believe that this could be anything important and they already had their hands full with routine stuff, but, like Robey, they knew they had to be sure.

The team was a senior technician named Corby and two assistants, Erin and Ruth. Corby was a tall, gangly skeleton of a man, with one of those long faces with a permanently dour, hang-dog expression. He had the biggest hands and longest fingers Eve ever remembered seeing on a human being, but those fingers were so dextrous that they could do things only micromachines were thought to accomplish.

"Girls, I want both monitor cover and security cover on both sides. Ruth, you over there; Erin, you on this side a few meters back of Ruth's position. Got it?"

They both nodded and picked up small hand-held devices from the scooter's saddlebags. Corby had a longer device with a complex readout screen in the base and a whole set of lights above. From the base, extending a good half a meter, was a long, smooth gun-metal-gray rod with a pale yellow tip.

Eve looked at the team and was impressed with how professionally they went into action. These people knew their business.

"Is there anything you know of this kind that wouldn't show up on our sensors?" she asked Corby.

"Oh, hundreds of things. Most likely, though, would be a security barrier. Wouldn't be much of a security system if it showed up on scans and pointed burglars right to it, would it? Might be a pain if the thing's on full with total body DNA recognition, so I'm prayin' it's off when somebody's inside. That's the norm."

"If it's on, could you still get in?" John asked him.

"Oh, sure," Corby responded casually, still tweaking his probe, "but might take a while if it's in good order and we ain't got a while." He twisted the probe and had some problems getting it to rotate to just where he wanted it. "*Ungh!* Either I'm gettin' old or this thing is. Okay now, though. You two stay back here on either side and provide backup."

"Backup?" Robey repeated. "You mean . . . ?"

"I mean backup. If they got a security vault this sophisticated then there's no tellin' what they keep in it, is there? God's welcome to call me home any time, but the devil, now, he gets a fight."

And, with that, he stepped down into the irrigation canal and began walking steadily along it, his frame tall enough that even somebody viewing him walking in at a right angle could see his shoulders.

He held the probe in both hands to steady it and walked slowly but deliberately forward, looking mostly straight ahead but glancing down from time to time to check that the footprints of his predecessors were still clearly visible in the soft mud.

The display lights kept dancing around, apparently guiding him or telling him something in a specialist's code, and the readout screen fed him more data, but he never stopped or wavered.

He walked straight into the barrier and it almost knocked him down. The probe, of course, touched it first, but it also acted as a conductor of some sort allowing energy to flow back to the handle base and then to the holder of same. The shock wasn't serious, but it was unexpected because he'd gotten no readout at all that anything was coming up.

"Brother, are you hurt?" Ruth called.

"Only my dignity, and maybe the seat of my pants," Corby grumbled, getting back to his feet. "Well, so much for the unlocked door theory. Here—somebody give me a hand up! We're going to see how far this thing goes."

Robey was the largest of the waiting agents and ran along the bank, past Erin, and gave the big, gaunt man the lift he needed to be pulled from the fairly deep ditch.

He *was* now filthy, covered with mud, but he looked more angry than embarrassed. "You women! Come on up here! Young man, you go on further on this side with Erin, and, young woman, you go along the other side with Ruth. Keep even on either side of the ditch. I'm going to make some adjustments. If anybody comes out of there, just freeze. They may not even know we're here or look back. If they do, then do whatever you must."

"That's the best instructions I've had in a long while," Robey commented. "'Do whatever you must.' I like that."

Corby paid no attention, adjusting his probe and then making a number of passes over the spot where he'd been shocked, only from the upper bank. "Got'cha!" he muttered to himself, smiling grimly. "Won't shock me again like that. Huh!"

"What is it?" Robey asked him.

"It's only three meters deep and it stops about twenty-point-three centimeters *above* the canal. Damned clever. When they need to irrigate it just runs right underneath. And that's their first line of defense, too. Got idiots like me standing in the wet grounding ourselves when we run into it."

Erin wasn't impressed. "You mean they're both squeezed into something about the size of a private bathroom? Sounds more kinky than threatening."

"No, I doubt if that's the case. The odds are it turns and goes into the bank and under. Second line of defense. A bit of a maze." Corby sighed. "Let's see if I'm lucky enough to at least be on the side that matters."

He began slowly passing the probe over the dry, hard-packed dirt and smooth rock in a broad sweep. "Nope. Not my day," he sighed, and looked over at the opposite bank. "I have no particular desire to jump back down into that muck or go back and walk around," he told them. "Ruth! Catch and do a sweep!"

With that, he threw the probe across to his assistant who caught it rather nimbly. Within a few minutes, Ruth was doing much the same as he but over on her side, and coming up with the same results.

"Sorry, Brother Corby, but there's nothing registering here, either!"

"Got to be!" he snapped, not so much at her as at the problem itself.

"You mean they really *are* in a three-meter-square box we can't see?" John asked him.

Corby brushed off the comment, too busy working the problem. The large hands waved in the air as he mentally worked out various theories. Finally, he called, "Ruth! Throw the thing back here! Got a theory to test before they pop back out!" She started to just throw it, but he yelled, "No! Wait! Not across the damned thing! Back here!"

He walked a few meters beyond where he'd worked out the "vault" or entrance or whatever to be, and then she threw him the probe and he caught it. Now the display started to flash as if defective, and they understood that Corby and his computerized probe were very much mentally intertwined at that moment. Finally, he nodded. "Got to be. Okay, people, let's see if we can crack this safe!"

He sent Erin back to bring him some more devices from the saddlebags and, incidentally, to hide the scooters in the corn. She then brought back a number of small cubes, no more than eight centimeters square, which he proceeded to put all around the invisible vault. Then he drew them even farther back, and close to the rim of the ditch on either side.

"Now what?" John asked.

"Now we wait, damn their eyes! I got other things to do!"

Eve, on the other side, just shook her head. "I never believed anything was truly invisible or could be. How is this possible?"

"It's not invisible, not in that sense," Ruth told her. "It's just projecting a false and very convincing picture of what you'd expect to see there. If you saw a visible vault there but found that you could pass your hand through it, you wouldn't think that odd, would you?"

"Of course not. A hologram."

"Exactly. Well, same principle, only it's not the *vault* that's the hologram, it's the area around it. Nonreflective, probably gives the signature of whatever we're seeing to any probes. The only time it might be detected would be when it opens, but that's for a very brief time and the energy involved would be so slight that you'd have to know where to look to detect it."

"But—where *are* the two men? Certainly not inside *there*."

"We'll find out when we get in," she said matter-of-factly. "Providing, of course, we don't blow it."

Eve was fascinated at the very idea of a vault. They didn't have such things in her area of *The Mountain*, nor would anyone need them. You'd have to have something of your own worth stealing. Only Doc and the security staff and the Ordained would have anything like that, and it wouldn't be something of this sort.

But how did these people get such a thing? And what did they own that had to be protected?

"The people farming here—they would have to know that this was here, wouldn't they?" Robey asked Corby.

The tall man nodded. "Sure. That's one reason why this is barren here. But they built it where they did so that it wouldn't accidentally be in the way of harvest wagons, big animals, that sort of thing. It isn't that unusual for even some of these lost and reverted folk to have remnants of the technology they brought here, or even to keep it hidden from us. The question is, what are they hiding and why do they think it's so important that they'd risk us finding it? If you're going to pretend to be a primitive, be one. Don't keep sneaking off and checking to see if the crown jewels are still there. It's like being so fearful of a pickpocket in a group that your hand keeps going to the pocket where you carry your valuables, thereby pointing out just where they are to every thief in creation. They aren't just hiding something from us here. Who cares if they do? No, they're up to something, and I'm afraid it's the devil's work."

There was some noise from the front of the invisible vault or entrance and on both sides the professionals hissed, "Down and quiet! They might not even see us! Let them get well clear!"

They barely had time to do this before there was a crackling and first Gregnar, then Alon appeared, walking back up the irrigation ditch. If either was concerned that they left the door unlocked they didn't show it, but each of them was carrying a heavy looking case full of what nobody else yet knew. Still, they didn't even give a glance backward, and might not have seen all that company anyway. Robey in particular noted with admiration that Corby's professional eye had placed them where the same illusion that masked the vault helped mask them from anyone exiting into the cornfield.

There was a danger if either went along the path and looked back, but that didn't seem to be a problem. When they reached the field, they said something to one another but neither gave more than a furtive glance around and then both men walked off in opposite directions, each carrying their new load.

"Give them a few minutes," Corby said quietly. "If they're any good at all and spotted us, they'll double back. I want to make sure they're well away."

It was a nervous five minutes, but then Corby decided that either the coast was clear or it no longer mattered. Getting up, he took his probe and pointed it at the unseen chamber, this time picking up whatever those small cubes had recorded.

"Got 'em! Not a problem, like I said," Corby exclaimed with satisfaction. "Fairly simple locking mechanism at that. We'll have no trouble playing it back. Robey, Toloway, come with me. Ruth, Erin, you cover for us. Anybody shows up, you know what to do."

Both women reached into the folds of their robes and showed impulse rifles. "Yes, Brother. We know what to do."

"Then let's find out what they're up to, shall we?" With that, he walked forward of the mysterious vault area and jumped back down into the muddy ditch. Steeling himself, Robey followed and managed not to fall on his face in the mud; Corby more gently lifted Eve down.

Corby then waved his probe to cover the whole area, invisible or not, and nodded to himself. "Step up, children, and watch that first step," he warned, then stepped back a couple of steps, almost knocking Robey over, and jumped forward and up. There was a crackling sound and he vanished.

The other two just stood there a moment, uncertain. Then Corby stuck his head out so that it floated ghostly in what seemed to be midair and called, "Well, come on! Or I'm going in without you!"

Eve shrugged, went to the edge, as it were, and allowed two long, large, ghostly hands to pull her in. Robey shrugged and, with a single hand up, managed to get into what turned out to be a spartan cube okay, although he bumped his knee and knew he'd have a bruise there if nothing else.

It was a *very* plain box, as it were, with no obvious way in or out. Dimly but adequately lit by a kind of phosphorescent glow emanating from the walls and ceiling, it felt more like a cargo container than anything else.

"*This* is what it's all about?" Eve managed, disappointed to say the least. "What were those two *doing* in here all that time?"

Corby gave a slight smile to both of them. "You haven't figured it out yet? Well, I'll show you, then." He walked over to the back wall and they now saw that there was a touch switch embedded in it about one meter from the floor. Corby touched it, and there was the sound of something engaging front and back, a kind of solid *chunk! chunk!* Then the cube began to vibrate.

"It's a lift!" Eve exclaimed, amazed. "But it's above the canal! How can we go down?"

"Well, at a guess, I'd say those two sounds were blockers coming down on both sides so that if there was any water in the ditch it would be restrained on both sides," Corby responded. "Once they're in place, it is likely that the base goes down and then swings away to allow access to the shaft. The reverse will happen when it goes back up. Some mud will fall into the bottom of the shaft, but I suspect there's a cleaner or drainage mechanism down there to keep it from building up too high. Ah! Not too deep! We appear to be here!"

There was a shudder and then a total absence of vibration, and now the forward entrance winked out, revealing a damp, rocky chamber lit much like the car. Corby walked out into it, and the other two followed.

It appeared to have been developed out of a

natural cavern left by eroding underground drainage over eons of time. The shaft and entryway were artificial, but the cavern itself was quite natural, much like those found in limestone and similar sedimentary rock regions on world after world. Lighting appeared to be permanent and chemical; there didn't seem to be any controls or power source, but half globes had been attached to the cave walls every few meters allowing for adequate vision.

"It would be interesting to see just what the other branches hold," Corby commented, "but this is certainly sufficient. I can see where the most recent traffic has gone—muddy traces—and they go into *that* branch there. Let us see."

Robey looked around at the eerie but impressive installation. "Now, who built this? And why? Certainly this is beyond these people!"

"Probably, but it isn't beyond their ancestors, the ones who came here and put up that temporary capital and landing area we first went to," Eve pointed out. "They were here with a lot of technological support for a number of years before things began to fail."

"Good deduction. I am impressed," Corby commented. "This, and perhaps others over the inhabited parts of the continent, was certainly done at that time, and, I would suspect, they wound up abandoning the tech center because they needed to grow food and they couldn't repair or adequately maintain their high-tech base. They knew what they were doing, though. Development here was probably very quick. Somebody brought the original settlers here and left, since there's no sign of a ship or wreckage. They then had to move fast with what they had just to survive. These are, perhaps, stores of things from the old days

that may be useful in an emergency, or it might—
oh, my!"

He stopped suddenly as they came into a larger
chamber, and they followed and then did the same,
astonished at what they saw.

"Weapons," Robey muttered. "Every kind imagin-
able."

Stacked in cases, and displayed on a wall that keyed
the crate numbers to the displays, were very high-
tech weapons indeed. No planet killers, but every kind
of hand weapon from guided projectile to disruptors,
small cannon, small and medium laser and phaser
weapons, even surface-to-air smart missiles.

"You could fight one heck of a war with this stuff,"
Robey noted, looking at display after display. "I don't
recognize a lot of them, but it's pretty clear what they
do. Some are high military stuff, I'd say."

Eve was looking at some of the crates. "Yeah, and
they've got enough power packs here to probably use
all of them, at least for a kind of last ditch Armageddon."

They stood there in silence for a moment, then
Corby said, "Armageddon might not be a bad term
here. Those two have been removing cases one at a
time, and I must assume it's been at least once a day
since we decided to land. The next question is, is that
because they don't trust us and they're preparing a
defense just in case? Or is this something far more
sinister?"

"The Festival Services!" Eve gasped. "They start
tonight!"

Corby nodded. "I think we need some more active
security agents down here, and some arms experts as
well. So long as my blockers remain in place they'll
think that anybody coming in or out of the lift will be

one of the authorized pair and admit them, so I'm not worried about access." He looked at his watch. "What I am concerned about is that we're going to be very vulnerable during that service, and it starts in less than seven hours."

The Doctor was *not* amused.

"You mean that this was reported *hours* ago and I'm *just now* learning about it?" he thundered. "Satan rides with every mission we undertake, and he's never more effective than when working on and through those I trust the most. We're going to have a major talk, all of us, and after that a purge, when this is all over with," he added ominously.

When he was angry like this, there was an inner part of his soul that seemed to come to the fore, particularly in the eyes, and send chills through anyone who was in his presence. This dangerous streak subsided, though, almost as soon as it showed up, as the leader of the True Church Universal switched to pragmatic mode. There were questions to answer, decisions to be made, actions to be taken before recriminations could even be thought of. Still, before turning to what they would do, he said, rather softly, "I want that idiot Cordish relieved of all duties. Put him on swab detail until I can deal with him."

"Yes, sir," an aide said crisply, and turned to give the orders to the ship above.

"And, Harry?"

"Sir?" the aide stopped and turned back towards him.

"Give the OD to Martin and put overall security control for the moment in the hands of Cromwell in Tactical Security. I want *Sinai* on full alert, understand? If they can materialize an arsenal, then they can also materialize combat ships. Remember Hanunka's Planet? This could be another trap like that. We've had a break by the grace of God and some young people who know how to do things right, so I don't want us caught with our pants down."

"Yes, sir. Tactical wants to know if the service remains on."

"Hell's bells! Of *course* it remains on! That's what we're *here* for! And I want everybody fully covered, but no weapons in sight, understand? If they think in terms of priests and nuns and kindly missionaries, I want them to keep that image in their minds. I'll be fine on stage. You just do your jobs in the crowd."

It was always tough to get these things together and operating smoothly no matter how self-contained they were and how many times before they'd done it, but knowing that some in the crowd might well have been armed and ready to pull something nasty made it all the tougher.

At least unless they made some kind of suicidal charge from the darkness they would be limited to small arms. Dressed as these people were, it wouldn't be hard to conceal a hand weapon but it would be damned near impossible to hide something big, particularly when the visitors were providing all the goodies and the people had to bring only themselves.

The service began with some jazzy religious songs and upbeat, fast tempo hymns as the people arrived from villages as far as forty kilometers away. Others, they knew, were gathering in big tents near their own villages up to five hundred kilometers from this point to watch everything on big screens. Except for not being able to see the band and preacher live, they had the same good food, treats, Bibles and hymnals as anyone there and, in fact, even those villagers at the *Olivet* site had a better view on the giant over-head screens than they did of the far-off stage.

It was clear to the staff that if these people hadn't seen a religious tent meeting before, they had a very good idea of what one was supposed to be, and so it was as disconcerting to them as it would be to a more technological culture when the Doctor came out and began. No prayers, no shouted "Amens!" none of the usual emotive stuff you'd expect with a revival. The boss just started talking, and that was, as usual, enough, once they had the language and dialect filters down as good as they did here.

There are some people who define the old Greek word *charisma*, and Doctor Karl Woodward was certainly one of them. The term meant "unmerited favor," but that never really did it, either. It was just that when Karl Woodward started speaking and you could understand him, you'd sit there and listen to him even if he was reading the technical manual on how to repair a gravity toilet.

"My friends," he was saying, in that deep, mellow voice that could go straight to your soul, "since I've arrived here everyone's been asking me and my people, 'What do you want?' Well, tonight I'm here to tell you, and it won't be what you expect. What I want is for you to listen to me and consider my words. Take the Bibles, those of you who can read them, and check me out if you think I misspeak. For example, we don't pray at our services, or have big prayer groups. Our Lord said that people who do that are showing off for other people and that their reward is that other people admire how holy and pious they are. But God doesn't really hear those prayers, because they aren't really directed at Him but rather at the audience. So we don't do that. You want to talk to

God, you go into some private place, off by yourself, and you talk to Him. You can pray, you can simply speak, do it any way you want, but do it in private. The Bible says do it in a closet, but we're not that literal. At any rate, we decided long ago that if you're going to believe in something, believe it and act on it, don't use it to show off. Still, we *are* here to bring you the good news of salvation through grace. We'll give you the truth, and the reasons why we believe it. We want you to listen. Those whom God wants to hear will do so. The rest of you will drift away. Our job is only to bring it to you. All we want is a few nights to present the case. After that, it's up to you."

It was the usual start to what would evolve into a stem-winding one-man performance, but with that sort of beginning it was notable that they were still sitting there, still listening.

Eve, John, and the rest knew that because their eyes weren't on the Doctor nor were their thoughts on what he said. They had plenty of time to learn at his feet, and to study what he said, because, believing it the truth, it never varied.

Instead, their eyes and thoughts were on the security channel and on looking for anything and anyone out of the ordinary.

Like men with guns.

I wish I knew what those men had taken out of that arsenal, John and many others thought as they studied the crowd. Some of those missiles could kill an awful lot of people and damage even their sophisticated defenses. God might protect His people from harm, but He did a much better job if you were wearing a bullet-proof suit, and He was known to kill hordes of His own chosen people just to make a point. As the Doctor was telling the crowd right at that point, "God didn't create us to have somebody to serve, He created us to serve Him. If you don't like that, tough."

It was not a message that always went down well, particularly with a poor populace, but it sure put pragmatism at the heart of the actions of those who followed these beliefs. None of the Arms of Gideon nor Tactical spread through the place thought that he or she was immune from harm just because they were on the side of the angels.

As Eve walked slowly down one aisle and up the other, she couldn't help but note how many of these people were checking the Doctor out when he threw out these unconventional notions along with chapters and verses. There was an exceptionally high literacy rate among these folks for simple cut-off farmers.

You could always sense, though, when the Word was getting through, and she felt that there was a fairly high percentage of people here who were really listening and nodding and muttering "That's right!" Not everybody, of course, but a fair number. Of course, they hadn't yet gotten to the hard part—of what God wanted of *them*—but that would be for later nights.

From a security standpoint, it meant that this wasn't an armed populace sitting there waiting for a chance to open up on their visitors. They were interested, or skeptical, or bored, but they weren't tense. Whatever Gregnar and his crew had in mind, they didn't include the village as a whole in their plans.

Speaking of which, Gregnar, Alon, and Krag were nowhere to be seen in this crowd, although, of course, they might well be simply swallowed up by it.

"Faith!" the Doctor was thundering. "Faith doesn't

mean singing hymns and looking holy! Faith is an *action*, it's putting yourself at risk for God's sake! God doesn't expect us to be like Him or become like Him—that's been tried since Adam and Eve way back when and look how badly *that* went! He's had to destroy most of humanity several times, and may have done in about half of it again if we think the worst of the Great Silence. Try as we might, we're gonna fail! It's not imitation that God wants, it's trust! Faith is trust! Look at me! I'm as much a sinner as anybody, but I trust the Lord and hang my body on His promises. I had nothing when I started—an itinerant preacher, living hand to mouth, bumming rides and meals from town to town, world to world, not a cent to my name. Now look at all this! Because I trusted Him, God decided that I was one to do His work out here. And here I am, the latest in a line of reformers trying to reach the unreachable and bring God back into the lives of people long forgotten by the rest of humanity. And when we bring the message to you all, then the Silence will be broken, and we who accept and believe will be taken in the wink of an eye to a new Earth and a new Jerusalem!"

He had been going for an hour and a quarter, and nobody could read a large audience from beyond the stage lights like Doc Woodward. He was winding up and leaving them wanting more, and when he was done these people would walk home or ride home on their animals or be taken home by Mission personnel and they'd be scattered too widely to pull anything.

And then it was over, and the old preacher got a lot of applause, and that was that. Eve and John met near the back, and he gave her a shrug. "Not tonight, looks like," he said.

"I don't know whether to be relieved or disappointed," she told him. "If they're not going to attack us during a service, and they aren't staking us out, then what's all this about?"

"We've got almost a week left," he reminded her. "And, well, maybe they just haven't had enough time to get all the weaponry out they need. Don't be so bloodthirsty. You *still* might get what you wish for, and worse."

V:
THE DESPERATE
& THE DEAD

A staff and strategy meeting presided over by Woodward himself was held deep into the night following the successful launch of the Mission Classes, as he liked to refer to them.

"We can't afford this kind of distraction," he grumbled. "We've got the Lord's work to do, and I sensed we made some real headway tonight. That means we're going to have to get to the bottom of these people's origins and secrets whether they want to talk to us or not."

Thomas Cromwell, chief of Tactical Security, was first to speak. "The problem is, we can't infiltrate them because they've basically kept to these small village groups where everybody knows everybody. And while everybody's civil and friendly enough, at least so far, they volunteer virtually no information. We've gotten more from hostile crowds than from this one. And there are no records, no depictions of their arrival, no legends that they've allowed us to hear, nothing. Even the kids don't talk."

The big preacher nodded. "It's not so much a closed society as a socially libertarian one. Everybody minds their own business, period. From what I've been able to tell from all the reports, while there are leader types there appears to be no civil authority, either on a village or larger level. Zip. And they have a brisk and well-organized trading system that brings things here and elsewhere that are needed in a smoothly functioning barter system, but nobody runs it. Nor is there any apparent crime, hence, no police. Governments began in ancient times because people got scared. Scared of the gods, scared of marauding tribes, scared of other countries. They organized collectively to mass their defenses, and, if that wasn't enough, they basically wound up selling their freedom to the meanest, nastiest group of killers around who got absolute power in a bargain that said these killers would protect the people from all outside sources of harm. Tribal chieftains, allied with priests and shamans, with their warriors evolved into princes and then kings and emperors, dictators and ruling bodies. The odd thing is, I sense real fear running through these people, but not what it is they are afraid of. And I see no evidence that fear, unlike all other times in history, has led to a breakdown in the simple village assignments based on work. It's bizarre."

They were silent for a moment, trying to figure out where to go, and Eve, who was a little scared herself just to be in this kind of company, nonetheless felt she had to put herself into the deliberations. "Excuse me, sir? Sirs?"

"Yes, child? What is it?" the white-bearded leader asked.

"They *are* hiding all this from us, and it's world-wide and deliberate. I can prove it."

"Go on."

"Those people who came tonight—they were reading their Bibles. They were following along."

"Yes?"

"Sir, there aren't any books! There aren't any records, computers, you name it. All those people could read our Bibles, *but they have nothing at all to read of their own!*"

"Well, I'll be damned!" muttered Woodward, thunderstruck at how he could define exactly how many angels were on the heads of pins and yet miss something that obvious. "Have you seen any sign of schools? Of where they learn to read?"

"No, sir. Not even the most primitive slate drawing boards or gathering halls. Children are basically baby-sat until they're big, and then, starting as young as seven or eight, they go off into the fields and help with the work or they do work under grown-up supervision in the villages."

They considered that. "Just how long do you think these people have been here?" Woodward asked them.

"Centuries. At least a century, maybe a century and a half, anyway," John Robey replied. "We had a careful examination of the original site, we dated the defense computers coming in at older than that, and none of the arsenal seems to date past the Great Silence. Besides, sir, this continent is quite well developed. You can't do that overnight."

"No, you can't," the Doctor agreed. "Still, there's something phoney here. I sometimes think it's too bad we *aren't* old order Roman Catholics. They know obedience to authority as well as anybody and, more importantly, once we had a few of these folks in confessionals we'd get the story." He sat back and sighed. "Well, unless you have anything else, we'll just have to keep thinking about this and hope we get another break. Anybody come back for more weapons?"

"No, sir," Cromwell told him. "And that has us a little worried. If they have that much firepower and they don't keep coming back to get more, it suggests they now have all that they require for whatever it is they're planning."

"Any idea how much they took out?" the bearded man asked. "Can we deduce it?"

"No, sir. Not from the way it's stacked and distributed, and the cave floor is much too scuffed up. Worse, I'm worried that with our mag scooters and small transports we've managed to give them the means they didn't have to distribute those weapons far and wide. Suppose they suddenly just decide to kill all the Arms of Gideon in their areas?"

"It would be ugly," Doc Woodward agreed. "Still, I don't think that's the problem. What would it get them? We still have this ship with potential unknown to them sitting here, and we have a more imposing presence above with a population and weaponry we've not allowed them to know the size of."

"Unless they think that, being people of God, we wouldn't retaliate," Cromwell suggested.

"Hmmm . . . Maybe I should preach a little tomorrow night on who Gideon was and what the three hundred did, eh?"

"It couldn't hurt," Cromwell replied. "Still, it would

make the additional point if, say, we began wearing conspicuous sidearms."

"No! Never! Not in an environment where we're only guessing at a threat and have people listening and interested! How can I teach them to practice faith when such a move would clearly show us doing the opposite? No, not unless we are actually under threat will a single weapon be shown or produced. But I want a solid aerial grid survey of this entire continent using our best equipment, understand?"

"What are we looking for?" Cromwell asked him.

"Anything that shows up that just doesn't fit. And let's get it started as soon as possible! In the meantime, we proceed as if everything is normal."

The survey began methodically, meter by square meter, from cameras in orbit guided by computers. The one problem even with the smartest computers, though, was that they were at their worst when told to look for "anything unusual." Even though this planet was inhabited by people whose ancestry was definitely Earth, it was another world, and not enough was known about it to give anyone, human or machine, enough information to really know when something was "normal" or "abnormal."

Still, as things went on as usual down below, and people went out in the fields to manage crops while others processed the harvest and still others cooked or looked after the kids, a few things *did* turn up, not close to the original landing site or the close-in villages but farther away, along the shores of some of the great internal lakes to the south and west of *Mount Olivet*'s landing site. The computers dutifully flagged the anthropologists, geologists, and other experts aboard the orbiting *Mount Sinai*.

"The remnants of older villages," chief anthropologist Morgan noted. "Not abandoned or overworked. They look to be definitely destroyed, probably by fire."

"There's an exceptionally fertile area right in along the lakeshore, too, very near those ruins," a geographer named Salkind put in. "And yet it's not worked. Nobody is living within ten kilometers of these ruins. Interesting. And just as fascinating, there's an exceptional amount of commercial-grade ore and some abnormal radiation readings in that area of the lake as well. I think we ought to send over a small expert away team and see what that's about."

"I agree," Morgan responded. "Why not you and me, and some military and forensic types?"

"Oh, I'd like nothing better," Salkind assured her. "I've been anxious to walk upon a real planet again after so long. I missed the last one, you know. Not much for me to do when all they're trying to do is capture or shoot us. At least, over there, there won't be any of the locals to even object."

The Doctor okayed the expedition on the condition that they take some experienced armed security with them. He was very uneasy about the secrets of these people and he didn't want any more ugly scenes just in case they misread things—as they had done more than once before.

The small team came down with full gear including waterproof probes that were smart enough to just let loose. Although none aboard the *Mountain* had ever seen a real fish, that's what the devices were called. Trained and obedient fish at that.

While others went to take forensic samples and to carefully examine the burnt-out ruins nearby, others set up the land-based part of the fish remotes. They used a flat panel rather than a hologram for most of this, as it was better in filtering out distortion in the water; if need be, they could plug into the board and connect directly with the fish and "fly" it for more detailed and true three-dimensional studies.

The lake was deep, dropping off from a narrow shelf to almost six meters in just a few steps and quickly plunging down to a dark and irregular bottom that at its deepest point was at least one hundred and twenty meters. The irregularity of the bottom seemed to be natural; either this was a system of huge caverns that had collapsed after being too weakened by erosion to support the upper rock floor or there were ancient volcanic flows down there. Evidence suggested the former, although at more than a hundred and thirty-four kilometers across at this point it must have been one *hell* of a collapse if that truly were its origin.

It was much too dark in the lake to use ordinary lights; the fish switched to sonar as their main guides and kept a wide spectrum sweep on all available frequencies for the rest. If you could see something visibly, they'd transmit it to the land-based screen; if not, they would interpolate it as a visual scene.

At about seven hundred meters out, they came upon The Object. It was about twenty meters down, although the depth around it at that point showed over a hundred meters, suggesting it was massive.

Little visible could be seen, but the outline translated from the sonar suggested a broad, smooth, metallic surface with no obvious opening. Laser probes showed it to be smooth, with no lake growths or sediment attaching itself to the thing. Whatever it was, it was pretty much the same as when it went in.

"A hundred meters tall, half a kilometer long. No

wonder it's all collapsed around there," the technician commented.

Thomas Cromwell studied the shape and orientation on the screen, chin in palm, then said, "Well, there's their ship. A ragtag Noah's ark, I'd suspect. It's an old model, one of a half dozen or so that come to mind. It's relatively small, too, but definitely interstellar. I'd say a converted corvette. Surplus military, probably cobbled together from junkyards or rebuilt from an abandoned Navy vessel. There's no sign of an energy leakage anywhere?"

"No, sir. Nothing."

"Then she's almost certainly cold. Even with all that armor there'd be *something*. I don't think it's hidden there or placed there deliberately. You don't come in and plunk yourself that deep in water, known or unknown, by choice. I think they crashed there." He sighed. "Well, at least now I think I can deduce some of the mystery here. If we had more people, more equipment, and more time we could go in, locate and pull the record modules and see what the log says about her, but I don't think it's practical at this point. It's possible they were removed anyway. Certainly they got the guns out, and who knows what else?"

"These people have acted like they're hiding some great secret," John Robey noted. "They've acted that way from the start. You think maybe they or their ancestors came in that thing, and that after they set things up they either discovered that the ship was too damaged to ever fly again or they just wanted it hidden where you'd have to be really curious to look for it?"

"No, I doubt that," Cromwell replied. "That's not the ship that brought most of these people here, along with the seed, initial two-year food supplies, prefab headquarters center, even crindin. You might stuff it all in, but it would be tight. No, this ship's more recent. From what we've found, probably a gunrunner to some of the independent worlds out there all paranoid about one another. I think it got chased here."

"You mean—?"

"That, Brother John, is a raider. Sleek, fast, probably modified with all the latest getaway gear and armed with enough weaponry to take on a small fleet, although not a Navy cruiser or its equivalent. I think if we cover the whole surface of the thing we'll find signs of a scrap, and a nasty one at that. They came up against something that was bigger and meaner than they were, or somebody just got in a lucky shot, something like that. Ambushed, most likely, when they were preparing to enter a genhole. They got in, managed some kind of maneuvers—I suspect that their captain was very good indeed—and somehow popped up here, off the charts. They were probably as surprised as we were to find an agricultural colony here. And, most likely, pretty pissed off at that, too. Can you imagine pirates suddenly having to become farmers?"

Robey thought about Gregnar, Krag, and Alon and compared them to the others. "I'm not sure they did—that is, until we showed up. Then they *had* to play farmer, at least long enough to lull us into a sense of, well, an odd cultural direction but nothing bizarre. But I didn't get the sense of the people in general being scared, and you have to figure these guys would become petty tyrants pretty easy."

"There's a fine line between fear and resignation at a situation you can do nothing about but cope," Cromwell noted. "They're pretty good at it, though. They had only a week or so to get everything ready, and they couldn't have planted all this and built all this in that time. I suspect we're seeing how the original settlers here lived, and mostly still do live. The question is where the raider crew survivors really live, and where the intermediary things we know must be here, from some kind of educational system to records, from books to computer learning systems, must be."

"This whole continent is underlain with caverns," Robey pointed out. "It's an interesting analogy for our own business, if you think of it. The power and the evil are below; the good but meek are above. The thing is, if you're right, what now?"

"What indeed?" Cromwell echoed. While it would be morally impossible not to intercede if, say, they found masses of people being tortured and killed, that kind of thing, this was much more insidious. To act in this circumstance would bring on a lot more death and destruction of the innocents than not acting, and nobody looked beaten or starved. In fact, they didn't even look all that unhappy, although looks could be as deceiving as these marooned pirates.

"Cromwell to Sister Morgan. Have anything yet?"

"More than enough," Ruth Morgan reported back. "Whatever happened here was deliberate. The place was leveled, the land in the immediate region was scorched, and we think that we've found signs of a mass grave. There's also a cemetery here but it's separate, and they even ran a disruptor over the markers."

"You heard our discussion over their ship?"

"Yes. At least these bastards can't get off. That's the best I can say about them."

Cromwell's bushy black eyebrows went up. "Tell me, everybody—put yourselves in the place of these pirates. After living here, in what is still certain to be primitive conditions by anybody's standpoint, for years, perhaps decades, what would be the one thing central in your mind? Or, at least, one of two things?"

That one was easy. "Getting out of here," John answered for all of them. "Without being discovered by the guys who chased you here first, of course."

"Exactly. And who's showed up with the only interstellar capable craft since they crashed?"

"Yeah, that's obvious. But what kind of thing do they think they can pull? I doubt if they realize that we *all* have implanted comm links, let alone the level of experts and expertise we do. And they might have every reason to think we turn the other cheek in all respects."

"Perhaps," Cromwell responded. "Still, desperation is a major motivator. They might well think that they only have one chance in a hundred, but that the alternative is possibly zero chances in a hundred if they let us leave. No, they'll try it. That's what the arsenal tapping's been about. And while they might underestimate us, they'll be prepared for a fight. The locals might even *help* them, just to be rid of them. We're certainly planting God's seed here, but, as always, not in everybody. Not by a long shot."

"When do you think they'll strike, then?" Albert Salkind put in, sounding worried. Geographers were good at charting running battles, but not all that good at actually fighting them.

"The next-to-last night, I suspect," Cromwell told them. "When they're apt to think we're complacent, taking security for granted because it's been so peaceful, and with us mostly intent on reinforcing the gospel. They know that *Olivet* will be relocating far away after the Sunday services, so that gives us one, two, oh, three days. Saturday. They'll make their move at some point on Saturday, and they will be extremely dangerous. They have only one real chance at this, and that means they will be as ruthless as possible. I think it's time we had a war council with the Doc."

Eve and John walked across the village square and out towards the distant but quite visible *Mount Olivet*. The sun was getting low in the sky, and soon the farmers would be coming in, the village communal kitchen would be serving a high fat, high caloric meal for them to work off the next day, and then some would head off for *Olivet*.

Most, of course, would not. After a few evenings the novelty had worn off, even though Doc Woodward seldom repeated anything even while always staying on message. If you didn't keep them interested you wouldn't keep them for the serious teaching.

Eve hadn't known John before this assignment; there were three hundred in the Arm of Gideon and the newer members tended to spend all their time in education and training and didn't really mix socially with the experienced officers. Still, she felt a sense of personal pride that she'd been accepted as an equal member of the team, even by the Doctor and his specialists, and certainly by John, who'd backed her up when everyone else was dismissing her suspicions as newbie paranoia. She didn't feel that the pride was ungodly or impermissible; this was simply an affirmation by others that she'd done her job.

It wasn't easy being a member of the Arm; you had to study enough theology to answer any question a new convert might come up and ask, and to minister to those who needed one-on-one treatment, but you also had to know a lot of general knowledge and be proficient in the skills of an investigator and first-contact specialist while also knowing all the technology that was at your disposal.

You didn't get much sleep even on the long interstellar voyages; you were always busy, always learning, always honing skills as best you could.

The most ironic thing was that few remained active in the Arm for very long, save the senior officers who had a particular feel for it and strong leadership abilities. Many just couldn't take the grind and dropped out and became security personnel or mission planners; some became specialists, experts in a particular field like Ruth Morgan's anthropology or Albert Salkind's geography. Some became ministers, both lay and ordained, to the large flock aboard the ship, while still others, often those who'd become couples while on assignments, wound up as missionaries, staying behind to grow what the Doctor planted.

Eve wasn't sure what she would eventually do. She loved this sort of thing, as she'd always thought she would, but she did not look forward to the next prolonged period of ship travel, of endless periods in artificial ship's time just doing the same things over and over again. And she knew that the day would be coming when that would be her fate, perhaps for years if she didn't become one of the dropouts. These settlers could be covered continent wide in just a few more weeks; there weren't all that many on this planet, after all.

The funny thing was, she thought she could remain here as a missionary if it was like it appeared to be, with these ramshackle farms and communal villages and smelly animals and smellier kids. There didn't seem to be any real threats to humans here, the insects and bacteria were just off enough that they didn't have much effect on humans, and with some medical equipment and training and a couple of medtechs this place would be one where you could settle down and possibly even live a long and productive life.

But it wasn't as it appeared. There was a second layer here, down beneath the surface, with guns and shielded vaults and endless caverns. She would have to see these people as they really were and this life as it really was before she could decide on anything about this place. Somewhere, among these seemingly happy and hard-working farmers were men and probably women who had destroyed those villages and all who lived within them, and done so merely to prevent anyone telling what they saw or interfering with the unloading of contraband and the technology to rule.

They were out here now, waiting to act, to do *something*, and many weren't even very shy about it. Gregnar had trimmed his long hair and bushy mustache and looked almost presentable as he sat there telling dirty stories to folks who were then going to march off and see if God was with them, and he seemed quite loose and friendly.

There was no good way to spy on everybody every minute, and the natives' loose-fitting cotton clothing could conceal almost as much as the Arm's robes actually did conceal. Still, it appeared that, if they really were going to do anything, they would be doing it with very small weapons. That wasn't totally reassuring; small weapons could do less damage, it was true, but they could kill a lot of folks within a reasonable range.

There had to be far more raider survivors than these three, but these three were the only ones they could be certain of, so they were closely watched. Eve had Gregnar simply because the big man had shown an eye for the ladies but also seemed to underestimate them. John took Alon, who seemed relaxed but was not as outgoing as Gregnar, and an Arm supervisor named Matthew Seldon, a long-time member of Doctor Woodward's inner circle and clearly the boss's man on this end, took Krag, who was acting the somewhat withdrawn loner. That didn't seem to have any real meaning, either, since Krag was usually that way.

In fact, the only thing really unusual about any of the three men's behavior this night was that they generally were inseparable after work, the best of buddies. Now, suddenly, each of them sat with his own group (or, in Krag's case, off by himself) and gave little attention to the other two. It wasn't much to go on, but Eve in particular felt that it was enough to say that they were certainly up to something.

I just wish we knew how many others here are their kind, and how many more of them will be at the lecture, she thought to herself. In several weeks of living among these people, not a single one had cracked or leaked *any* information that couldn't be clearly observed.

And now it was dark, save for the torches in the village and the bright light of the *Olivet* on the horizon. None of the three seemed in any hurry, but, finally, Gregnar finished his last ale and seemed to give a knowing glance to the other two—or was it just the watchers' imaginations? He banged down the heavy wooden mug and then got up and started to walk out of the village, towards the distant shining lights. Eve followed, trying to be as nonchalant as she could and also look like she was just going in the same direction. John watched her with a wry smile on his face, noting to himself that she wouldn't fool anybody. It didn't matter; these guys certainly knew that they were being shadowed if indeed they were grounded raiders from that crashed ship.

Heck, it might even deter them from action, and, Security felt certain, if they didn't act tonight it was unlikely that they would be able to act tomorrow. That was as good as prevention or active intervention.

Alon moved off next, never once glancing at John or any other robed people in the area, confident and secure. He walked into the darkness, and, after a few minutes, John followed, looking as relaxed as his mark. He wasn't that worried about losing his man in the darkness; like the other two, and most of the other Arm members down there, he was wearing tiny computer-controlled infrared contact lenses that allowed him pretty good night vision when he needed it.

He wasn't on the road ten minutes when Alon proved that he was more than a hick farmer and much the pro. The native suddenly darted off into tall grain almost like he was sneaking back to the cache, and John, losing sight of him for a moment, wandered over in that direction, thereby revealing himself.

Robey no sooner got into the tall wheat, though, when he suddenly felt something dark and wet. "Hey!" he yelled out, startled.

"Oops! Sorry! Didn't think anybody was lurking in here," Alon responded in an obviously pleased, almost smug tone.

The big man had sent a message to his shadow, and in the most primitive and smelly of ways.

Pulling his pants back up, Alon marched quickly

out of the grain and rejoined the crowd heading towards the service.

Doctor Woodward at times could be as much the virtuoso of cussing as he could be the voice of the living God, but Robey mentally was trying to outdo the old boy, although much of it was self-directed. *Don't underestimate these bastards*, he warned himself.

He began even more to wish that he knew just what sort of weapons they'd removed from that underground arsenal.

"Umph! I'm about halfway to the ship and people keep bumping into me and stepping on me," Seldon reported through the intercom. Since the system was actually implanted, it was nearly impervious to interruption; even people standing right next to you could hear nothing. To the Arms, though, it was as clear as day.

Still, it wasn't telepathy. You had to speak, at least softly. *"You're lucky,"* John whispered back. *"I just got peed on and that s.o.b. has the bladder of ten men!"*

"I'm getting kind of roughed up and pushed around here, too," Eve reported. *"And they don't seem to be running into each other."*

Soon other Arms randomly distributed through the three hundred and sixty degrees that could be used to approach *Olivet* started reporting their own jostling and shoving, and several were tripped up.

Eve saw a bunch of young women talking and giggling among themselves as they approached her, then essentially engulfed her. She was pushed, shoved, and started to say something when she felt a slight tingling and an enormous numbing rush inside her body. Then things went very dark.

One by one, Arms stationed outside of the main lighting area throughout the meeting seemed to meet the same fate. It was so fast, and so innocuous when it happened, that there wasn't a word on the intercom that anything untoward was happening.

Martin Luther Grady, the Guardian Angel up in the security seat on *Sinai* in stationary orbit above them, was not quick to sense anything untoward, but he did begin to note a lessening of traffic. Not the sounds of the crowds and the excitement of the occasion, but the agent traffic. There were also a couple of times when somebody seemed about to say something and then got cut off.

"Rose, get me biotelemetry on a random sampling of Arm personnel below," he ordered, frowning. There was just *something* . . .

"Nobody missing," Rose reported, "but—*huh!* Now *that's* weird! A whole bunch of them have virtually the same ritual breathing and relaxed state, almost like they were *asleep!*"

"Or unconscious!" Grady opened the full channel. "They are making their move! A number of our people are down in the darkness! Repeat, they are knocking you out, probably by injection!" He turned back to Rose. "How many so far?"

"Twenty. . . . No, twenty-two. Oops! There goes another one!"

"Break out of the crowd, drop surveillance!" Grady ordered. *Lord! How many have we got down there? Sweet Jesus! A hundred and four!* "How many now?"

"Thirty-seven!" Rose reported.

"They're in among the crowds!" Seldon reported. "We're up to our armpits in people going to the teaching! There's no way we can—*what? Ouch! Watch—*"

"Thirty-eight," Rose said needlessly.

"Head for the lights! Fast as you can! Nobody illuminated is being taken!" Grady told them. *"Run! They're pushing you, push them!"*

"Fifty-three," Rose reported.

Grady sighed. "Get me Doctor Woodward on the secure line," he told her. "And give me a full infrared screen of the area. I want tracings of anybody, awake or asleep, that's going anywhere but *towards* the teaching. Understand? I want the location of every single sleeper!" He turned and flipped a switch. "Tactical, assemble full military SWAT now. They have taken massive hostages!"

VI:
TRUTH &
CONSEQUENCES

"I can't believe the whole population's in on it," Woodward told his staff over the intercom when apprised of what had been happening. "We have a full house plus tonight, and even in some of the remote villages where they're set up to watch on screen we've got people sitting there waiting for me to start even when it's clear that somebody's nabbed most of our people there."

"True, but that's the one advantage they have over us," Grady responded. "We don't know who *they* are in the crowds so long as they look like and act like everybody else."

"What about the infrared taps?"

"No good. Well, we've got some, but they don't last long. That area must be honeycombed with disguised cave openings. No real problem, I don't think. We're trying to trace them through the intercom links, which, of course, stay open, but like the arsenal caves the inside's heavy with magnetite and similar minerals that really scramble direct transmissions. We have a SWAT team ready to go down in. Once they're down there, they should be able to pick up the comm links fairly easily. What are your instructions?"

"Wait," the Doctor ordered. "We can't get everybody at once, so our best bet is to let them make the first move. Still, I want as much information on what's down there as possible. We've been looking all over for the caves; we knew they had to be *someplace*. Now we know. Put some probes down as relays and then send in some ferrets and let's see what we've got. In the meantime, everybody's going to have to pretend that there's nothing going on in the congregation, so I'll give them my usual. That will service the needs of the people not involved in this, and also pin down any who are from interrupting the ferret operation. When you've got information, we'll talk again. You can act on your own, using your best judgment while I'm on, but if there's any shooting, any injuries or deaths, I want to hear about it even if I'm in mid-sentence, you understand?"

"Yes, sir! I've got a couple of likely openings spotted. When you start, we should be pretty clear outside and able to commence operations."

At that a door hissed open behind Grady. He turned and saw Thomas Cromwell himself standing there in full battle armor, with the cross of Saint George on his front and back. The armor was standard Navy tactical; it was smart and able to act on its own to protect its wearer if need be, and nobody was going to get a sleep dart through it, that was for sure.

"You heard, Brother Cromwell?"

The big Tactical chief nodded. "I'm going down with a small team now. You put me where we can most likely get some information fast. Doc's good, but the whole service is under two hours complete with music. I don't want that mob letting out while we're right in the middle."

"Very good, Brother," Grady responded. "We're pretty sure they've been taken to some sort of central location, but it'll be fairly deep. Still, if you drill and drop a line probe into a ferret hole it should reach at full power."

Cromwell nodded, turned, and walked back out and down to the shuttle site. The rest of his team were already there in suits similar to his but without the cross front and back. The cross was Cromwell's own trademark, although it could vanish very suddenly if it singled him out as a target.

In the twenty-six minutes it took to land the team and its equipment, the rocky plain had been pretty well cleared of people, which was just fine with Cromwell. He knew that there had to be guards posted but he didn't care. If any humans were around and attempted to flee or suddenly vanished down a hole, they would regret doing so very quickly.

The "ferrets" were a land-based version of the "fish" used at the lake, better suited for going along solid ground than through liquids. They were small and made out of the same malleable material as the combat suits, so they could morph quickly into shapes and sizes needed to get through very tight places, cling to the tops rather than the floors of buildings, ships, caves, or whatever, and take on characteristics useful for camouflage. Like the fish, they were best monitored with screens and then taken over and run by direct hookup to a human brain, and the tactical unit used a set of small screens for this purpose. The suits could link with the ferrets for a full virtual reality experience, transferring the consciousness of the human to the ferret, but Cromwell did that only when necessary. It took somebody out of the fight here, and if there were armed enemies around, that might be fatal to them or to those protecting the one linked in.

In the security command center on *Olivet*, in back of the stage, they were gathered around watching the same thing on bigger screens, which were also being uplinked to the orbiting *Sinai*.

The five-member tactical squad referred to itself only by Greek letters—Cromwell, of course, was Alpha— to save time and make no mistake as to who was talking to whom. They had jumped from the shuttle and set up their gear even as the shuttle rose rapidly into the sky and vanished. Nobody was going to take one of those things if it could be helped, and the computer pilots would kill any unauthorized passengers or even destroy themselves and their vehicles before allowing anyone to endanger *Sinai*.

The natural "at rest" coloration of the suits, originally made more than two centuries ago for Navy special teams like the one Cromwell had once run, was the usual gun metal gray, and so were the ferrets. In the darkness, away from the just starting "teaching," or service, they were virtually invisible and, thanks to the suit, they gave off no heat signatures. They did, however, have to have a place to go, and until now there was no evidence of the hidden part of this society no matter how obvious it was that it had to be there. Now they did.

Cromwell just wished he had more than half a dozen, and he prayed that the ones he had would return safe and sound. While there was some self repair built in, if these went there was no way to get more and little in the reference as to how the things worked anyway.

There was no question that this was one of the openings even though it didn't register from space or from any appreciable distance. Standing on it, you got a fairly steady anomalous energy reading that generally meant a steady-state power grid below. Great shielding, though, Cromwell thought, then took out what looked to be a large pistol. He put its barrel flat to the edge of the area now showing energy below and said, "Gamma, bring me a probe terminator." One of the others reached into a pack and then handed him a disc-shaped object perhaps thirty centimeters across which he clamped to his suit. He then fired the pistol.

There wasn't any sort of explosion; instead, there was a whirring sound and when he felt the bit fall free of the covering he relaxed the pistol and pulled it slightly back. A black snakelike line continued to issue from the barrel as the probe dropped as far as gravity would take it. When it stopped, Cromwell twisted the barrel and removed the other end of the snake, then took the disc and attached it to the line, then let it go. The disc provided a solid anchor for the probe, which now was acting much like a real snake, moving around until it acquired the best signal. When it seemed satisfied, the center of the disc glowed a dull red for a few seconds, then went inert again.

"Good signal," one of the team reported.

"Very well, then," their commander responded. "Release ferret."

From the probe a small, cigarlike shape seemed to flow out like liquid mercury, then started speeding ahead down the tunnel, which appeared to be lit by those glowing stripes similar to the ones used in the arsenal cave.

"Good visibility, good audio, but not much of a clue as to where anybody went," Beta commented.

"Give it time," their leader said soothingly.

"Junction!" Gamma called out. "Split ferret?"

"No, not until and unless we have to," Cromwell told them. "Best guess, leave it up to the ferret. It has better sensors than we do."

The ferret unhesitatingly chose the right tunnel and went on at maximum speed. Those little things could really *move*, Cromwell reflected, not for the first time.

"Observers! Two in the bush to the left, one sixty!" Delta called to them in the way only they could really hear.

Cromwell wasn't about to go for subtleties when his people were being grabbed. He turned and looked straight at the interlopers using full night vision and saw the pair, a man and a woman, both middle-aged and both butt-ugly, he thought, but not otherwise distinguishable from the rest of the settlers. Except, of course, they both had standard military issue energy pistols in their hands.

"Take 'em both on my command," he instructed. "If they're going to take our people then maybe we should have a few of theirs."

Before he could give the command, the woman rose up, trained her pistol right on him, and fired. There was a brief beam that struck him dead on—

and had absolutely no effect whatever. Battle suits were *not* robes.

She seemed absolutely baffled, and Cromwell said, "Now! Both of them!"

Delta fired two short autoguided bursts and both of the settlers dropped.

"Why in the *world* would they think those things would work on combat suits?" somebody asked, as two of them went over to check on and then restrain the pair.

"It's damned dark out here, that's why," Cromwell reminded them. "That's why we picked this location. They may have better natural night vision than we do, but I'll bet you that they couldn't even tell we weren't buck naked at that distance with just their eyes. I'm impressed that she hit me at all. That's damned good shooting."

"We'll have to pray that the Doctor has the quality of mercy in him when he interrogates them, too," Delta commented, picking up the pistol and examining it.

"Oh? Why?"

"This is a fairly old model, but unless I'm really misreading this she had it on a force high enough to kill, not just knock you cold."

"Huh! Well, search 'em thoroughly for weapons. Archangel, you're sending a pickup team, I hope?"

"On the way," said the controller for the team high in orbit above them.

"We've got something on screen!" Beta called to them. "Alpha, I think you will want to see this."

They all did, but with one standing picket and two binding up the prisoners, only Cromwell and Beta were able to take a look at that point, along with, a fraction of a second later, Archangel.

The ferret had climbed up the wall and now was slowly positioning itself on the ceiling for the best shot.

The cave had expanded into a large chamber, originally natural but now enlarged and regularized, that was quite a different level of existence than topside. While not luxurious, it was perfectly modern, a series of cubes assembled together into a kind of apartment building or office complex, it was difficult to say which. There was lighting in there, and some people around, and in the center was a regular circular depression with three concentric levels that seemed like some ancient forum.

The people looked pretty much the same as they did topside, but perhaps cleaner and a bit less conditioned than everyday farmers. All carried sidearms similar to the ones used by the two who'd come upon the team, held in casual holsters worn outside of their loose-fitting clothing. There seemed no sexual hierarchy; both men and women had the sidearms and also the arrogant expressions that they backed up.

"They didn't do this in a few days or weeks," Beta commented. "They've been here for a very long time. And they got a ton of the stuff out of that ship, didn't they?"

Cromwell nodded. "And this is just one of them. I wonder how extensive this cave system is, and just how many complexes like this there might be? Those ships like the one we found were basically automated, but as raiders they often carried a hundred or more people, sometimes what passes for families among them. Give them a hundred, and perhaps fifty years, and you've got a fair-sized elite here."

"Holy—! Just *look* at that!" Delta commented, coming over to look.

From one of the caverns emerged a small mag tractor pulling two flats loaded with crates of something or other.

"If they have that kind of mobility, why strong-arm the arsenal?" Beta wondered.

"Security. I bet few of them have full access to that lift. If they did, they'd have knocked each other off by now. At least we know how they're getting trade goods they need in when they need them without obvious wagon trains. I doubt if they have too many of the tractors, though. That one looks like the kind they'd use to load and unload their ship. I suspect they have no more than four or five, tops; that would be enough for their needs but not for everybody else."

"But why have everything set up down there? It must have been rough to build with just what they had, and it also has to be maintained. Most of the caves are natural, and there have to be some regions where they're unstable," Delta said.

"Indeed. Can't hide the farms and farmers—everybody has to eat, and there's precious little in the way of synthesizers here, I suspect. Not for an expanding population. No, these people aren't hiding from us," Cromwell told them. "They're *in hiding*. From whom is the big question. Works nicely as a trap for suckers like us, and we may well not be the first, but that's not worth *this*. We'd have come down if they'd had a nice civilization aboveboard. No, they're hiding from somebody in particular. Somebody they think that, after all this time, might still show up any moment. Makes you wonder."

"Well, they're through hiding from *us*, anyway," Beta commented. "I just wish we could see signs of our people down there. I don't like the idea we got shot at full strength."

"They'll have them well away from here," Cromwell assured them. "But within limits. I have this feeling that these people just don't understand who and what they are dealing with when they attacked us."

"Yeah, but this would sure be one time when it would be handy if we believed in praying in public. Easy to pick 'em up, and it would drive *this* crew nuts," Beta commented.

Deep down, though, Cromwell knew that his team was very concerned, probably as concerned as he was. If the ferrets couldn't find them, then some good people were bound to die on this miserable dirt ball.

In the darkness there was first a soft nothingness, then a tingling, growing pain that seemed to come from everywhere inside her, blossom, and then explode into a bodywide network of pointed needles or spikes stuck into her. She gave an exclamation of pure displeasure that seemed to die in her throat and then her eyes popped open.

The jabbing pains subsided after a moment, but her joints throbbed and there was a part of her head that felt like it was being struck by a dull but forceful mallet every few seconds. She was on her knees, she realized, and stark naked, a fact which greatly embarrassed and worried her. What had they done to her? What might they have done while she was unconscious?

She tried to move, to rub her painful joints, but she found that she could not. First, her wrists were bound behind her, held in some kind of restraint that also went around the ankles. She was unable to shift, get up, or unwind from the uncomfortable pose. There was no slack; the restraints were solid, not chains or flexible materials.

There *was* a chain, loosely around her neck. She tried to turn and see what it was connected to, but, that proving impossible, she looked around and saw many others in the same situation and pose. The chains appeared simply riveted into the wall of the cave, but the loops proved to be a choke chain. You move or twist, the chain gets tighter. You get back into the proscribed position, the chain loosened through a series of carefully managed loops along its length. The chain could also lock into place within its "lax" zone, wrapping as it did around a similar waist chain before going to the wall. This is what kept them from falling forward or over. Somebody who knew what they were doing did not want anybody trying any tricks whatsoever.

These stocks or whatever you call them weren't put here for us, she thought, looking around carefully. *This place was* designed *as a holding prison. Good old Greg's not so nice down here, I bet*. The thought did not make her feel any better.

There were perhaps a dozen others in the room—it was difficult to tell with her limited movement—and all had familiar faces. They were also all females; she wasn't sure if that was a good sign or an ominous one.

Some were still unconscious; others were awake, but that was about all that could be said. They were all gagged; that was why even her cry of pain had been muffled. Still, the communications system for the Arm was implanted in each of them; she listened for any sign of being hunted or any news of what was going on, but there was nothing, just a slight hissing if you concentrated. Shielded, too. They seemed to have thought of everything.

Within half an hour the miserable pain hadn't

subsided, but just about all the others were at least awake and already through her own process of discovery.

Everything seemed to drag into eternal boredom; there was nothing you could do, nothing you could say, and nothing left to see. There were no frames of reference, nothing. Eventually, most discovered that if you had to relieve yourself you just had to relieve yourself; it grew foul and smelly in no time.

Finally, somebody entered. He was a younger man, dressed like a crindin handler, wearing gray cotton clothing and heavy boots that looked like they'd been taken off one of the male members of the Arm and probably were. He hit the stench and turned up his nose. "Ew! Yuk!" he muttered, then left, returning with a long hose of the sort used to wash the big animals. He turned and shouted down the cavern, "German! Pump!"

The hose was inactive for a few moments, then it gushed water, which he used to wash off each of the women in turn, breaking now and then to use a homemade push broom to get the mess into the center of the room where there was an actual drain-hole or some kind, masked until he pulled it up by a slate rock fitted cover.

"Okay!" he yelled at his unseen companion. "It's bearable!"

He looked around at them and had a leering sort of grin on his face. "Pretty. Different from most of the girls we got 'round here. Maybe I'll take me one of you if this don't go good."

Just try it with me, Eve thought grimly, daggers shooting from her eyes. She, or any of the others, for that matter. *Let me get one arm free and you'll never want a woman again*, she thought with absolute confidence in her ability to do the job.

The herder type left, though, taking his equipment with him, and shortly another came in, this time a tall, middle-aged man with a neatly trimmed beard.

"All right, ladies, listen up!" he said in a tone of absolute command. "You are currently in no position to haggle. I think we've made that clear. In fact, we've tried very hard not to underestimate you. There wasn't any plan to go this far, or even disrobe you, but after we searched and found the incredible amount of stuff you were hiding, including the guns and power packs, we just had to assume that you were fully trained in combat and control. Disappointing for people who say they're from God, but after listening to your boss's messages I can understand it. Now you understand this. We're desperate. We can't get off this hole and we sure as hell don't want to die on it munching grass. We knew we couldn't make much of a deal after you explored the crash site, so here we are. Be very convinced that we will do exactly what we say and what we feel we have to do. I suspect that we may have to do some unpleasant things to some of you, maybe even kill a few, to demonstrate our resolve. If we loosen up your restraints and you violate any of the rules, and I mean *any*, you're number one on the list. Holy people like to talk about martyrs who are tortured and killed for their faith. You may get that chance. We will need a few examples before the others to establish the limits of your faith. Who's first? Any volunteers?"

He was playing with them, of course, but he seemed very different than the chief of a raider band might be imagined. Cultured, calm, knowledgeable, and apparently born without a soul, and all the scarier for it. This was not a man who would *ever* enjoy ravishing a captive. This was a man who would enjoy watching it, maybe even recording it and replaying it over and over at parties.

"All right," he sighed, "now that we understand each other, here's the first choice in the rest of your life. We have food here. It'll be served by women, not men, so relax on that score, but don't take any of *them* for granted, either. One at a time, your gags will be lifted and you will get drink and food. If you say anything, and I mean *anything*, all that will stop, and you'll not get any more. Understand? No more water, even. But don't worry, it won't last long. You'll become an early example. Or, you can relax and wait. This could be over in a day or two, one way or the other. Just also keep in mind that none of you and your people, and we've got almost a hundred of you in various locations, will survive unless we get what we want."

And, with that, he walked out.

If he'd intended to frighten them, it only took a look in the eyes of the others to show that he succeeded. Eve suspected her own eyes looked much the same. It wasn't just the threats—those they already took for granted—but the coldly pragmatic way he warned them that got them. To him, torture, kidnap, murder, were all just business, and he almost certainly lost no sleep whatsoever over them.

He was certainly as good as his word in delivering what he promised. He hadn't been out of the cavern a minute when three women entered. They looked hard and tough, but so did just about everybody on the surface, so there was nothing obvious to set them apart from the villagers. That was the insidious part of this. You couldn't tell one from the other, if, in fact, there was something to tell. The two different populations had been deduced primarily from the size of the crashed spaceship and the subtle differences in genetic makeup of the majority of villagers versus the nonmatching polyglot of the few others. But who really knew?

One thing was for sure: the short, slender, long-haired woman in the patterned cotton dress had a pretty mean-looking pistol that wasn't of a familiar type to Eve, at least.

A second woman was unarmed but had a medical sensor in her hand and passed it completely over the first captive woman, then checked the readings. "This one's okay, but she'll have some problems walking or doing anything complex for a while. They all will, most likely."

"Not our problem. Okay, Miga. Take off the gag, give her a drink, then feed her. *You* kneeling, you remember what happens if you say just one word, understand? *One word!*"

The frightened woman nodded, and the third member of the trio removed the gag and allowed the captive a number of deep breaths. Then a jar was lifted in front of her, containing a large gravity straw, and the woman drank, first hesitantly, then, after a few coughs and some spitting out of liquid which the experienced woman administering the drink was ready for, eagerly and in gulps.

After that, the drink was removed even though the woman clearly wanted more, and a kind of homemade granola and honey bar was hand fed to her. She was allowed one intermediate and one ending drink, and then the gag was replaced and it was on to the next woman.

"Faith!" the one with the gun sneered at all of them. "Easy to spout about until it's live or die time or worse, isn't it?"

The comment stung them all far more than the chains and restraints. It *was* far easier to assume that you would die for your faith, or suffer any affliction for it, until you were faced with the choice. Most of the apostles had been brutally tortured and murdered in the end, or executed at least, but they all did have the advantage that they had seen the dead and risen Christ. She began to realize that, for all the teaching and training, "evil" was a word long out of fashion and used mostly to cover the scope of a crime. Nobody really believed in evil anymore; they believed in "wrong" and "bad" and "psychotic."

I have the honor by the grace of God to be the first of my generation to face true evil, she thought. *And I don't know if I have the guts for it. Please, God! Tell me what You want me to do?*

The same thoughts had to be going through the others here, and the others in other caves around the region if the leader's claim of a hundred captured was true.

I will not deny Him, she resolved, *even if death is the end.* But denial wasn't the demand or the claim; it was rather to simply go along and not make waves. Was it enough to refuse to do something that they weren't asking her to do anyway?

One by one, the process done with the first woman was repeated with the others, often with pauses while someone went out to get the jug or stash of granola-style bars refilled, and, during the whole of it, not one of them, not even Eve, had done anything at all save what they'd been told to do.

When the feeding was done and the three underground women were gone, Eve felt a blackness, a hole in her soul, where confidence had once stood. The fact that none of the others had done anything, nor could they claim to later, having done nothing in this public exhibition, made it somewhat worse, but God would know. God would also forgive, but not forever. This was but the beginning of their trials, and at some point she would either have to demonstrate her faith or watch it shatter.

Even so, she wondered now if anybody among the captured had actually made any gesture of resistance, however futile.

Cromwell didn't even consider taking the pair of would-be assassins in for a nice questioning. He had the team take them not up to *Sinai*, since that would be the last place he'd want any of these people, even as prisoners, until he knew them a *lot* better, but rather to *Olivet*, still on the ground, still brightly lit although, this long after the service, pretty well deserted. The guard was there, well lit and monitored from inside and from above, to insure that nobody else was going to be snatched, but that was about it. The shields around the ship were certainly more than adequate for the rest; if they weren't, then the attackers would have seized the ship and its leader instead of random acolytes in the dark.

Now the male captive was in the infirmary, hooked up to a bank of medical monitors and being intravenously fed a very efficient blend of drugs that made him friendly, happy, and otherwise not thinking very much.

"Hello," said a friendly sounding deep male voice.

The man opened his eyes and saw the huge form and bearded face of Karl Woodward, looking not stern or angry but rather fatherly. The man's lips formed a childlike grin.

"Hi," he responded.

"Are we friends?" the doctor asked him.

"Yes, sure. Friends . . ."

The deep tones suddenly sounded wounded, hurt.
"Then why did you try and harm and kill my children? Why did you take my children away? Is *that*
what friends do to other friends?"

There was a sudden sorrow in the man's expression now, almost like he wanted to cry. "Didn't wanna
do it. It was—orders. Just orders. Nothin' personal,
friend. We don't wanna hurt nobody, see?"

"Then why did you take my children?"

"Nothin' personal," the man repeated, drooling a
bit. "See, 'cause we gotta get outa here. Got the big
one. Know where the treasure of treasures is. But we
can't get to it. Stuck here, eatin' *grass* and drinkin'
sheep dip beer. Cap said you wouldn't take us. No
room. So we make room . . ."

"Cap? Who's Cap? Did he give the orders?"

"Yeah, sure. Cap always gives the orders. That's
what cap'ns do."

"Where is this captain? I'd like to talk to him."

The man gave an uncomfortable shrug, seemingly
unaware that he was lying strapped down on a medical table connected to all sorts of tubes. "Somewhere
down below. We don't see him much, y'know? Like
most cap'ns. They just pass down the orders. Ours
not to reason why . . ."

"Stow the ancient quotes. Where did they take my
children?"

Another shrug. "All over. Dunno. Lotsa places.
Booby-trapped places, see."

"What if *we* took hostages?"

"Wouldn't matter. 'Less, o'course, you can find the
ossifers. Rest of us, all expensable."

"You mean expendable?"

"Yeah, that's it. Exprendable."

"The villagers—are they crew, too?"

"Not most of 'em, no. They was already here. Stuck here long, long ago. Got conned, y'see. Old con. Used t'do it myself in the old days. Take their stuff, drop 'em nowhere while you fake a fight, lose the fight, then they're stuck. You spend their money, nobody remembers they was born."

Woodward looked over at Cromwell. "Pirates all right. It's amazing that we can learn the basics of subatomic physics, the magic of faster-than-light travel, and still the human soul stays right where it's always been."

Cromwell nodded. "Amen to that."

Woodward turned back to the captive. "Were you ordered to attack my children out there just now? You and the woman?"

"No, not like that," the man managed. "See, we was just—just—we was kinda rear guards, see? Slow down anybody chasin' till they can split up the hostages and get 'em set up."

"You figure you did your job?"

"Oh, sure. I mean, I guess so."

Woodward sighed and stepped back. "Keep working on him. I want every detail his rather empty head contains, no matter how small. What about the woman?"

"His partner, more or less," Cromwell told him. They were having an expert female security interrogator work with her in another room using pretty much the same techniques. "More vicious because, we think, she's of the first group. She managed to snare one of them and dominate him and get entry into their better society, but she's done it by being meaner than they are. I have a feeling that taking her out of circulation might gain us some local friends."

"Well, we've tried finding local friends," the Doctor noted, "and it's gotten us nowhere. No, I don't think this is a time for being diplomatic. Those stranded pirates were *helped* by many of the local villagers. You can see it on the recordings. No, I think it's time we fought the devil on some of his own ground. Tomorrow morning I want every single child in the closest and surrounding villages picked up. Babies to maybe ten or eleven. All of them. Bring down some of our child-care people to help out with them. Treat them fine, but keep them inside here, out of sight. Don't bring any of their babysitters. If there's any resistance, knock 'em cold and leave 'em where they fall."

"You really think that's going to do anything to help *our* people?"

"Tom, I have no idea. What I *do* know is that nothing in your ferret operation here or the other one to the north showed any children underground. Men, women, yes, but no kids. And the kids up here are all getting educated, whether they're pirate or villager. Let's see if we can at least get our pirates to talk on a timetable of our choosing, huh? I also want this village locked down. They can stay inside the village, but nobody leaves. Nobody goes anywhere outside. If they want to leave they're going to have to do it underground and probably with us watching. Let's see what *they* think when they see their kids taken away."

"But surely we're not going to do anything to the children!"

"Of course not! You know that, and *I* know that. But do *they* know that? If we can't pressure those bastards underground one way, let the villagers do it. Sometimes you can fake even the devil out."

He paused a moment, then added, "I'd like you and all the Elders to meet me in the Meditation Room in one hour. I believe that, before we act, we must consult a higher power. Only with His will and strength behind us will we have a good ending here tomorrow."

VII:
MOUNTAIN
MOVES FAITHS

The question really was, when was faith truly faith and when was it a synonym for doing something stupid? How many cult types in human history had jumped off cliffs or taken poison because they were convinced it was the act of faith God wanted?

It was so easy to go through these problems in classes, to imagine yourself in this or that position, but it was like contemplating death: you knew it was possible, but there was always the chance that an exception might be made.

The one problem with martyrs was that they were all dead.

Not that she didn't believe in God with all her

heart, but her group taught that it wasn't as simple
as that. Believing wasn't enough; you had to *act* on
that belief, and you had to do it without God's instructions from the omnipresent parallel dimensions called
Heaven. Get it wrong, and you wind up with all the
cultists of history in that other set of extra-dimensional
ether some called Hell.

If she spit food back in the faces of her captors next
feeding, would it mean martyrdom or degradation?

The pirate leader seemed almost disappointed by
the lack of real resistance. Captain Morgudan Sapenza
had actually attended all but the last of the Doctor's
lectures, and he'd been quite impressed with the old
patriarch. Sapenza hadn't been raised Christian, but
there was a lot to like in the old man's tough and gritty
brand of it, and some good common sense as well. His
mother had believed in seven Heavens and nine Hells;
his father allowed as how there might be something
else to life but that it wasn't worth looking at because
all it did was cramp your style. He was his father's
child, and always had been.

He finished off a beer and lit a cigar. He knew
the damned things were bad for people but he'd
gotten this far and that was pretty far indeed, at least
until he'd wound up against this damned dirt ball of
a wall.

There was suddenly an awful commotion down one
tunnel and everybody's hands went to their sidearms,
but it was soon clear that it was just a woman with
a really big mouth almost hysterical about something.

"What is it?" he shouted to the woman as she tried
to shake off restraining hands and run right to him.
"Let her go!"

She ran up to him. "The children, sir! The children
from Village Nine!"

"What about them?"

"They came this morning and they *took* them! Took them all away to their big ship! Troopers with guns, not holy folks in robes!"

He sat up. "Just calm down. Sit, get a drink. We'll take care of this!"

Now she allowed herself to be taken away, and he started to think hard. He hadn't expected *this*. These people were after his own heart. They thought ugly.

He had only pragmatic regard for the kids; he had none himself that he knew of, but some of his people had them and they wouldn't be easy to control if their kids were suddenly taken up to a Holy Joe education never to be seen again. It was time to start playing the hand he'd dealt. "Megak! Tollya! Front and center!" he called in an authoritative tone.

Two ragged-looking members of the band, one male, one female, came over to him and waited expectantly.

"We haven't gotten any would-be martyrs or principled sacrificial lambs, it seems," he said, "so we're just gonna have to use what we got and pick a couple at random. Tollya, go to the nearest holding pen and pick some woman at random. Meg, you do the same with one of the men. Keep 'em sedated, treat them like your worst enemies, because from what I saw they're probably very well trained and could break your necks if given half a chance."

"Sure, Cap," Meg replied. "But where do we take 'em?"

"Clinic. We got a few leeches left, and we may as well use a couple. Just make sure they don't break 'em. We can't spare them."

Megak grinned. "Leeches, huh? Why don't you let

me pick the woman and let *her* pick the guy? Get better results."

"Never mind that! I don't want them harmed, just leeched. I'm gonna have to talk to this Doctor and I think he's one tough son of a bitch. They also got a few people up there with full combat gear. Three or four of them could wipe us out if they could find us and their people. You keep *that* in mind, too! The odds are we're gonna suffer for this, but it was take a chance or learn to love wheat threshing. Now—*go!* They're starting to pick up their own hostages, and we can lose some real support at our backs as well as much of the village if we don't get cracking!" He turned to a woman standing by. "You contact that Doctor. You tell 'em we'll talk in—oh, make it an hour. I don't want this to drag on, and that should be enough time for the leeches to set in."

"Right away, sir!"

"Gerta—use human runners from outside town. Do *not* use any comm links. Not yet. They'll be ready to pounce on the slightest transmission."

He'd hoped to be able to use the hostages' own links, but they apparently had a receiver implanted. Not practical if you wanted to use it yourself. He thought a moment. *Or was it?* Wouldn't the pair he would have with him be perfectly okay for that?

The native woman came in and looked around, as if thinking about something, or perhaps judging each of the hostages on some unknown level. Finally she looked at Eve, who was closest to her and to the cave opening, shrugged, and gestured for two very large men with a crude wooden cart to enter. "May as well take that one," said the woman, pointing to Eve. "She's small and light and nearest the exit."

Eve wasn't sure whether this was a good or a bad thing. Certainly unhooking her from the wall and harness was both excruciatingly painful and wonderful at one and the same time, but she was then placed, still bound, on the small cart. One of the men pulled it, while the other man and the woman made certain she stayed on the wooden bed.

They went through the small complex of modern-style cubicles built, or rather stacked, along both sides of a wide cavern within the cave, and she felt both ashamed that they could see her nakedness and yet curiously detached from it. It was hard to think about such things and be that concerned about them; she hadn't broken, but she was very much on the edge.

Down one of the caves that led out of the cavern complex, and into a "room" that was certainly carved out of a much smaller natural opening but was anything but natural now. It looked quite familiar in its basics—a clinic, not the kind of place you went for major operations or diagnostics but the kind of place you went when you just felt a bit off or had a splinter you couldn't get out of your finger, that kind of thing.

It did, however, have a fully reclining surgical bed that had seen better days and perhaps better years. It looked as if the entire population had used it repeatedly, and it had been inexpertly reupholstered far too many times. Still, it served. A medic, or at least somebody in a medic's gray tunic, came over, gave her a cursory examination while still on the cart with a diagnostic wand, checked a few readings, and then picked up a small pressure syringe. He set the dosage and then injected whatever it was into her behind. She didn't feel it, not even the pressure of the thing against her skin. She was that numb.

Within a minute she was drifting off, the residual
pain ebbing away, and she felt some relief and a pleasant feeling of floating through the clouds.

Once she was unconscious, they undid her chains
and the two big men straightened her out, something
that would have produced unbearable agony had she
not been sedated. Now they lay her on the surgical
bed and the medic performed a far more extensive
series of tests.

"You all can go now, prepare the male. This won't
take long," the medic told them. "However, you
should tell the Captain that neither one of them are
likely to be physically able to walk for some time."

"He won't like that," one of the men warned.

The medic shrugged. "Then he shouldn't truss them
up like this. You can't get full muscular function back
easily or quickly after such abuse any more than you
can stop a storm by telling it to not get you wet. If
reality was like that then he could just will the
damned crashed ship to fix itself and take off. Now,
go."

"You sure she's not gonna wake up and maybe do
some harm in here?" the woman asked.

"Were you listening? Odds are this girl couldn't lift
her arms or walk two feet at the moment. I'm sure
if we had a full ship's hospital we could do wonders,
but we don't even have a real doctor here, so forget it. Besides, the shot I gave her is good for an hour
or more at her weight. My only danger from her is
if I spend that hour talking to you and then turn my
back on her."

With that, they left, leaving him to his business.

There was bruising and cramping for sure, but
nothing that couldn't be overcome if she went through
a series of exercises over the next day or so. With-

out the automatic machines to do that, though, he could only rely on the leech.

He had often wondered who had invented the ghastly things, and he was sure that he never wanted to meet them. They certainly were an unfinished product. An artificial parasite, programmable, controllable, and knowledgeable about the human nervous system. He pulled down the full body probe and passed it over her from head to foot, then back again. The data piled up in the medical computer he normally used to see about internal injuries and breaks and the like and gave a three-dimensional hologram of the woman. He could even spot the implants in her head and admired the workmanship. If only *they* had that kind of skill!

Then he reached into a drawer and pulled out a small sealed container. There weren't many in there, and there were no more when these were gone. He put the container directly into a special socket made for it in the medlab computer console, and said, "Download human schematic." What the probes had learned, which was quite a lot, was compressed, condensed, and passed down to the leech.

The damned things scared him a bit, not so much for what they did but for what they probably could do in their finished, polished form which must be perfected by now somewhere in the human side of colonization. This thing could turn a complex human into a far simpler machine. Very limited usefulness, really. He could imagine, though, that whatever mad scientist or madder government or agency had been working on these must by now have one that fused with and reprogrammed the host. You'd seem the same, but you'd be always totally loyal to the leader, you would be obedient to all law and authority, and you'd turn in your own mother if she deviated. And that would be just for starters. *This* was bad enough, but at least it was basic and as easy to recover as to implant.

Maybe somebody had blown up the gates going back to the Mother System. Maybe they didn't want a virus of slavery spreading so quickly. That sure would explain the Great Silence.

He turned her over on her side a bit. She gave a mumbled protest but didn't awaken, and he didn't need very much area. He looked over, saw green, and removed the container from the programming slot, then turned it and positioned it just so against her neck. When he had the exact spot he wanted, he pushed a small switch at the end of the container. The thing quivered, and something small and black and sluglike went from the container into her body at that point. He withdrew the container, noted the clean but small and almost antiseptic-looking wound, got some cotton and alcohol and cleaned it off, then patched it with artificial skin. In a few hours there would be no trace of it unless you were looking for it, and even most medical diagnostics would miss the leech as it virtually merged with the spinal column just at the back of the head where it emerged from the brain. And you'd need the code and the container to transmit it to get the thing out.

One of the men who'd brought her in came back. "You all done, Doc?"

"As much as I can right now. I want you to take her to the recovery area, lie her flat, and find and bring me her robe and put it in there. Make sure there's nothing in it, of course."

"Oh, they all been stripped. Kind of a shame, though. You gonna dress her? I mean, she looks—"

"Never mind. There's enough of that around as it

is. We want control, nothing more. When you've done that, bring in the male."

I've been here too long, the medic told himself. *I'm beginning to care again.*

For Eve, it was like coming out of a sweet, motherly embrace back to a colder and harsher consciousness. Still, there was no pain, and perhaps for good reason. She found herself barely able to feel much of anything at all, almost like she'd been bathed in some painkilling lotion that had made her skin dead and nonreceptive.

She was lying on her back on a basic straw mattress, and that was interesting. She tried moving, but nothing at all seemed to work. It was as if she were paralyzed; perfectly awake, but unable to move or even feel much of anything at all.

The thought brought momentary panic. What if they *had* paralyzed her? It didn't take much—you learned that in martial arts classes. Naturally, when *The Mountain* was whole and everything and everybody was on ship's routine you could use the medical labs there and grow new connections, but down here, like this, it was a particularly frightening idea.

The big men wheeled in another figure, this time a man, and for a moment she was afraid that it was John Robey. She tried to move her head to see, but she simply couldn't. She was blinking, she was breathing, even swallowing as needed or required, but she could control nothing at all.

They'd put him next to her, so it wasn't possible to see much beyond his legs and feet. He was a hairy guy, anyway, and appeared to be, well, large if that which was partly glimpsed was what she thought it was. Still, there was no way to even tell when or if he was awake, let alone communicate with him. It was as frustrating as the cave where they'd been chained, although, she had to admit, less painful.

The medic came in after a few minutes and examined each of them professionally and clinically, top to bottom. She was somewhat embarrassed by this but could hardly protest. What good would it have done had she been able to, anyway? This was the man who'd paralyzed them both, wasn't it?

He finished, stood back, and unclipped a small rod-shaped device from a utility belt and held it like a small portable microphone. He pressed two buttons on the side and then said into it, "Legs up in the air, backs flat against the bed."

To her complete astonishment, her legs went straight up vertical to her hips and held there.

"Legs together. Yes, that's right," he continued. "Now, because I know you know what this means, I want you to use only the legs and do a bicycle movement with both. Slowly, now. Yes, that's good."

In both their cases, their legs were going back and forth as if riding some sort of imaginary bicycle or exercise machine. What was amazing to her was that she barely felt it, and had nothing to do with it.

"Excellent. Keep doing that at that rate. Back remaining flat, arms up in the air parallel to the legs. Now close fists. Bring the arms down bending at the elbows until the elbows touch the bed. Good. Now raise the arms up and at the same time open your hands completely and rapidly wiggle all your fingers. Good. Now repeat that action until I tell you to stop."

It was effortless exercise, but also frightening. Whatever this man told them to do, they had to do! How elaborate it was she couldn't imagine, but it was a kind of torture she might have imagined a demon to wield. But, of course, demons misused technology better than anyone, didn't they?

While there was still the overriding numbness, there were twinges here and there in both the arms and the legs, which told her that the pain that created them must really be horrible.

The medic nodded. "You may stop now. Arms down at your sides, hands flat against your sides, legs down in rest." He did a physical check of both of them again, and seemed satisfied.

In fact, the medic was surprised. They were in far better shape than he'd expected, or than he or most others here would be after this long in those restraints. The Captain might well be able to use them in fairly short order.

What a pity it would be to hand the controller over, though. This kind of thing might be worrisome but it gave *such* a rush! Power always beat every drug he'd tried.

"Well," he sighed, "since you're in such good shape, let's see how good." He brought the small tube near his mouth and she could see that he was actually holding down the buttons. Apparently one was her, one was him, and both buttons operated both of them at once. "Arms vertical, hands forward, fingers closed," he instructed. "Now, sit up and try and touch your toes."

The first couple of tries she couldn't do it; then, with an effort she could feel, she rose up and, with several rocking motions, managed to touch her toes. Since she had nothing to do with the operation, she tried to see if the man was doing it, too. If so, he wasn't to her stage yet.

She could hear him breathing heavily, and then

there was a mighty heave and he managed it, more or less, although he couldn't keep his fingers on the toes. It was very possible, though, that he couldn't before they'd done this to him. Different people were assembled in different ways.

"Very well, now arms at rest, pivot to your right on your ass and sit with your legs dangling over the side of the bed."

She found herself doing it, although it required a little bit of adjustment. She was now facing the young man, who was in fact quite handsomely put together but still sitting with his arms reaching to his toes. He looked familiar, but not anybody of her age or classes and not anyone she'd worked with before.

The medic repeated the instructions but with a turn to the left rather than the right, but she found that they had no effect on her, only on him, as he pivoted and then sat facing her. There was some life, and recognition, in the eyes, but little else. Eye movement was automatic as needed, just like the use of the arms and hands for balance, but it was nothing either could control.

Walking proved more difficult, and the first time she'd been told to try it she'd had to reach out and grab the bed to keep from falling. Still, the medic kept at it, very professionally, until she managed to walk across the room to the wall, turn, and walk back to the bed. Her companion had even more trouble, but managed eventually to get it, too.

She wasn't a really large woman, and both of these men were unusually tall; her companion in misery must have had twenty centimeters on her, and probably thirty kilos as well. The medic was even slightly taller than the Arm man, but thinner. Still, her level of total helplessness was compounded by standing there feeling dwarfed by the company. She had never felt so totally helpless in her life.

Well, Lord, if you are testing me, help me to pass my test, she prayed to the only one who *could* help her at that moment.

He had them do knee-bends and push-ups and several other exercises to check them out, but when it became easy and virtually effortless to do what he instructed, he tired of the game. It was clear that they were in remarkably good shape, even if visibly bruised where the chains and restraints had held them.

It was also becoming clear that whatever had been used to turn them into nothing more than automatons had serious limits in the number and complexity of instructions that would work with them. Simple things, from "Walk forward" and "Stop" to the slightly more complex "Follow me" worked fine, but any complex series of actions had to be told one instruction at a time and then combined into a sequence that would then be repeated ad nauseam. Even "Mop the floor" was tricky, since without any judgment they would just keep mopping the floor interminably until told to stop. If you couldn't simply define when and where to stop, it didn't work out. Still, she had to wonder if some of the limits weren't more than enough.

What would happen if they were told to take these guns and go back to the ship and then shoot anybody they saw who was with the Doctor? She wasn't sure there wasn't a stepped sequence of orders that would allow that to be done.

She also had to wonder how long it might be before she was sexually violated. It seemed to her that these kind of people would be unable to *not* do that, sooner or later, when they had somebody like her who couldn't resist. Particularly because the medic would have discovered right off in his probe that although the subject was well into her twenties she was still a virgin.

The same sort of thoughts had kept going through the medic's own mind as he got them into condition to do whatever the Captain had in mind, but, damn it, he couldn't and hope to still wake up the next day. Not now, not yet, and certainly not without the Captain and Committee's permission.

It was time to hand these two over and at least get a pat on the head for being competent.

And the Captain *was* pleased. Very much so. He sensed the medic's reluctance to give up the control stick, which was simply one of the leech containers set up to control up to four units from one panel, but he also understood it and grinned. "Maybe later. We have a lot of girls we can have fun with."

"Not like that one," the medic replied. "At least, not with more than four more without doing extractions and reprogramming. Oh—and I brought their robes. Didn't bother to put 'em on yet, though."

"Save it. I had been thinking along one set of lines, but now that I see these two I think perhaps I'll go a different direction. What could be more intimidating and frightening to Woodward's bunch than to see two of their own naked and totally obedient to the bad guys? They might even think that the rest of them were that way, too, and since they probably wouldn't know the method they have no way of knowing if we can't do it to everybody. A little misdirection and your mark's ignorance of your own capabilities can do wonders."

"I dunno," the medic sighed.

"Eh? What?"

"They sure as hell know we can't get off this rock without 'em."

The Captain looked like he was going to have one of his infamous and dangerous flashes of serious temper, but he caught himself right off. "That's okay, Doc. Trust me on this one. Go now. I'll take it from here. But, if you like her looks, hell, if it don't go well you can have your fun."

The medic gave a slight shrug and left.

The Captain came up to them and walked around them, examining them from head to toe as if they were some kind of strange animals or specimens. He'd used leeches before, but rarely in recent years. Too much chance of them getting broken. He'd paid dear for these decades ago on the black market in Ceberan and he never felt he'd been cheated.

He dreamed often of Ceberan, its vast bazaars and haunts and other pleasures, and what they could give to anyone who had something of serious value to trade.

Fate had played a nasty trick on him since then, giving him the address to riches beyond all his wildest dreams and then marooning him here, hiding from the others who knew not *what* he knew but only *that* he knew. After almost thirty years on this dirt ball ruling over a bunch of yokels, he was desperate to get out, to get *anywhere* but here.

It was still going to be damned tough. The only saving grace was that it should be easier with a loopy and tough evangelist than with a Navy cruiser or, worst case of all, some of his old comrades. Friendships died awful easy when you had the goods. A lot of his friends had died pitifully easy at his hand for those very same goods, in this case a piece of information.

"Follow me, you two," he said into the controller. "Walk behind me but walk where I walk and stop or turn when I turn."

He walked over to one of the lower cubicles, one on the end of the big row, and they followed him dutifully, unable to do much else.

For the next hour, the Captain prepared them. He was used to giving orders to subordinates to carry out, yet here he did not wish to relinquish the control rod at all and thus he was an active overseer.

The quarters were more like those of an officer aboard a ship than a real home, but the unit actually had running water and a small sit-down sort of ship's shower installed. He had the male slave lather and wash her completely off, and then she him, and, lastly, she also was commanded to do the Captain. He was a bit more imaginative at that point than she'd expected, and Eve feared that this was where he was going to go into her. He didn't, but he did force some oral acts that she found repugnant even as she did as ordered.

After, he fed both of them from a private stock that apparently came from far on the eastern side of the continent, but which was very well preserved. They were tubular fruit and a kind of thick gruel in a bowl eaten with a spoon, but they appeared to be sufficiently nutritious, washed down with a blend of some sort that was thick but filling and also quenched thirst. He clearly wanted them well prepared for whatever he intended to do.

Eve felt totally alone, totally helpless and humiliated, and she knew that the poor guy who shared her fate probably felt the same way, but, still, she had to admit, she was very curious as to how this bastard thought kidnapping even a hundred of the Arm would get the Doctor to move one millimeter. The Doctor got mad, and sometimes he got even, but he just about never compromised.

That didn't necessarily cheer her up. It pretty much implied that she was going to be stuck down here with these monsters permanently.

"Please, sir! He's my only child! He did nothing to you or your people! He's only a little boy!"

The woman's agony was apparent in her face and her trembling and tears, but Karl Woodward understood that the reason why the small group of all women had been sent was because they would be the best way to tug at his conscience and his heartstring. And, to an extent, they did just that—he could understand what they were going through.

Still, he knew that the children were not only in no danger, they were having the best meal and playing with the most toys of any point in their lives, and they were being carefully looked after. The older kids were being held apart from the small ones, but in a theater-type setting with, again, toys appropriate for their ages, holographic entertainment modules with content suited to their age groups, and, hell, even an automated beauty and makeover station from the makeup department. With the older ones all girls, this was a very popular place.

They also had good meals, good tasting drinks, and ice cream and candy. Heck, the kids were in a little heaven and probably mostly worried that it was all going to end too soon.

These moms and grandmas, though, they didn't know that, and that was what kept him firm, stern, and all business.

"Stop all this wailing!" he shouted to them in that

Voice of the Almighty he could call upon when preaching and teaching. Most of them stopped, or at least wound down to sniffles.

"Now, the first thing we're gonna do here is get some things straight," he thundered. "Over eighty of my people were kidnapped last night, kidnapped even though they'd done nothing but help you and your villages and shown you kindness and Christian charity. For all I know they may be dead, or tortured, or worse. And some of it was with *your* doing. Village women, not these Pirates of Belial! *Laughing* village women at that! Want to see the recordings? Maybe I can match faces to faces here. Didn't know our cameras saw in the dark, did you? I can see it in your faces! So, I wondered, if *they* can take my young people and laugh, then what can I take from them to shut off this laughter? And then it struck me! I can take their children to replace the ones you've taken!"

There was more wailing and gnashing of teeth and sobbing; he almost felt like he was in some kind of Biblical scene. What he didn't hear was confession, contrition, or much else.

"Now we can trade them back, or not. Your choice. And your problem. You have no concept of how huge a ship I've got up there. This is a mere lifeboat!" That wasn't true, but it *was* only a tenth of the complex. He and Cromwell and the rest of the Elders had spent all of the night before praying that they didn't blow this, that they did it right, that there would be no loss of life and that they would foil Satan's attack. He had to trust God after that, and play it out, have faith that his actions were God's directions. Otherwise, he would have been living a lie.

Nevertheless, no matter how it turned out, *Not my will, but thine, O Lord*.

"Now, then," he continued. "Let's stop all the games. You and this planet have descended into the grip of Satan, who is wherever air is, as he is the Prince of the Power of the Air. You've sold your souls, and now you don't seem to like living with the consequences. So, if you acted on instructions of the Father of Lies, then who gave you those instructions? The truth, now, and none of this minding my own business crap. We minded our own business and *you* attacked. Very well. Now *you*, your children, maybe this entire foul *planet* are my business. So you tell me *exactly* what I want to hear. You tell me who your people are, how they came here, why, and then why you threw in your lot with a bunch of shipwrecked pirates. Pick a spokeswoman and let her speak for all of you. You have certainly learned *nothing* from me or from God in the past week, else you would have approached me very differently. Now you stand before me as my enemy, both physical and spiritual. I will hear the truth!"

And, eventually, that's what he believed he received.

They were called the Seeders. A few of the original members, now very old, were still alive, but most of them had been born later, after the group had raised just enough money for supplies and paid a none too reputable independent freighter for passage to a habitable region not on the standard charts.

This world, which they called simply the Foundation, was where their group had been brought. Quasi-religious, they were not truly of any specific faith but rather a generalized gathering of like-minded and unhappy souls looking for some way to start over and forget the rest of the universe. Their group was of a type historians called the Naturalist Movement, in which much of the advances of humankind over the ages was viewed as evil, negative; having virtually used up and fouled up the mother planet Earth beyond nature's ability to repair, they saw the colonization movement as simply an extension of the same, to find all the pretty, natural worlds and screw them up, probably destroy them, as well. They would raise their families there in a natural way, promoting natural ways and harmony with the land and raising their children to think that way as well.

Like most such groups, they had been organized around a charismatic leader whom they called Mother Tymm. She must have been, in her own way, quite a character and dominant personality, and she received her marching orders through visions and dreams and trances. It was a curious mixture of traditional religions, old shamanlike spiritualism, and Oriental mysticism. It was said that she'd given the captain of that first freighter precise coordinates for them to have popped out here, even though this was at the end of a genhole network and had been forgotten and uncharted because it was established just as the Great Silence fell and things fell apart. That, too, Mother Tymm was supposed to have foreseen.

They set up the space defenses as best they could, but they'd even bought those on the economic level where they had no idea what they were getting or whether any of it would work or last. Then they'd established the main landing station, just to get things up and running, and Mother Tymm and a few of her councillors had left with the freighter promising to return quickly with additional seed and livestock and full title to this place as well as sufficient spare parts to keep the landing center active.

But she'd never returned, and, for almost a century,

neither did anybody else. Without their leader and
her closest advisors there wasn't even a lot of organization, but they had a firm belief that, like Jesus
and the Second Coming, Mother Tymm would some-
day, somehow, return. Until then, they abandoned
what they could not support and ran the towns and
the cottage industries and the farms the way she'd
set them up.

They ultimately *were* discovered, but by a ragtag
old tent evangelical group out wandering the stars and
searching for Heaven. They hadn't paid the group very
much attention or taken them very seriously, and the
ship they'd come in was much too small for any practical uses, and the evangelist hadn't even *heard* of
Mother Tymm, so they let him show up, gave him
the cold shoulder, and he eventually took the hint and
left. When that happened, somebody found and
turned on the defense grid, such as it was.

Only a few years later a Franciscan priest and two
nuns showed up in a ship even smaller and more
austere than the evangelist's. They refused to even
allow them to land, but they tried coming in anyway. One of the defensive units managed to target
them, and while it didn't destroy them it made their
ship inoperable. It came in at the wrong angle and
burned up in the atmosphere. Those who'd warned
them away said they heard them praying all the way
down, and then they heard the screams before they
were cut off. At that point several muscular types
smashed the last of the system communications
equipment.

That's why they didn't even know about the pirate
vessel until it screamed through the atmosphere and
overhead a bit over thirty years ago and crashed into
the lake. Locals assumed, though, that the ship had

been downed and destroyed by the same defense grid and felt a great deal of guilt about that.

But the ship hadn't been harmed by the defense grid; its shields were in fairly good shape and the defense grid by that point was not. They also had begun to believe that the only people left with interstellar spacecraft were preachers and missionaries. They quickly found out that this latest group to come in had survived the crash, but not by prayers and hymns.

In point of fact, the newcomers' ship had been badly shot up, and it was clearly on the run. Down and unable to repair it or get it back up, they had no choice but to sink it in the lake and then set up here until somebody else came along to get them out of there. They had no idea how long it would be.

The colonists originally helped them transfer their huge cargo, only to discover that once the newcomers decided to put it down in the extensive caverns and allow nothing of their technology to show, they also didn't want anyone knowing just exactly how they'd set it up or just where they'd put it, so they massacred all the colonists who'd helped them, and everyone else in the district surrounding the lakeshore near the crash site. Then they irradiated the ground for kilometers around so that nothing, absolutely nothing, could be grown there, and thus there would be no more villages in the area.

And then, oddly, they struck a deal with the colonists who did not see or know of this at the time. They were hiding out, all things below ground, and there most of them would live and do whatever they wanted as well. They wanted to be as sure as they could be that any newcomers to Foundation would see only the original colonists. Some of them would also work with the locals, but more in the nature of advisors than fellow farmers. "Efficiency experts," their leader called them.

They would harm no more villagers—everybody knew that their "tragic mistake" on landing was a lie, but the colonists could hardly do much about it and pragmatism was the best course—but would consume some of the food and drink as a "fee." In return for that "fee," they would train and allow the use of the complex learning system they had along with its practical library, which allowed much of the network of irrigation among other things to be improved and developed and which, also, gave their children an education and practical skills, and they would handle the one area most needed by the colonists: medical and pharmaceutical skills and goods. They also established a far more efficient and motorized underground trade route system so that foods that normally could never reach, say, the nearby village, would now be readily available and some could even be stored. Refrigeration units, power units, and the like from the ship were established underground for that purpose.

They mostly lived in this region because there were only a few hundred of them and because in this area the strata and oddities in the magnetic fields and other things the women didn't understand made it possible for them to hide from the most sophisticated scanners.

But the thing that had brought everybody up short and made the alliance a willing one after some early roughness was the reason why they had been in a fight, and what they had that everyone else wanted.

A little piece of knowledge. Something stolen, most likely, but something among the most valuable snippets of knowledge in the entire known galaxy if truth be told.

Mother Tymm had prophesied from the start that even Foundation was but a way stop, a stepping stone. That the true Naturalists would actually meld with the forces of nature, the deities of the Garden, and that their children and grandchildren would walk and live in perfect harmony with nature and the natural and supernatural upon the world of Paradise among the Three Kings. And she'd further prophesied that this would come about from the Tree of Evil imparting to the Knowledge of Good, and that Darkness would take the Seeders to the Light.

"Are you telling me that this pirate leader claims to have the location of the Three Kings?" Karl Woodward responded, incredulous. Cromwell and some of the others behind him were beyond that and almost into derision. Every charlatan anybody ever met claimed to know the location of the Three Kings, and every cult and nut group and even some perfectly normal, natural, and straightforward political and religious groups always seemed to fall for it.

"And because of this prophecy you think that these men and women of darkness are the ones that are here to take you to the Three Kings?" the Doctor asked them.

They nodded. "And that is why we live with them and do as they say and protect them as they do what they must. We are sorry that it was you, but whoever it was becomes part of the prophecy, don't you see? And they have kept their word to us for a very long time now."

"But what makes you certain that they *really* know where the Three Kings are any more than we do?"

Woodward pressed. "These people are in the grips of the Father of Lies."

"We know, but Mother Tymm did not lie, and her prophecies came true. Something these people had, something real and physical, convinced those who made the bargain that this knowledge was there, and after that, since it was impractical to show it to everyone, there was and is a measure of faith involved. You spoke on just such a topic."

"Physical proof? You've not seen this proof, though, or know what it might be if it really exists?"

"No, but we have Mother's prophecies, in her own hand. We believe in them. They have always been the true guide."

This was a rough one. Christians certainly weren't the only members of a belief system that acted in faith, and the old Biblical axiom was that the test of a prophet was that his—or her—prophecies came true.

"I'd like to see and read the writings of this Mother Tymm," he told them. "But, for now, I have a more immediate problem. Where are my people being held?"

"Honestly, sir, we don't know," the chief spokeswoman assured him. "We are not allowed in most of the cave complex, save the parts that are part of their bargain with us. The caves run forever, almost. Hundreds and hundreds of kilometers. And they have some slow but steady transport down there that can carry loads. Now and then they treat us to tropical fruits of a kind that we know some of the farthest villages can grow but which no one here has ever seen because they spoil long before they can get here by crindin wagons. They do not grow them below, so they must get them from those same villages, yet they

are always just ripe. If they can cover that distance,
and underground, in that short a time, then your
people can be anywhere at all."

Woodward sat back and sighed. Much of the history
and background was now out in the open, but nothing else had changed. One shoe was on the pirates' foot,
the other was waiting for the scoundrels' to drop. If
they went into the caves in full combat armor following the ferrets then people would die, some of the
combat gear might even be lost due to clashes with who
knew what sort of weapons, and, in the end, you could
only find hostages dead using the brute force method.

They still had to continue to drill holes in likely
areas and send the ferrets in and hope they got lucky.
Until then, they would have to wait for the bastards
on the other side to make a move.

"Sir?" the chief spokeswoman for the group called
out.

"Yes?"

"Our children—what about the children?"

"Nothing has changed, at least not yet," he
reminded them. "What happens to the children
depends entirely on what this spawn of Hell hiding
appropriately below decides to do next."

He suspected that they wouldn't have long to wait,
and he was right.

VIII:
IS THE DEVIL
A GENTLEMAN?

The note was in a scraggly hand, clearly the work of someone who wrote down very few things and those mostly for his own use.

"Dear Doctor Woodword," it began, misspelling his name and getting him irritated right from the start by so doing. "I am Captain Morgudan Sapenza, once of the proud ship *Amandal*, now, as you know, half sunk in the great lake, but still master of her crew and systems. I am sorry to have had to do this, but after all this time we have become desperate and feel we have nothing to lose. This is a backward planet, but we have some comforts of civilization below and we have many modern tools of our trade. We must talk, but your own ships and company can easily do me great harm and then where am I? So, you will have to come to where the messenger here will lead you. It is not far and you have my word that no harm will come to you nor will you be touched. You may bring a fully armed bodyguard to insure this. I will wait for you with a way for us to speak. If you do not come, I will leave at least one of our guests from your company there by two hours before sundown today, or rather I will leave the body and you shall see how this person died. The next time it will be two. Then four an hour after that. And so on. I am sorry, but it is the only way I know of to insist that you come. Until then, I remain, *very* sincerely, Captain Morgudan Sapenza.

"P.S. Nice move, but I have no kids."

Woodward shook with rage, and he looked ready to kill the small villager who'd brought the note. Cromwell carefully retrieved the message and handed it to a technician. "Any clues and analysis, Sister— and move on it!"

The aide took the sheet with gloved hand and dashed off to the lab.

"And where are we supposed to meet this—this *creature*?" Karl Woodward thundered at the messenger.

"Please, sir! I'm just a villager. Not one of *them*! I even dunno what the thing says. I never learned to read, which is why he took me, I guess. If we don't do what they tell us, our families—gone! You got to understand!"

Woodward seemed to soften for a second, but only for that brief flash. He had only the word of this little man that the messenger wasn't really a certain captain himself, or the chief torturer. The Father of Lies was the greatest actor in all creation.

"I didn't ask you to throw yourself on your knife," the Doctor reminded him. "I asked where this meeting was to be held."

"Just over that knob, in the crindin pasture," the little man told him. "The exact spot I'd have to show you."

"Near one of their tunnel entrances, I assume?"

"Oh, yes, sir. There's about a dozen around here, and one inside the village barn. They don't use this one much, though."

"What is your name?" Woodward asked the little man.

"They call me Ziggee, sir," he replied. "Kind of a play on a silly name."

"All right, Ziggee, you can show us your neutrality by going over to Brother Cromwell there and, on the map he has of this area, drawing or pointing to just where all these entrances are. And if we ever find out that you left out *just one*, then you will be treated as an accomplice and dealt with. Understand?"

The little man nodded nervously. "Y—yes, sir."

The Archangel up above studied a close-up of the area and reported, just to the Doctor, "Looks fairly flat, some dirt mounds and, sir, a *lot* of, well, crindin fertilizer if you know what I mean. No energy scan, but we'll nail it the moment it opens. Depending on where he stops, call it twenty or thirty meters of fairly flat field."

"Can you cover it all?"

"Yes, sir! We could shoot gnats from this altitude at an area that clear and defined!"

"Well, I don't want you to shoot gnats, but you might be called on to shoot everybody who's not us. Full stun from above at the first sign of problems. If you have to, shoot *us*, too. We'll wake up. Just make sure nobody else can wake up sooner. Brother Cromwell will be with me as bodyguard, and in full armor. I assume we can leave him standing."

"Sir, in that armor, he can take a heavy shot from us."

"Oh—and one more thing," Woodward added, as loud as he could.

"Sir?"

"If our native guide pulls anything at all, even tries to run or hide, smite him, level one, no permission required. You got that?"

The little man looked up from the map. "Hey! Wait a minute, Doc! What's this smitin' stuff?"

Cromwell towered over him and grinned. "Basically, my son, you will either share our fate or they will burn you to a crisp if I don't do it first. Got that?"

"Y—yes, sir," Ziggee responded miserably.

It took them less than an hour to prepare. Cromwell had his recharged suit ready for him, its crosses blazoned, and Woodward, while looking normal, used his large bulk to disguise some lightweight sophisticated body armor. It wouldn't really handle a head shot, but it had come in handy elsewhere before. He also put on his black frock "preacher's coat," which had loose sleeves fitted with smart laser pistols. Once on, all he needed to do was mentally command them to deploy and he would be shooting with both hands.

And, just before Cromwell sealed his suit, the two of them went back into Woodward's quarters and took a communion together, imploring God to be with them and the captives.

They were just emerging when a young male member of the Arm rushed in. He seemed nervous and a bit awed at the sight of both leaders so close up, but it didn't stop him.

"Sir? Doctor Woodward?"

"Yes, boy?"

"John Robey, sir! They took my partner and almost got me, but I got in here just in the nick of time. I've been going crazy, sir, praying that I could be a part of the recovery."

Karl Woodward smiled and put his big arm on the young man. "You will, lad, you will. But not in *this* business today. I simply have no role for you in this."

"But, sir! We were assigned to this very village. We were the advance team for right here, and I've been living here, with and among these people, for weeks now. I know the land and who's who. For example, I know that this little man's no member of this village. I've never seen him before."

Woodward's busy eyebrows went up. "Indeed! Is that so? Hmm . . . What about this crindin pasture?"

"It's fairly flat, that's true, but if there's any caves underneath they have to be pretty deep. Crindins alone can weigh over eight hundred kilos and when they're done for the night they pretty well wander over that area. Most of this is soft limestone, but that area was picked as the pasture because it's more like a granite extrusion or table. If he takes you there, they won't be popping up out of the ground."

Cromwell and Woodward exchanged glances. "Maybe we *should* take him, Karl," the security chief said.

"Could be. Can't hurt. All right, son. Not even Tom here can watch me, that weasel, and all our backs at the same time. Keep your pistol armed and in your robe sleeve pocket, and keep it aimed at our shifty little friend in there. Got that?"

"Yes *sir*! Thank you!"

"Don't thank me, son, until it's over," Woodward cautioned him. "Usually, when you face down the devil, it hurts like hell even when you win."

Cromwell looked at the old man and sighed. "I wish you weren't going at all. I know how these kind of people think. Take out the head and they'll be able to take over the body."

"*Our* body was hung on a tree twenty-two hundred years ago and He screwed 'em up good by coming back," the Doctor responded firmly. "If I don't walk out there, where's my demonstration of faith?"

"But only one person came back from the dead," Cromwell noted. "And I don't think there's anything in the promises that an exception will be made for you or me."

Karl Woodward smiled. "If I die, I'll just find out the answers to all my questions and the counters to all my doubts and fears that much sooner. I've already lived seven times the length He did; half of me is regenerated or regrown, the other half should be. But I didn't found *this* ministry. I came along when Doctor Chernyn was called to the Lord. And if God needs somebody else to carry on after me, He'll provide him. No, Tom. You don't run from the devil; that's playing *his* game. If I never taught anybody anything else I sure should have emphasized *that*. You go out, face him nose to nose, and when he's not looking, you twist his balls." He reached down, put on a floppy old hat, then searched around and found a cigar.

"I've stayed off these since they regrew half my heart," he said nostalgically, "but I've kept 'em fresh. Now's as good a time as any to have one." He fumbled in a drawer, found an old hand-carved container and from it took out a battered old cigar lighter.

He lit the cigar, puffed on it to make it catch full, and leaned back, his expression almost as if he were witnessing the Second Coming. Then he suddenly bounded into action.

"All right, people! Go get that little snake and let's go spit at the devil!"

Cromwell's armor was an intimidating sight, and the malleable "shell" that formed around him and protected him also could take on some qualities at his very thoughts. It was shining now in the sun, gleaming silver, and it was impressive.

John Robey had on the crimson robe of a security officer. He liked the look, even though he was, of course, as vulnerable as ever in the thing. It took years to learn how to mentally merge with those combat suits, and probably many more to learn how to use them properly. He would have liked its protection, but not unless, like Cromwell, it was second nature and second skin. Instead, he watched Doc Woodward, and he was impressed. He'd never seen the old man so up, so seemingly confident and almost eager for some kind of action. He was taking this whole thing seriously, but, somehow, you got the feeling that the old boy was enjoying this, at least on some level.

As Ziggee led them up towards the village and then to the left of the great barn, Cromwell was already in full sensor mode and on a scrambled tactical frequency he was certain nobody but his people could pick up.

"Top floor barn, facing the pasture," Cromwell ordered. *"I think it's a good spot for a sniper."*

"What shall I do if he's up there, sir?" Alpha's voice responded.

"Oh, terminate anybody who has a weapon. If they

*have any gear, though, try and keep that intact. Keep
it quiet.*"

They were in the pasture now, and Ziggee was
looking around as if searching for some kind of
marker. Either that, Robey thought, or he was afraid
of stepping in crindin dung. It didn't smell all that
bad out here, but there was a lot of it.

Woodward sensed that the little weasel wasn't too
sure of himself. The Doctor glanced at his watch and
noted that it was pretty much on the nose when the
meeting was supposed to take place.

"Apostles, this is Archangel," came a general frequency call to all of them. *"I've picked up activity
about twenty meters to your right. I'm also reading
hostile powered weapons in the barn and in the last
house facing the pasture."*

"Got it," Alpha responded. *"Delta and I will take
the barn, Gamma the house, Epsilon will hold between
as backup. Move!"*

Ziggee finally stopped in the middle of the field
and scratched his head, then turned back to the trio.
"Honest, sir, this is about the place. They was supposed to put a marker here, but I don't see it."

"I hate it when demons aren't punctual," the Doctor growled, "but we'll wait a little bit. Who knows?
There may be surprises in store."

Almost on cue there was the curious and unique
sound of an energy pistol firing on full power, and
suddenly from the small lift door at the top of the
barn something pitched forward and fell the nearly
fourteen meters to the ground.

"One down," Alpha reported. *"One running like all
the demons of Hell was chasing him. Shall we pursue?"*

"Negative. Anybody who runs like that doesn't need

encouragement. You two stay up there and cover us instead. Epsilon move to back up the house entry.

Since Cromwell was in his suit and on a high security frequency, he alone could speak back and forth without anyone else hearing. On the other hand, Ziggee was beginning to look back at the body that seemed to be still smouldering on the ground and the little man didn't look too good at all.

A second set of three sharp electronic blasts came from the house. Within seconds, it seemed to catch fire, with smoke coming from the small back window.

"Two more down," Epsilon reported. *"I don't think we can put this thing out on our own, though."*

"If it doesn't look likely to spread, let it burn," Cromwell told them. *"If it does, allow the villagers to put it out."*

Woodward looked at the silvery suit of armor quizzically. "Tom?"

"Nothing, sir. Uninvited guests are taken care of, and we may have a midday cook fire over there."

"Hey!" Ziggee yelled, a real nervous wreck at this point. "You ain't supposed to do that!"

"Neither were you," Woodward responded, still enjoying his cigar, now already about half smoked. "Now, your Captain what's his name can come on out in the open like us, fully armed, and bring his best soldier with his best equipment. Then we'll be even. But snipers taking beads on us from hidden places—*that* will never do."

"I—" Ziggee started to respond, but he suddenly stopped and just stared, apparently taken as off guard as the three from the ship.

"Doctor Woodward, so nice of you to come," said a woman's voice. They all turned and saw Eve, naked as the day she was born and still showing the bruises of her bonds and captivity, standing there woodenly.

"Eve!" Robey shouted. "It's me, John!"

Woodward put his hand on the young man's shoulder. "That's not your Eve, although she's certainly dressed like it."

"You are correct, sir," said the figure. "I am Captain Sapenza. I am using this body for several obvious reasons, including the ones you just so ably demonstrated. They were not amateurs, either, that your people took."

"Neither are mine," responded the Doctor.

"Eve" laughed, but it was a hollow, wooden laugh, like the voice, without body language to reinforce it.

"In addition to the safety this method affords me," Sapenza through Eve continued, "it also demonstrates that I am not without resources myself, even if I do not have anything on the scale of yours. I wish to demonstrate that we are not merely talking potential death of your people here."

Cromwell was inaudible to the rest, but not to Archangel above. *"Archangel, is this a broadcast or is she truly possessed by something?"* This was new to him and he didn't like it.

"If it's a broadcast I do not have a way to find the frequency or method of transmission," the controller in orbit above them reported. *"Either this captain is inside the body or he's got some method we know nothing about."*

Woodward sighed. "Well, I am impressed, I admit, although the shame she must feel is not reciprocated by looking at a very attractive if mishandled and mal-treated female form. Possession of even the most holy isn't unknown to us in history, but only her body is in danger, not her soul."

"Her soul, if there is such a thing, is as much in my possession as her body," the Captain responded. "Conditioning, hopelessness, trauma—all that can, in the hands of experts, be simple to do. We've had a lot of practice with just some of these dumb peasants. You don't need gimmicks, technology, any of that. You just need a damp cell, some chains, a bare light, and a feeling of total and complete impotence, and to stop them when they go through the possible suicide phase. *Anybody* can be broken, Doctor. *Anybody.* Even you if I had you, or, for that matter, me if you had me and went that route. And when you break, you're damned. Isn't that right, Doctor?"

"You are under the control of and in the power of creatures you do not even believe exist," Woodward told him. "And, to them, you're just another tool, just as this poor girl is to you."

"Well, then, you'll just have to deal, tool to tool, as it were, won't you?" Sapenza came back.

"All right, then, what's your proposition? It's hot out here and uncomfortable to boot."

"Direct and to the point. Too bad, really. I enjoy drawing things out."

"Then let's do this sitting comfortably in air conditioning and with decent drinks," the Doctor retorted.

Sapenza laughed. "I really do enjoy dealing with you, Doctor. Very well, let's be at it. We want off this rock. Our ship's disabled and beyond our ability to fix, but *your* people might know how to do it. If not, they know where to go to surreptitiously get the parts. I want a working ship again, Doctor. I want off this dirt ball. I'll give your people the codes and anything they need to gain full access to the ship. It's underwater, but I know you can get to it, and if necessary lift it. Some of my staff and your staff will work together. We've already done a major damage assessment, and it's not that huge a job—if you have the parts and equipment to do the fix. As it is, for us, it's impossible."

"And for the eighty-seven that you captured I am supposed to do all this?"

There was a pause, and then Sapenza, through Eve, said, "No, Doctor. The eighty-seven captives are to keep your people from coming down here and tearing through our underworld. You can raise hell with us down here but you can't save them by doing that, and after all these years we have nothing at all to lose."

"And if I just leave them?"

"You'd really do that? Leave this pretty girl to all the folks down here who want to have some fun with her?"

"There are times when you have to make hard decisions in doing the Lord's work. I'm not your typical Bible thumper, Sapenza. In fact, I'm not an evangelist in the traditional sense at all. I come, I teach, I see if it takes. If it does, I leave some to plant and nurture. If it doesn't, I curse the world and all its people and move on. That is my job. If I leave them here, God will treat them as martyrs. He will take them to His bosom when their time comes no matter what you make of their physical flesh here. But you, and your people, will still be here and still be stuck, and your very existence will be entirely in *our* hands. Either we can find the Navy, or whoever you were in a battle with and are still hiding from all this time later, or whatever, or we can blow the controls on the genhole as we leave and you'll be marooned here *forever*. Which would you prefer?"

Sapenza sounded genuinely shocked. "You would *really* do that to so many of your own young people?"

"As opposed to what? Selling our souls? I would have to pray a lot over the decision, but I suspect I could still sleep."

"Well, Doc, that *does* make it a little easier on me, though, doesn't it? What happens to them is your fault, your choice. And, as I said, they are only to insure that you don't come down here. They are not my hostages in this matter."

"No? Then what else do we have to talk about, Captain?"

"You. When we first crashed here, we removed some of the heavy weapons and concealed them in an effective defensive grid. They're good weapons, many of a kind rarely seen even in the old days, and they have their own internal power packs. Fusion and directed antimatter steam, for example. Your soldier boy there can probably tell you what those things can do."

"What are you threatening, Sapenza? To shoot down my ship in orbit?"

Sapenza gave another pause, although it was unclear if it was for effect or if he was really nervous or just thinking furiously. Finally he said, "No, I'm not sure we have the juice for that, and definitely not the space combat computers. Even a lucky hit would probably be diluted enough to bounce off your shields. These weapons weren't really designed as surface weapons. But they *can* take on more limited targets, and they power on in seconds. They can take on a stationary or nearly stationary object very well, even of some great size, and concentrate enough to go through the best shields in that scenario. And I think we could knock down your ersatz lifeboats, your shuttle craft, with disposable weapons, since the shuttles really don't have any effective energy shielding."

"He's talking about *Olivet*," John Robey gasped. "Sir, he's got the ground ship targeted!"

In his head, Cromwell, on the secure band, hissed, *"Shut up you idiot! Just play along and don't panic!"*

Robey felt properly chastened, but he couldn't quite figure out why he was being called on the carpet for that kind of outburst. They *were* trapped, weren't they?

Weren't they?

The Doctor thought for a moment, then said, "All right, tell you what. Send me your experts on your ship with the codes and I'll have maintenance and engineering take a look at it. I assume I can bring a few people down and shoot a few back up to their labs?"

"Of course. But no one from your *present* ship goes up, including you, and nobody comes down to this area. You have one shuttle. That should be sufficient to get anyone you need over to the lake in plenty of time, and back as well. We'll be watching."

"I'm sure you will," Woodward told him. "So, shall we meet here again tomorrow, same time, same place, and compare notes?"

There was a pause, then, "Yes, that will be sufficient."

"In the meantime, you will treat my people as your prisoners, *not* as your property!" the Doctor snapped. "I see what you've done to this girl even *before* you worked your evil on controlling her actions. You will find a cave with one entrance you can guard or close off, you will give them sufficient food and water, and you can post guards to keep them from getting out. If you can't do that much, then I swear to God that

I will blow up your ship, my ship, I don't care, and no matter what happens you will *never* be able to turn a back on any of us. Understood?"

The Captain wasn't used to this kind of attitude, but after counting ten to keep his own temper in check, he then chuckled and replied, "All right. We'll try it. But if any of them make a break for it or cause any harm to *my* people, they will pay and it will be on your head, not mine."

"If you can't do your part of the job, then send them back!" Woodward said acidly.

Eve turned and woodenly walked off into the field, oblivious of what was lying on the ground, and reached a point about ten meters from them. She then took one more step and seemed to fall into a deep hole. Robey, unable to restrain himself, ran to the spot, only to be unable to find it even though it was so close.

"It's a rock door, boy!" Woodward called to him. "Relax. I think we are on the way to resolving this."

Cromwell seemed much more relieved, and, after doing a fresh check for bugging devices in the Doctor's offices, he seemed almost relaxed. Robey was anything but, with the image of the tortured and manipulated puppetlike Eve fresh in his mind and, he knew, likely to haunt his nightmares.

The Doctor was a bit angrier inside, an anger that bubbled up from time to time, but he, too, seemed more confident.

"At least we know he can't control most of the hostages," Cromwell commented. "I'm sure you noticed that."

Woodward sat back in his big chair and nodded. "Yes, when he began to object to a normal incarceration, it was pretty clear that whatever he did to the girl has severe limits. We're not going to have to fight some sort of zombie army."

Robey just shook his head. "Sir, what's the difference? I mean, if he can target us here in *Olivet* and he can shoot down the shuttles, then he has *us* hostage, too."

"Not at all," Cromwell told him. "In fact, until now I wasn't certain of just how much relative power and equipment he might have. Now I know. It's why he keeps our people. Deep down, even he suspects that we're in no true danger here. If it wasn't for them, we could just curse this place and go."

"Then why deal with him? Wouldn't they be just as well-off passing over to the Lord as being like— like *that*?"

"We're going to try and save them all, or as many as we can, son. That I promise," Woodward assured him. "Right now, we're going to play along a bit. Rather interesting that they held out the old Three Kings canard here but never mentioned it out there. I wonder if our pirate captain realizes just what a miserable spot he's in?"

Robey respected these two men, and if they didn't seem worried then he saw no reason to stew on their behalf, but he realized that eighty-seven lives were still at stake, maybe a few more on their side. "So what do we do now?"

"We pray, as always, and trust to the Lord," Karl Woodward told him seriously. "And, later on, our engineers and technicians will go with *their* engineers and technicians, and maybe by midnight we'll know just what kind of weapons they had on that ship, which ones they removed, and just what their targeting and energy capabilities are. By morning we should know more about that ship, and have its schematics analyzed, than the original crew probably knew. And by the end of our meeting tomorrow we should have access to their underground information, particularly if we can reclaim your woman friend. I can't guarantee we can free her from whatever infernal device they're using on her, but I *do* think that we may well be able to listen in on them."

"And then," added Thomas Cromwell, "the Lord will enable His terrible swift sword."

It was difficult to say if Eve was any better or worse than the day before, or even if she could feel such things, but at least the old pirate captain was learning. This time she had her old robe on, and it even looked like somebody had cleaned it. It didn't take away from the woodenness of her actions, but it did seem to give her a little dignity.

Woodward, Cromwell, Robey, and several others had spent the entire night in the strangest gathering Robey could ever have imagined, a kind of combination prayer meeting, strategy session and technical argument with experts up on *Sinai*. He was out of his depth from the start and he knew it, so he mostly tried to concentrate on prayer and, as they kept urging him, getting some sleep. He couldn't do much of either one, though. They had all those comrades, including the outgoing and intelligent Eve made little more than a robot, and they had weapons from an interstellar combination warship and freighter mounted in a defensive ring so that they could blast anything trying to land that they didn't like—and, of course, anything taking off as well. It seemed like a standoff, and that meant exactly that. The Doctor would never make a serious deal with these evil people, nor could anybody trust them in the first place even if you tried. And they could blow *Olivet* to hell, or Heaven, or wherever, leaving those on the ground stranded as much as the locals here and those up above helpless to do more than take a measure of revenge.

But if you looked at Woodward, you'd swear that there wasn't much to worry about. Robey began to wonder if being almost two hundred years old wasn't pushing the envelope on the mind. They could repair, regenerate, or grow new almost any part of the body these days, but just because you could replace brain cells didn't mean that you operated like you did in your twenties, or thought as quickly and clearly. Science had moved the bar on longevity and quality of life by a great amount, but there was still a bar there.

Cromwell, somewhat the heir apparent, was different. There was no question the man was a true believer, a fanatic, and in top physical and mental form for taking on all comers. But his own dark and violent side was in some ways as scary as that pirate's, and there was also some of the same "the end justifies any means" attitude to his actions and beliefs. Everybody at least knew about Karl Woodward, once considered one of humanity's smartest human beings, a genius in any field that interested him, professor, lecturer, researcher, who, after the Great Silence, one day announced that he had deduced through research and logic the truth of Christianity and embarked on his new crusade, alienating just about every one of his old intellectual colleagues who thought he'd gone over that fine line between genius and madness and also alienating just about all of traditional Christianity by rejecting most of it as "corrupt and stupid."

Woodward was also convinced that the Great Silence was at the heart of current day religion; that in fact humanity was in the "post-Apocalypse period" on Earth and that was why they'd been cut off. Not being on Earth, not being there for the Second Coming, they had denied themselves a part in it. Now the rest of humanity was in a desperate war between those evil forces not involved in the matters of Earth and those other celestial civilizations who were waiting for them.

Robey had been born and raised to believe that, as had the other young people of *The Mountain* and its mission. Now, though, he was beginning to wonder if maybe Woodward wasn't as divinely inspired as he seemed. It was very easy to believe within the ship's society and within a traditional missionary frame. It was getting a lot harder, with real evil beneath them and around them holding real guns.

Now, out in the sun once more, facing his former partner under the control of that evil, he felt no sense of holy mission, none of God's presence, only a kind of hollow and hopeless sense of inevitable doom. Even his one instruction from Cromwell, his one job, as it were, in whatever they were plotting, was conditional and not exactly something that he thought would do any good.

"Well, what do you think?" Captain Sapenza asked them. "What do your people tell you?"

"Your engines are shot. Your bubble's cracked clean through," Cromwell told him. "There's no repair for that kind of thing. You have to replace the entire aft engine system, and there's little chance of finding one of those in good shape that would fit your system these days. The only thing salvageable is your freighter module, but that was never intended to land intact like that. There's no way to get it back up. But you knew that, didn't you?"

"We—*suspected* it, but without the kind of diagnostic equipment and experts you had, and the scanners, we didn't know for sure. Well, that leaves us with Plan B."

"Which is?" Woodward prompted.

"You'll have to take us all with you."

Woodward laughed. "Oh, really? And why should we do that? We've already established that you do not have sufficient hostage incentive for that."

"I *will* kill them, or worse," Sapenza warned him.

"I'm sure you will. People have been doing that to Christians for a very long time, and, unfortunately, in an abominable twisting of belief on its head, so-called Christians have been doing it to others. Still, we have a word for it—'martyr.' Those who break and voluntarily go with you lose their souls. Good riddance. Those who don't and die for it will find themselves welcomed at the new temple in Jerusalem and become written as saints in our newest testament. Or, to put it another way, you blew it, *Captain* Sapenza. You have nothing to offer. Rot in Hell."

Sapenza surprised him by responding, "Why, *this* is Hell, nor am I out of it. If you're right, and Earth's Last Trump already blew, then *both* of us missed it, Doctor. Not just me, but you, too. Look around, Doctor. *This* dirt ball is the kind of place you get when you think you got the One True Faith and you follow that one with the real truth blindly down any road and right into the sun to be consumed! *That* is your history, too. You don't think old Mother Tymm didn't believe it just as much as you believe your position? From *my* perspective, the only difference between you and your followers and she and her followers is that yours haven't yet been led into their own circle of Hell yet. But when you do, when you do, then don't take me along with you. If you're going to Hell anyway, Doctor, you should have a really good time before you get there."

The Captain's words seemed to be having a serious effect on Woodward, who stood there, grim-faced, for the first time looking very old and not as cocksure of himself and all his views. For Robey it was even more devastating, putting into words what had been gnawing at his soul since the hostages had been taken.

"What exactly are you proposing, Sapenza?" Woodward asked in a hollow tone.

"Mutual mistrust and cooperation on that basis. I have a hundred and sixteen people here, plus your eighty-seven. We wire ourselves and those hostages together and we come aboard your ship over there as a group. Put us in one of the big rooms you have there—the thing's designed as a traveling cathedral, after all. You seal us in there. We'll have a floating dead man switch between us. Anything like a gas or energy attack, anything sudden, we all blow up. Or, we come aboard, and you feed us and take us out of here."

"To where, exactly, do we take you?"

"It's been a long time. I don't know what's still going where. If we can get to a place where we can get a replacement ship, fine. That's good enough. At least some kind of civilization where I can bargain what I have."

"And what do you think you can bargain for the likes of a ship? Even if we took you in this fashion and there was no double cross, we can't take your cargo, your booty, whatever."

"Don't be stupid, Woodward. You were supposed to be a bright guy. With a diminishing supply of ships and repairs there's little material that can be traded for anything big these days, although we'll try and deal the salvage on my poor ship there. But I wasn't kidding about having something of incalculable value. Knowledge that is worth more than anybody can pay for it."

"You're not going to come up with that Three Kings nonsense again," Cromwell put in.

"Oh, but that's exactly what I've got, sir. I've got the Three Kings. I've got their location, their general descriptions, full navigational information, requirements to force through to them, and some sampling that indicates that they at least partially live up to their reputation. You see, we found dear, sainted Mother Tymm's vessel. *She* had the information. Where *she* got it from, I don't know. I don't think she'd ever been there, but she sure knew somebody who had. The data modules were scouting reports from a Vaticanus class scout. And, there were—samples. All the stuff the old legends never gave, but otherwise totally consistent with them."

"How do you know she didn't just create these out of her visions?" Cromwell asked him. "If she could astronavigate, it wouldn't be that outrageous."

Eve reached into her robe pocket and pulled out an egg-shaped object about the size of a child's fist. She stretched out an arm straight in front of her, offering it to them. When neither of the older men moved, Robey stepped forward and took it from her, then stepped back.

It was smooth, smoother than glass, smoother than just about anything he could remember. It was also slightly warm; not hot, but certainly above body temperature, and it didn't seem to be warm because it was next to anything. The colors of the thing were spectacular, a kind of crimson wash against a pale yellow; but although he could not catch it doing anything, the mixture seemed to move, so that you couldn't quite find the same pattern or design if you looked away and then looked back at it.

John Robey stared hard into the egg-shaped thing and, somehow, half inside the thing, half inside his head, a shape, a *picture* of some sort, seemed to form and then sharpen into realistic three-dimensional clarity. He saw it, cried out, and almost dropped the thing. Cromwell moved quickly and caught it, then looked at it quizzically.

"What was it, son? What did you see?" the security man asked him.

"I—I saw *her*. Eve. She was—screaming. In agony. It was—*horrible*."

Cromwell looked at it, turned it over in his hand, and shook his head. "Weird," he muttered. "Doctor?"

Woodward took the thing, examined it, and nodded. "It's just as the old stories say. There's supposed to be some of these on Vaticanus, but of course a lot of the physical evidence was suppressed. There was always the hope that they could find the place again while convincing everybody else it was just a legend."

He stared into it as Robey had, and for him, too, a vision coalesced, although clearly not the same one the younger man had seen. He looked at it, seemingly transfixed, fascinated by its image which seemed revealed to him alone.

Suddenly, he broke away, as if awakening from a trance. "What did you do to get this, Sapenza? Murder the crew?"

"Nothing of the sort! She'd been dead and so had the small crew of that ship for a century and a half before we lucked onto her, and that was only because we'd just had a professional disagreement, let's say, with a former partner over some financial matters and then discovered he had bigger guns than we did even though we had a faster ship. We went through gate after gate at top speed, so scrambled even we didn't know or care where we were going. We gave 'em the slip somewhere in the system, and came out an old gate and almost crashed into the wreck. Who knows how long it was there, or how many other ships might have gone past without even noticing it? Sheer luck, or chance. We did a salvage and strip, and the first thing we did, of course, was retrace its course to see if the colony was worth a look. As you can see, it wasn't, but that last shot we'd taken and the stress of all that gating at speed caused the bubble to burst. We've been stuck here ever since. The Curse of Mother Tymm, you might call it. What with all the informational stuff, the Three Kings artifacts, and the Reverend Mother's own personal possessions we were able to convince the yokels that we were the guardians until the dear Mother returned. She won't, of course. Not in *this* life. Besides, she'd be almost four hundred anyway. A bit old for anybody's taste."

"Why did she die? And why did she leave the colony here?" Cromwell asked.

"I can tell you that there's no gate at the Kings. It's a free wormhole and its got a lot of energy. You'd need shields ten times stronger than what that old bucket of hers had. I think they tried it, but they found out in time that if they went through they'd wind up as the galaxy's smallest neutron star. So they dropped here, figuring it would support the colony for years until she could get what she needed to go through, and she left. The thing must have been half torn to pieces by the first attempt. It was imploded. Ugly. But, at least, intact for all that. If it had exploded we'd never have figured out what it was."

And there was the whole story. It rang true, felt true, sounded true. And it had one particularly problematical side effect.

Maybe these soulless and evil people really *did* know the way to the Three Kings.

"There's no way we could take them under those conditions he laid out," Cromwell noted on the secure channel. *"We'd wind up killing all of us, and destroying the full* Mountain *as well. I say we go with our original plan. Then we'll see what sort of bargain can be struck at the point of* our *weapons!"*

Woodward continued to finger the egg for a few moments, then he sighed and seemed to nod to himself. After a moment, he took out another cigar from his pocket and lit it. As he puffed, he stepped back a bit from the others.

"Okay, boy, this is it! On my count, it's shoot and run! Three . . . two . . . one . . ." And then, shouted loudly, "Now!"

IX:
THE DEVIL IN IRONS

It might have been that after all this time, Captain Sapenza was just too rusty, but he'd clearly made an amateur's mistake and now he was going to pay for it. With the security team sweep having made certain that there were no unwelcome snipers about as had been planted the day before, the primary danger came from who and what they could see and from the single entrance/exit they already knew about.

From the moment Doctor Woodward had signalled the "go ahead" with his cigar, things pretty much automatically happened. As the Doctor stepped back, Cromwell's combat suit sent a strong stun charge straight into Ziggee, dropping him before the little man even was aware that anything was wrong. At the same moment, Robey tapped the small button just inside the sleeve of his robe and felt the pistol shoot into his hand. He didn't have Cromwell's computerized super accuracy but he didn't need it; his job was to shoot Eve at maximum stun.

Even as she took the force of the blast and seemed to collapse like some kind of marionette whose strings were swiftly cut, Cromwell had swiveled and fired a series of strong blasts directly at the cave opening. Large rocks and part of the shattered door blew up and out with a bang.

Woodward now crouched and ran forward, picking up the limp Eve as if she were a rag doll and then running back towards the ship. By this point, he was under protective cover from three of Cromwell's snipers and from Archangel orbiting above.

Neither Cromwell nor Robey stopped. They both went forward, Robey behind the armored Cromwell for protection, making as fast as they could for the opening to down below. Reaching the still smoking spot, Cromwell jumped into the hole as Robey undid the sash of his robe in order to remove the portable ferret monitor strapped to his chest, put it on the ground and activate it.

"*Damn!*" he heard Cromwell swear, and knew that not everything was according to plan.

"Problems, sir?"

"It's Englar. Will Englar. The bastard was using *him* as a secondary remote! I'd hoped to see Sapenza, but he's rusty, not dumb. All right, I'm going to bring the boy out. He's probably under control, like your girl, but he's also hurt bad here. Get him back to *Olivet* as fast as you can!"

"Sir? You don't need me for the ferrets?"

"Come on, lad! Take him! My people are coming in to reinforce as we speak! Your job's over!"

Even as Robey struggled with the big man's limp body, he heard the sounds of explosions off in the distance. The other teams were in and probably ahead of them.

It was obvious to him that he just couldn't get Englar back to the ship alone. The guy was bigger than he was, limp, and bleeding from several wounds. Eve was a lot easier to handle.

"Need help with a wounded man here!" he radioed on the general frequency. "Bleeding, time of the essence!"

Within a couple of minutes, even as the rest of Cromwell's team was going in, two brown-robed Chief Ushers were at Robey's side, one with a litter. With that, and a man on each end, Robey realized that he had nothing else to do.

Well, the black-clad security people didn't have those fancy Cromwell-type suits on when they'd gone down that hole, he thought. Cromwell wanted the combat suits spread out among the different teams going in all over the area.

"Archangel, hook me into Secured Tactical," he called. "I'm going in."

"That's not authorized, Brother," the monitoring security officer responded.

"Look, I've just about had it with these people and the only one I've been able to shoot so far is my partner. I'm going in. If you don't patch me in, they'll probably shoot me thinking I'm a bad guy, but I'm going in!"

"Very well. We'll patch you in, but this will be reported to the Doctor."

"Fine. I've been with him the last day and a half. He may not approve but I think he'll understand. Going in!"

He jumped down into the hole.

It was clear almost immediately that they'd jury-rigged some kind of comm link using the two captured and controlled Arms as the last links. That way, Sapenza was in no immediate danger from the kind of move they pulled, and their own people had taken the brunt of it. So be it.

Whatever the chemical was that they sprayed on these mostly natural caverns to illuminate them was effective. It wasn't exactly daylight, but it was pretty easy to see and to navigate through the area.

Mostly, that meant seeing where Cromwell's people had been. At various hollows, where "rooms" had been cut out or enlarged from natural expansion, there were signs of skirmishes and even a couple of bodies. Villagers from their looks, which meant Sapenza's crew in this case.

There was no fooling around at this point, either. People with any sort of weapon in their possession or near them were stone cold dead; those without weapons were mostly out in heavy stun, to be collected by a mop-up team that was even now being deployed from *Olivet* and going into each of the openings.

The first time, Robey stared at the open, lifeless eyes and death expressions and tried to get a grip on himself. Stun, even heavy stun, he'd seen and done, but people deliberately killed was new to him. The fact that they appeared to have been almost surgically selected and almost certainly dispatched with incredible speed was a tribute to Cromwell's skill, and a scary look inside the old soldier's soul. There were all sorts of legends as to who and what Cromwell had been before joining *The Mountain*, but only here was Robey faced with the probability that some of them were true.

Robey snapped out of it and turned and started running down the cave as the noises of various light weapons could be heard echoing in the distance. No more looking in at each room or musing about life and death; what was happening was happening ahead, and if he didn't get there soon he might wind up with the mop-up team.

"Archangel, how far ahead is the security team?" he called, then suddenly realized that the same coating and mineral structure that had protected Sapenza's empire from being detected also had him cut off from anybody else. All of a sudden he was aware of how alone he really was.

This was brought home to him when he suddenly came out into a larger cave only to see a half dozen smaller tubular caves leading away in different directions. There were no signs, no "You Are Here" plaques, nothing. Like the cave where these people had hidden their arsenal, he and possibly the rest were in a Minoan maze without benefit of string to find their way out.

He was about to pick one at random and trust to Providence when the distinctive electronic sound of rifle fire reached him from the second cave entrance to his right. He quickly moved towards it and saw that somebody had chalked an "X" just at its entrance. He hadn't noticed it because it was rather light and from any distance just mixed with the mineral's glimmerings but now he realized how the mop-up team was supposed to follow. Entering, he ran down the cave at full speed.

Some of the cave segments were much larger or wider than others, but the longest was no more than a few hundred meters before it opened into one or another chamber. In this one, the chamber it opened into was impressive indeed; it was, in fact, almost an entire small town in and of itself, complete with a couple of echoing barking dogs.

These looked to be offices or apartments of some kind, and they looked prefabricated, not something that anyone would expect or even be able to make on this rural backwater of a world.

Cubes stacked atop cubes . . . How did they get them in here? he wondered. Was there another lift like the one used at the arsenal? Or did these construct themselves from programmed modules once you got them down through a cave opening?

He didn't have much time to ruminate or explore. An armored head suddenly shot out from a second-story window of the complex and Cromwell's unmistakable voice, icy to the point of freezing anything it touched, yelled, "Robey, what the *devil* do you think you're doing here? Go! Get out of here! Get back to the ship! It's *important*, unless you want to stay on this miserable rock with the surviving ones who did this to us!"

Robey suddenly had the awful feeling that he'd slept through the meeting or something. "But where do I go?" he called back. "How do I find the way out?"

"Use the chalk marks! Keep to the right and look for up arrows! The rest will be obvious! Now *move!*"

He wasn't quite sure what all the fuss was about, since so long as they didn't have the location and control of those defensive naval guns everybody was stuck here anyway, but you didn't argue with Cromwell. Next to the Doctor, he was the most formidable power anybody who grew up in the mission ever knew or could conceive of.

"Keep to the right. . . . " Sounded simple enough.

An "X" on the far right cave confirmed things. Now
he was on the trail of Cromwell's heavily armed squad,
although he wasn't sure what the security man was
doing hanging back. Looking for anything useful in
that previously hidden headquarters, most likely.

Still, he was so concerned with getting out at this
point that he almost ran straight into a firefight.

They were shooting back and forth from cave openings across a small chamber just ahead. He could see
two of the security team firing what they called rifles
but which were, if at full power, more like portable
laser cannons of the sort Cromwell had used to initially blast the opening pack in the pasture. Return
fire seemed to be smaller hand weapons, pulse blast-
ers and laser pistols. They were no match for the
security team's firepower, but so long as they could
shoot across the open space there was no way anybody else was going to cross.

One of the black-clad squad glanced back and
noticed him and seemed about as thrilled by his presence as Cromwell had been. Still, he was one more
gun if need be.

He crouched low and tried to see what he could.
"Where are they?"

"Just stick your head out there and you'll find out!"
the nearest team member responded. He was surprised to hear a woman's voice, particularly one with
that kind of toughness. The Doctor really was kind
of sexist, but somehow he'd never let that get in the
way of pragmatism, and Cromwell only wanted to see
you in action.

"They're blocking that one tunnel on both sides,"
the woman continued. "We don't know why. If they
don't have an escape hatch in between they're virtually committing suicide and they have to know that."

Robey could see the problem. You couldn't use gas down here for obvious reasons, particularly not with hostages and idiots like him wandering about, and you couldn't just turn limestone into marble using the laser cannons because you didn't want to block access.

"Cover your ears and open your mouth!" the woman told him sharply. "It might not save your ears, but you deserve that much for being where you shouldn't!"

He barely had time to do as instructed when the two of them used the targeting computer modules on their rifles to calibrate and time two shots, including ricochets. This was a new one on him, but he noted that before they started their computations both members of the squad had put on ear mufflers.

The light was almost blinding as it was, the initial sounds the twangs of laser weapons, but when the shots, one after the other, struck the cave where resistance was mounted there was a noise louder and more prolonged and more intense than John Robey had ever heard. His ears literally hurt as if somebody had stuck sharp objects into them, and for a moment he seemed to lose consciousness and then come back with a horrible and persistent ringing all he could hear.

The squad members, having no such problems thanks to their mufflers, now moved, removing the head gear as they did so, and advanced, military style, across the cavern to the targeted cave opening.

There were several more shots that Robey could tell only by seeing the flashes, and then nothing. Curious, the pain in his ears subsiding although not the ringing, he decided to follow. If he was on the way out, then his best route might well be by following those two.

They had shot to kill, that was clear, but the expressions on the faces and the huge amount of blood evident there made it even more dramatic. They weren't bleeding from the *coup de gras*, that was for sure. They were bleeding from their ears, noses, and mouths.

Almost subconsciously he reached up to both his ears and put a finger in each, then looked at them. No blood, thank the Lord! But he was aware that he did in fact have something of a bloody nose. He hoped that was all.

One of the squad said something to him, but all he could do was reply, "I can't hear! Ringing in my ears won't stop!"

"That's a good reason why you should do as you're told," he heard from the implant radio. It was the woman on tactical. *"Stay close and don't stray or get in the way!"*

There was only one side opening off the cave, and they reached it at just about the same time as two other black-clad security team members met them coming the other way. It was frustrating not to be able to hear them talk, although if they made any calls on the tactical frequency the implant would give him the same as they were broadcasting, which was something.

The woman from his side and a guy from the other side of the cavern flattened on either side of the door, then, at a nodded signal, rifles at ready, spun around and went into the chamber.

Traffic was quick. *"Father, use the ferret line!"*

"Go ahead. What have you got?" Hearing this way wasn't like hearing normal speech, but he was pretty certain it was Cromwell just from the tone and manner of speaking.

"We're going to fire straight up from this position. No access doors nearby that we can find. We need everything you got. Looks like thirty, forty of our people. Mostly dead, but some are still moving. This just happened!"

"Then speed's of the essence. We're moving now. Make your opening!"

The other two security team members moved down to where the cavern opened into a chamber and, with precision and their rifles on full power, aimed at the same spot above and to the left of them and just kept firing.

The whole complex shook as if undergoing a minor earthquake, and molten rock began to form and then ooze down. They had to be very careful that they had as straight an angle as possible while being just enough off not to get caught in this white-hot residue.

At about twelve meters beyond the chamber roof there was a sudden buckling and then the two beams shot out and made open air.

"Cease firing and clear that area. We'll enlarge from above and then get people in. Any resistance?"

"All dead," the security people reported. "We'll establish a parameter at the other end, but we need more people, all kinds, as quick as possible!"

Above, having picked up the flash of the laser canon and the deformation in the rock, Archangel targeted the position and gave a surgical blast with a naval grade disintegrator. It reamed a hole about three meters around all the way to the chamber and also eliminated the still heated edges left by the blast.

At least forty people from *Olivet* ran for the opening as soon as it was made, carrying bales of netting, ropes, whatever they could find. It was still a little dicey working around the remnants of molten rock below, but that was localized and the security team quickly sprayed it with a yellow chalk dye so that nobody was going to go into those piles by accident.

Robey had kept well back while all this was going on, but he'd also taken advantage of the action to look into the liberated chamber that the pirates had fought so hard to guard.

There were bodies, and parts of bodies, and the awful smell of charred flesh all around. He was suddenly thankful that he couldn't hear their groaning, the ones left alive, and he pulled back and felt suddenly very sick.

Almost since he could speak he'd been taught that man was saved only by grace and that evil was always lurking about and victories were always partial, but he'd been taught, too, that there was only one unforgiveable sin, and that was denying God to save oneself and going over into the service of evil. All else was supposedly forgivable if sincerely repented. Well, he didn't *want* any repentance on the part of these bastards! Not now, not ever. All he wanted for any of them, *any* of them, was that they be resurrected in indestructible bodies but in the Lake of Fire, roasting eternally without hope.

Somebody tapped him on the shoulder. He saw an usher, ashen-faced, and the man pointed up and tugged at Robey's sleeve. The Arm of Gideon nodded. He had seen more down here than he ever really wanted to see, more than he should have seen.

He climbed up the netting, even though it was no easy task, and into the sunlight without even thinking of the exertion and effort. He was trying very hard not to think at all.

❖ ❖ ❖

Thomas Cromwell, too, had seen enough, even though few here realized that he'd seen even worse in the past, *much* worse.

Using magsleds helped along by good old-fashioned guide ropes, they managed to evacuate the wounded, anybody still alive in that massacre chamber. *Olivet's* hospital, though, was already overwhelmed; it was adequate for the basic things the staff and a transitory group might encounter—the usual aches, pains, accidental breaks, that kind of thing—but not this kind of heavy-duty work. Things had improved a bit after a couple of bad previous landings, but nothing had compared with this kind of damage.

"Sir, I think we'd better move everybody out," one of his squad told him as he looked at the aftermath of the killing room.

"Eh? What, girl? Oh—what's the hurry, now? We still don't have His Nibs and the top henchmen off our earlier ferret recordings."

"Yes, sir, but we believe now that they've gotten far enough back that they are in a position to flood this entire cave complex. We came across the watertight doors with automated devices on them and we haven't been able to solve the security there. We think they're going to blow them. Please, sir! There's nothing left here now!"

He looked at the dead bodies, a low priority until all the living were evacuated, and muttered, *"Until the sea shall give up her dead, in the sure and certain belief in the resurrection and life to come . . ."* Then he seemed to snap out of it. "Very well, Sergeant. Get everybody out *now!* You, too! Complete evacuation. Everybody to *Olivet* unless you want to stay here with these—these *people!*" He made the word sound like the worst kind of vermin.

Olivet could only mark time, and then for only so long. They had twenty-six critically injured and probably dying if they didn't get help, and while only three of the women were dead in the other chamber discovered over a kilometer away on the other side, the damage to them mentally and physically was going to take a lot of work. He didn't have the total score yet, but he estimated that, deaths alone, they'd lost about half the hostages and most likely would lose some more. He couldn't imagine any of the others coming out of this without severe spiritual and psychological damages.

He also knew what this would do to the Doctor. Karl Woodward was a great actor, as all teachers and leaders must be, but Cromwell knew him better. This would break his heart, for all his words about martyrdom and New Jerusalem.

Cromwell was just about the last one out, and barely in the nick of time. The explosions could be heard both below and above, and the waters from that distant lake started flowing down through the network, washing through all they struck, on the way to even deeper pools that would lead eventually towards the far-off ocean.

They had worried about this flooding almost since they started planning the taking of the underground complex; teams had discovered the other ends, nicely sealed, when exploring the area around the downed ship and the burned-out villages and they'd guessed what the seals were for. Initially dry and airlocked so that they could be used to bring in all of the downed ship's cargo and weaponry without any local prying eyes left to say what it was or where it went, they then became nice last-ditch suicidal defenses. The only thing was, anybody triggering them would have to be in either an upward elevation region of the caves or outside on the surface. Cromwell's battle computers had taken a good guess at how long this would take once operations commenced, and as it turned out they were rather conservative, but it had weighed on his mind since the start.

The only reason he'd gone for it at all was that these sorts of people were criminals, not zealots. Captain Sapenza hadn't sounded like a man of much faith, even if a man of great nerve, and he certainly couldn't have sustained that kind of live conversation via Eve from much of a distance.

So, Captain, where are you now, eh? At the control center of one of those twelve ship's naval guns you removed and built into this region, I'd say. Waiting.

Waiting for *Olivet*, its crew, tactical squads, Doctor, and all the rest, to take off in a desperate attempt to get those injured ones to hospital.

Cromwell looked around at the region, the village, the now packed-up *Olivet*, all the rest, and nodded to himself.

"Everybody on board? If not, five minutes. Five minutes or you learn to love it here." He called on all frequencies, then walked towards the ship with a slow, deliberate military gait.

"All the children been set loose and returned to Mummy?" he asked.

"Yes, sir," the reply came. "We told the villagers to remain inside the village today at the risk of being burned out or worse, and they've complied. All the kids are back, but in the big barn, where they're still more or less under our monitoring."

As Cromwell went up the ramp and heard it close behind him, he asked, "Anybody here or above discovered those bloody guns yet?"

"No, sir. They're pretty well hid. We can guess at a few, but there's no way we can cover them all. Remember, they had thirty years to disguise them, and deploying, setting up, and hiding those guns was the number one priority. They were certain they were still being chased."

"All right," the security chief sighed. "I just hope the engineers are right on what sort of guns were removed and what their limitations are in planetary mounts," he said. "Otherwise, this is going to be a very short trip."

"Stand by for motion!" the ship's intercom warned. "Secure all loose items, strap in if you can or hold on. Thirty seconds."

Even Robey, who had yet to get rid of the ringing or hear much of anything else in spite of some treatment, knew what it meant when he felt the vibration in the deck and he was suddenly almost overcome with sheer panic.

My God in Heaven! he thought to himself. *I'm about to be blown up!*

It was one thing for the Doctor to have full faith in miracles, but having the same sort of faith in engineers and their computers was quite another. And only a miracle would keep this ship from being blown to bits in the next minute or so.

John couldn't help it. Unable to move, to run, to do anything much at all, he instead just sat there in the Arm's quarters and stared at the clock on the wall.

When first one minute dragged by, then another, he began to doubt his senses, then wonder if in fact they were really going anywhere. By all rights they should be dead by now.

Now he desperately wanted to see where they were, how far they'd gotten, how far it was to the safety of the union in *The Mountain*, but he dared not move while the red flashing danger light was on or his hearing might well be the least of his problems.

He couldn't understand what was going on. They should be well up in the planetary stratosphere by now, essentially in space, yet the vibration continued at its maximum and there was a fair amount of buffeting, the kind of ride you got when you were maneuvering to land rather than blasting off at full speed.

Something was definitely wrong, yet it was impossible to tell what when you were inside such a massive flying structure.

When the clock passed the twenty-minute mark, he knew that they weren't headed up to *Sinai* and he suspected that they weren't headed up at all. The back and forth rolling and jerky motions were continuing, and even getting a little worse.

Suddenly, he realized what they were doing, what they *had* to be doing.

Olivet had taken off, all right, and it had gone straight up—for maybe a couple of meters. Then, with the landing sensors on, they had been moving not up but *sideways*, following the topography at just that couple of meters height. Somebody smart had figured out that you could not depress those naval guns so that they'd be useful as surface-to-surface weapons; instead, they were aimed at creating a crisscross defensive pattern that would be certain to nail any spaceship either landing or taking off.

Olivet was doing neither, but there were at most only twelve naval guns in place and they were large and required separate fire control positions when not networked into the ship as designed.

He could see the engineers now, working out the most effective and broadest pattern for total defense. Now, extend that from the lake area and their ship over to the village and perhaps even to the original colony headquarters site and you were already short a gun or two. Get beyond there, towards the other side of the continent, even a few hundred kilometers, and you would be out of range. Then you could launch on a trajectory that their firing patterns could not be altered to nail without moving the guns. Move those big guns and their power supplies and you were a sitting duck for Archangel.

It was a long, rough ride because this sort of lateral movement was something *Olivet* was never intended to do. But as a former orbit-to-ground-to-orbit cargo shuttle it had that capability, at least theoretically. Now it was more than theory, but it might well be a couple of hours before it could move beyond the curvature of the planet, far enough away so that even an orbital trajectory wouldn't be anywhere in the line of sight of the armorers staffing those gun emplacements.

Robey let out a breath and relaxed as well as he could. Only the faces of those poor devils maimed and murdered kept him from feeling exhilarated at the now obvious escape. He wondered how the downed pirate captain was taking it. Certainly it would not do to be all that close to him physically right at this moment, he bet.

In point of fact, *Olivet*'s lateral motion was barely fifty kilometers per hour; it was too massive to move any faster at such a low level, and the whole lateral movement capability designed into it was to make it move several meters one way or the other, not long distances. There was always the danger that the small engines would burn out before they made it far enough to feel safe; these were not the big engines designed for orbit, after all.

Still, while one was showing real signs of strain and another was giving intermittent readings, the movement was steady and solid as a rock as far as the bridge was concerned. They'd built these lifting bodies, as the engineers called them, for harsh conditions on planets never intended for humans and far from space dry-dock and repair facilities, and it was sure showing the quality of its construction now.

They didn't need to complete the journey before Captain Sapenza knew he was licked. The ship was already well out of sight over the horizon, and the captain had no planetary tracking equipment or orbiting satellites to tell him just where the fleeing quarry was nor how far it could go.

"They blew up the arsenal at the same time," Gregnar told him. "That lift shot so far in the air it came down five kilometers away in the middle of a maize field."

"Figures," Sapenza commented in an almost disinterested tone.

It was only when Almarie, his longtime chief woman, started nattering that he showed what was going on inside him.

"Yeah, sure. Kidnap 'em. The Holy Joes'll freak and give us our ticket. Torture a few to make 'em scared. They scared real good, didn't they? You couldn't have tried it straight with them first? Maybe cut their throats later if it didn't work? *No!* You hadda screw 'em from the start! Now we're *stuck* here! You happy now?"

Sapenza sighed and said nothing, but he took out a small pistol and shot her at point-blank range on maximum blast. Her whole form shimmered and then there was only the smell of burnt flesh and a little pile of gray powder where she'd stood.

Gregnar and the rest moved back several steps.

The Captain turned towards them and they all froze, half expecting this to be their last moments anywhere. Instead, he said, "Can we still contact them?"

"Yeah, boss. They use standard frequencies. You just call them and if they're out of range it'll be intercepted by their orbiting ship and passed along," somebody told him. "But, boss—you start broadcasting, you tell 'em just where we are."

"Who the hell cares *now*?" he asked them. "Get me to a transceiver."

They quickly brought him to a communications terminal inside one of the camouflaged gun emplacements. *Not a shot fired*, he thought ruefully. *Maybe their God really is somebody. Or maybe we just blew it.*

"Captain Sapenza to Doctor Woodward," he called. "Patch me through if he's available, please, anyone who picks this up. Repeat, Captain Sapenza to Doctor Karl Woodward."

"Just a minute," came a young man's voice over the speaker. "We'll hail him and see if he wants a patch."

Woodward did indeed.

"Well, Captain! If you hadn't killed so many innocent people I might well be in a very good mood right now," the Doctor responded. "As it is, I'm royally pissed."

Sapenza couldn't help but smile. Who'd ever have thought that his match would be a pot-bellied white-bearded evangelist? He almost felt like the whole damn universe was sniggering behind his back.

"Good to talk to you directly, Doctor," he responded in his calm, businesslike but friendly tone. "I don't suppose we can talk repentance?"

Woodward *did* manage a chuckle. "I would and could discuss it with you all day if need be, but it's between you and God. It doesn't cut quite so much ice between you and me at the moment, though. Problem is, unlike the Almighty, I don't have any way of knowing the sincerity of repentance."

"Yeah, well, maybe I'm sorry I tried it this way, or that anybody got hurt, but I have to admit that I'm mostly sorry it didn't work."

"Well, honesty is a good starting point," the Doctor noted. "So, what can I do for you now? If you want to tell me who you've been scared would find you all these years I'll be happy to go look him or her or them or it up and give them your regards. I think a more fitting punishment would be to simply blow the genhole gate controller by timer after we leave. What do you think?"

"And isolate forever this colony population, so they'll never have a crack at their utopia?" the Captain responded. "Could you really live with *that* on your conscience?"

"Quite easily, considering their easy and facile collusion with you and your people against us," the Doctor replied. "We came here and delivered a good bit of the truth to them. We also have left a great deal of study materials, Bibles, written and computer material and the like for those whom the spirit might call to discover and perhaps build upon here. The rest—they had their choice, us or you, and they clearly parked their ethics and morality at the door and listened not to me or the truth in the Word. No, Captain, I would not lose a single minute of sleep doing that. Those who might accept the truth won't need the return of their dead matriarch or the Three Kings; they will have a better deal. The rest don't deserve any better than this."

"You sound like you're serious."

"I am *quite* serious, sir! While I would have liked to have reached the rest of these people directly, I can no longer afford to do so. I can't know what goodies you've booby-trapped near and far, or who is who and what is what. I depend on the Word to get there the way God intended. It will spread, and be heard by those who have ears to hear. Faith comes by hearing the word of God."

"Faith . . . " Sapenza repeated, more to himself than to the Doctor. He was thinking. "You know something, Doctor? I *will* propose a deal to you, in spite of this, um, *unpleasantness*. It's a good one, I think."

"What can you possibly propose that we could take seriously, Captain?"

Sapenza sighed deeply, then said, "I really *have* got the Three Kings, Doc. You saw the stone. Mother Tymm's ship broke apart, it's true, but on the way *back*. She was a nun, a Mother Superior or whatever they call them, you know. Catholic nun. She somehow got or solved part of the puzzle. She got there. She even sort of broke with her church, or at least didn't let them know. She took her group and she was going to ferry them to Paradise. She got there, but getting back killed her. Divine justice, maybe, or maybe she just didn't have *quite* enough faith."

"I'm not going to take you out of here, Sapenza," Woodward warned him. "Nor any of your people. The corruption after my own folks see these poor souls would be too great, and we couldn't watch our backs often enough even if we stuck you in space suits and hung you on the outside. You all get to live, which is more than you deserve, but not to move."

"I understand that, Doctor. All I'm asking is for a reset to the previous status quo."

"A what?"

"I give you the Three Kings. You leave and do with that knowledge what you want. Go there, give it to somebody else, destroy it—it's all up to you. The Kings are even a little in your theology. See? I did too listen! You're better off and better equipped than Mother Tymm. Hell, you're better equipped than the Colonial Navy from the looks of it! You might make it there, and back. You might make it there and want to stay. I can't use it. I *can* give them to you."

"In exchange for what?"

"Well, as much as we could get, I suppose. At the very minimum, you leave, don't mention this place to anybody, leave the gate as it is, and simply go your own way. We're worse off than we were by a long shot, having lost most of our weapons and all of our creature comforts, as it were. This way, at least, we won't be at the mercy of anybody else and we won't be so cut off that, one day, we might not still get off this giant turd."

"I could just say 'yes' and then roll out the welcome mat," the Doctor pointed out.

"Yeah, you could, but you're not like me. You're a man of honor. If you swore an oath to God that you'd keep your word, you'd keep it. That's the minimum price."

Karl Woodward was still thinking about it when the engineering computers decided that they were far enough away to launch on a south trajectory and safely attain orbit with no vulnerability to the big guns.

He was still thinking about it many minutes later when, at orbital velocity, *Olivet* made the turn that would reunite it with its interstellar-capable big brother.

There was never any real doubt in the Doctor's mind that the offer would be accepted, but if Sapenza could not be brought to account by human judgment, at least he would have to wait a bit and sweat.

There were people on *The Mountain* who were opposed to any deal and who, in fact, urged Wood-ward to blast the radio and the entire region north of the lake tubes, but this just made the Doctor angry and sad at the same time.

"Have you learned *nothing* here? Is my whole life a failure?" he thundered. "Do you so easily give your-selves over to hatred and vengeance? We *protect* ourselves! God can't abide wimps! But the moment, the *moment* we turn into our enemy then we might as well *become* the enemy! God knows that in my own heart I can never truly forgive the bastards, but I am content to leave their ultimate fate to God's judgment! This is not the Navy! We aren't in the business of *taking* lives! God will take care of them and bring justice! *Our* job is to look ahead to His new work!"

Have I been deluding myself? he wondered. *Don't they truly understand* anything? *Damn* them! Act in *faith*, not out of vengeance and hatred. Somehow, sometime, when he wasn't looking, the devil had snuck back aboard and corrupted them. He hated that reali-zation more than he hated the dead and wounded. They were supposed to be better than that.

"All right, Sapenza, you have a deal," he told the pirate below. "But what you initially stated is what you get. Nothing more, and nothing less. I will trust to God that you will rot here, and leave it entirely in His hands whether or not you do. In exchange, you send all the pertinent details, a copy of everything you have on the Three Kings. Agreed?"

"Agreed," the captain responded.

"You sound too self-satisfied," the Doctor commented suspiciously. "Don't alter or edit the material. We *will* test it out, and if there's any funny business you will be on the map of everyone in creation as quickly as we can manage it. That's understood?"

"Understood."

"Then what the hell's making you so smug, Sapenza?"

The captain paused a moment. "I think, at least, I've blown a lot of your confidence in your own faithful," he commented. "I'd bet on that. But I haven't laid a glove on you. I'm doing you no favor, Doctor, but I suspect you won't take my warning. Keep your faith and erase what I send and forget the Three Kings. That's my good deed advice of the day. If you do, you may wind up living the rest of your life and dying in self-deluded saintliness. But if you go to the Three Kings, like Mother Tymm, you're going to find your faith is far too simplistic and no matter how smart you are, deep down you're just like your people who you think have failed you. This is my revenge, Doctor. I tell you that right up front. And you won't even believe it until it happens. When it does, when your faith fails you, *then* think of me, stuck here, but laughing! I'm sending the data now as we speak, Doctor. See you in Hell!"

X:
HEAVEN HAS
THREE CIRCLES

The hospital facilities on *The Mountain* were among the best; even when Woodward would skimp and save things he always made certain that the medical division had the best.

Up until now, this particular expedition had not been the most profitable. In fact, after treating the wounded and doing all the long-term work necessary to get the former hostages at least physically back to par, together with the losses in equipment and supplies that were more routine, *The Mountain* and its mission were in some trouble.

Near the end of every mission cycle, they'd had

to return to civilization and endure weeks or months of refitting, repairs, and the like so that they could go out again. During that period they would spend much of their time anxiously fund-raising, but, the fact was, if they didn't bring back something from the missions themselves there wouldn't be enough to do the job with what they could raise elsewhere.

Doctor Woodward, it was rumored, was considering something far more radical before going in to a refit they could not possibly manage. He would never give up what he considered his commission from God, but even he had limits in that he couldn't bring himself to just go begging like so many denominations and missionaries did.

So while everyone else was getting well, licking their wounds, straightening up, and into intensive Bible study and work on the meaning of faith, the Doctor, alone save for one of two of his closest friends, was studying the uploads from Sapenza and thinking.

"Our science and engineering people have seen this?" he asked at last.

Thomas Cromwell nodded. "In one sense, it's pretty straightforward. In another, it's like nothing we've ever seen. Still, the risk is in the going and, if that thing can't be stabilized, very much more in the return. The question is whether any computer ever made can predict that writhing, snaking monster of a natural wormhole and get it *exactly* right. That's what we think happened to Tymm's ship. She was essentially shaken to death. It was certainly an ugly way to go."

"We run those kinds of risks all the time," Woodward responded. "We just did something like that from a risk point of view. There are times when you trust to your people and your machines and leave the rest to God. For some reason, God didn't want her to have it. I have to wonder if perhaps all this was to put it into our hands."

"Sapenza seemed to think he was doing us no favors," Cromwell pointed out. "The question is, what didn't he tell us? What does he know that we don't? He admitted not trying it himself. Not with the ship he had."

"Oh, I suspect that his ship was better suited to threading this wormhole than ours, and certainly better than Mother Tymm's," Woodward commented. "But he didn't find Tymm's ship, he just stole it all from the ones that did, and at some cost in battle. I think he was backtracking Tymm based on this data when he got ambushed by somebody else who knew at least part of the story."

"Do you really think this ship can get there, and back?" Cromwell asked him.

"I do. I believe God has a special assignment for us and that this is part of it. No matter what, it would prove the existence of the Three Kings for certain and would allow us to pick up things of substantial value that could be used to virtually make this ship over. And if one of them is as liveable as legend has it, then we may well also find our own home."

Captain Jorge Lime, one of the three rotating captains of *The Mountain* and also one of the Elders, shook his head. "I don't know. This whole complex, all these people—in a wild hole. It would truly require a miracle to go both ways."

"Then we'll pray for a miracle!" the Doctor shot back. "I'm sick and tired of all the people on this ship, which is in itself a miracle that shouldn't exist, suddenly having no faith at all in God's hand or His plan for us! I think we have to do it for that reason alone!

I'm sick and tired of having to keep demonstrating faith, but I certainly expect it from my leaders! Are you saying that you will not take us there, Captain?"

The captain felt stung by the remarks. "No, sir, I am not saying that I will not take us there, but I am laying out the facts and the odds. If I were to take a pistol, fully charged and tested, point it at your head and pull the trigger, the odds are you would have your head blown off. There is a fine line between faith and common sense in some of this."

"We'll make it, at least one way!" the Doctor said emphatically. "Whether or not we can make it back, or even are meant to, is something for God to decide."

Even so, after they'd all left to pray and think things over, he couldn't help but dwell for a moment on the enigmatic figure of Judas.

Not Judas the Betrayer, but Judas the Prideful. Judas never did understand the message, but he was pretty sure of the messenger. The Messiah was supposed to rise up and liberate the Jewish people from the yoke of the House of Herod and of Imperial Rome. Instead he kept refusing and talking all sorts of things, even accommodation with the Romans as in the exhortation to pay your taxes. But when He took a whip to the money changers, *then* the fire and fury had come out. Judas decided to push his Messiah to reveal Himself, to rise up and be a leader. If they arrested, convicted, and went to crucify Him, *then* He'd have to move, right?

And so Judas the Prideful decided that, since he didn't like how God was doing things, he'd push Him into a corner so He'd see things and do things *Judas's* way.

There was always the danger that a leader could

go past that point, commit the same sin as Satan, and be damned. Woodward worried about that constantly, with his own ego and his own arrogance. If they only knew how alone he really was, how much doubt he always had to fight.

In the end, what Judas did was what God already had planned. He damned himself but managed at the same time to save countless souls yet unborn. Ironic, but that, too, was something he always had to live with.

He *had* to act on faith, no matter what! Otherwise, this was all a waste, and he was just another hypocrite and charlatan or self-deluded false prophet.

He understood the physics of it—that was one of his fields of expertise, and one that he understood well. He did *not* understand the full data about the Three Kings. Three planet-sized moons around a gas giant well into the life zone of a G-class star. All three with both temperatures and atmospheres that would support human life or any life as they knew it.

The old monk who'd first discovered them hadn't wanted to name them after the Kings; he'd wanted to name them after Dante. Inferno, Purgatorio, Paradisio. Those, too, were interesting choices. Hell, Purgatory, Heaven. Woodward's own beliefs didn't allow for a Purgatory, but he could see its appeal as analogy.

Why had he changed his mind?

Why did Sapenza think that the Kings would crush his faith?

He *had* to go. Deep down he felt that was a given as sure as anything he'd ever believed or thought in his whole life. He had to go as a demonstration of faith, not just to the crew of *The Mountain* but also as much before God and to himself.

Three Kings. Three was the number of God.

◇   ◇   ◇

John Robey stared at the sluglike thing in the tray and shook his head.

Robey still had temporary direct sensory implants so he could hear while his new eardrums bonded and settled in, so it made everything and everybody sound a little tinny and distant, but it was good enough to keep him functional.

"That's the thing?" he asked.

The medtech nodded. "In a way, it's not much different from our ferrets and fish. Same general material, actually, although the thing is designed to do a bit different job. Sloppy, really, because it can't get in through the pores but has to essentially drill a small hole, and so much is taken up with medical instructions on how to deploy I'd suspect there's little in the way of independent instructional ability, but it sure does the job. The only way we could get it out was to suspend the two of them, remove the things and the collateral brain stem and connectors, and then replace the removed natural parts with cultured cloned duplicates. It's always a bit tricky when you're working that close to and partly in the brain, but it looks like things will work out. I just wish we'd had the codes for this little critter. Then it would have been simple to just tell it to detach and leave."

Robey continued to shake his head in wonder at the thing. "What kind of sick mind would come up with something like that?"

"Oh, this is very old technology," the medtech responded, oblivious to the other's moral tone. "They've got them down to preprogrammable injectables now, I hear. Lots of spy and black market type stuff in them. That's the kicker. If it had been one of the newer ones I could have pulled how to reprogram it from our database; it's these old development types that are the problem. They were lab stuff and changed almost weekly."

Robey was appalled, not just by the callousness but also by the thought that these things had been "perfected" and could be bought by the likes of Sapenza on the black market. "So that's the future for the rest of us?" he mused, aloud but as much to himself as to the other. "Just slaves, perfect and obedient? Programmed like cleaning robots?"

"Probably not. Not worth it," the tech replied. "However, it's a reminder of what's out there. There's stuff that would make you wake up convinced beyond any ability of anybody to talk you out of it that you were the Red Queen of Wonderland and everybody else were rabbits. We exist in a kind of balance, Brother Robey. The main reason we're who and what we are in this day and age is that most of us aren't worth the trouble to somebody to screw around with."

Now *there* was a comforting thought. "What about Eve? When will she be—back to normal, I guess is the way to put it."

The medtech sighed. "Probably never. Oh, *physically*, with some physical therapy and a decent monitoring program, she'll get back to normal, but *mentally* . . . Well, this sort of stuff does things to you. I've seen it time and again. We've got it with many if not most of the former hostages we rescued. Some of them had particularly ugly times. Most of the women were raped, some brutally and repeatedly. The kind of therapy that erases that sort of thing also erases part of your mind and memories."

"You don't mean Eve was—"

"Oh, no, actually. No rape, not in the usual sense

of the word. But both of them, the man as well as the woman, will have an even harder thing to overcome. They just spent a long period as passengers in their own bodies. I don't think you or I could really understand what that feels like, how helpless and insecure it makes you. Just like that—*zap!*—and you have no control at all, period. To get over that, to fully get your nerve back, to sleep well after that, it's almost impossible. When something like that happens in normal planetary situations we use a kind of sophisticated device that creates a data worm that goes into the mind and simply deletes that whole experience. You wake up and it's an hour before it happened and that's that. We have no such things here. The Doctor believes that such things subvert the whole system of good and evil in the universe. It removes choice and will. So, she's going to have to learn to live with it. If she doesn't, she'll be no good to anyone, least of all herself."

"Can I see her?"

"In a few days. She'll be in an induced coma for a while yet, then be brought up slowly. Leave your extension and we'll give you a call when you can see her."

Great! he thought sourly, heading back towards the quarters for his group. *Just great!*

"Attention! Attention, brothers and sisters!" the ship's intercom suddenly announced. "At zero six hundred all personnel are to be in the *Olivet* section cathedral, a sector chapel, or in a ward room where video is available to hear an important talk by Doctor Woodward on the future of this mission. This will be repeated for all shifts. All personnel are required to attend and to listen. The lives and very future of everyone here is at stake. Do not take this one lightly.

This announcement will be repeated every half hour until zero six hundred."

Robey frowned. That was odd. It was one thing to have services or classes, but these kinds of announcements were pretty much saved for initial briefings after taking off on a new long mission or before coming into a major port. It was very rare to have this kind of required mass meeting while underway in midmission, as rotten as this one had been up to now. The Doctor was known to be displeased with the assembly for its depression and lagging faith under these conditions, but that wasn't handled like this.

One thing for sure: it would be the only topic of conversation aboard until the appointed time, and there would be few not present or glued to a screen.

And when it came, it was vintage Woodward plus.

He spent the first twenty minutes just haranguing those who'd doubted or given up during the battle of wits on the planet. He was careful to note those who stuck with him and his decisions and those who helped make the hard choices, but he was very upset that many, if not most, of the youngest and "best taught" had talked compromise with evil or had simply conceded the victory. So many of these were in the parts of the Arm of Gideon that was not taken hostage. Gideon had slain thousands with a mere three hundred warriors because they had the power of faith, he reminded them. Complacency and lack of faith had done the damage here.

"We came out of this with several positives, however, which I will now put to use," he told them. "First, we triumphed over a festering and ruthless evil force because enough of us had faith enough to believe that God would not allow us to fail. We are tougher and better for it as well, for we've been slapped down and shown the cost of taking it all for granted. We are constantly being tested, because we're the last hope the remnants of humanity have, and not many of them will awaken in New Jerusalem. Nowhere in the Bible does it say that things will be easy," he reminded them. "It only says you'll be able to win if you're willing to put your body where God requires it to be."

Old stuff, mostly, but essential as a pep talk for what was coming. Everybody knew that this was merely a prologue.

And, finally, he came to the subject of the gathering, and it gripped them when they saw it.

"Ever since a monk discovered them, the location of the Three Kings has been closely guarded, lost, or in the hands of evil men whom God would not permit to reach them. They are there for us. Remnants of the holy empire that was, and the one that will spread and become part of God's universe once more. Prophecy told us long ago that *we* were the inheritors of the Three Kings, and that we would eventually be shown the way. Now that prophecy has been fulfilled. I intend to go claim that promise, which will require an ultimate test of faith. Let me show you why that is so, and the price of coming up a bit short."

The old video of Mother Tymm's ship, battered and derelict, with the grotesque vacuum-preserved corpses of some of that crew, opened the second phase of the talk. It was sobering stuff.

To navigate via wormholes required precision computers and a ship whose systems were in top condition. Genholes tended to be "easy" in that they were either artificial or artificially enhanced and maintained; their paths internally tended to be straight, their

courses predictable and mapped. Short of a cata-
strophic failure, the genhole system established by the
old Combine and still in use at least on *this* side of
the Great Silence was almost like a railroad network
of centuries past, and no more dangerous.

"Wild" holes were something else again. They were
natural; they expanded and contracted without warning, they were not a consistent internal shape, and
they weren't all that consistent in how or where they
emerged. A very strong one such as the one charted
in the Three Kings data recordings made it certain
that it would be a very nasty, rough, and perilous ride
to the end, but that it would wind up where you
wanted to go, in the Three Kings system.

The pressures on such a hole, though, and particularly the forces that came to bear on the ends, made
it much like a dangerous serpent. They writhed and
wriggled and danced, and particularly within a strong
solar system which would tend to concentrate the
pressures and forces of nature trying to close or tame
such a hole, much like a hose left on the floor or
ground as the pressurized material streamed out.

If a ship merely grazed by a hole wall, the forces
returned on the ship might be enough to destroy it
and would certainly be enough to damage it. That
was why your systems had to be in excellent shape,
always adjusting to keep the ship centered in the
tunnellike hole. Shields could help lessen the damage, but they were like cardboard in terms of really
being able to protect a craft that made such mistakes.

Even so, *if* your ship's systems were good enough,
if your guidance and navigational computers were the
best and properly programmed, trained, and maintained, and *if* that wriggling end wasn't pointing too
close to something solid or the heart of a star, you

had a chance of making it to the system. The original Vaticanus scout, Mother Tymm, and perhaps others had done that much.

"Our computers and engineers have done a full analysis of these recordings and all the relevant data accompanying them and then compared them to the last status checks of our own ship and equipment," Woodward told them. "They tell me there is a seventy percent chance of making it through with no serious problems."

It *sounded* reassuring, but the only alternative to getting through was to die like those in that first video, and a thirty percent chance of the loss of all aboard was more sobering.

And getting back—*there* was an even greater challenge.

"It appears that the hole is very nondescript at this end," Woodward continued. "In fact, while it's in the middle of nowhere, it's one of hundreds of such in that region actually on the charts. It's listed as a dead-end anomaly because no probe sent into it ever sent data back from a position beyond it. It's apparently an easy entry but gets very rough very quickly. It is also, apparently, quite long. We shall have to maintain ourselves inside it for almost six days."

That caused some gasps and murmurs within the groups watching. Most genholes bypassed our universe and its laws almost entirely, curving away into something far different and then coming back. Raw holes were always much longer, sometimes minutes, hours, days, even weeks or months. There was no way to tell, but *six days* in an environment that was constantly trying to murder you . . . *That* was another thing to be very uneasy about.

"Back should be no more difficult than going, except

that this is a system dominated by gas giants and the forces that create the other end of the hole are part of the physics of the system itself. Gravity is in a delicate balance in all such systems, but when you're dealing with one this complex you often have a hole that drains away or adds just enough for it all to work. *That* is our spitting, wriggling hose. Appropriately, our serpent, keeping us on one side of the gate. To enter, we would have to be perfectly centered inside a constantly moving and probably not wholly predictable target. Miss, and you die. Go in even the *slightest* bit off center, you spend six days bouncing off the hole walls. You saw the results in the opening sequence to *that*. And that brings me to the challenge to this congregation."

Most of them were uneasy at this, many were appalled, and only a few seemed ready for this sort of challenge and that may have been bravado. Still, there it was, all laid out, leaving only the Doctor to put it in the starkest, simplest terms.

"There they are, people!" he thundered. "Three crosses. How good is your faith? Who's going to be the first to climb up there and yell, 'All right! Nail me here!'?"

There was some murmuring and a lot of wide eyes and open mouths at this, but, more, Woodward could feel the sense of unease sweeping through just the church part that he could see. They didn't like this. They didn't like this at all, and the older staff seemed to like it less than anybody else.

The Doctor let it all ripple around and sink in, waiting for the proper time to continue. Finally, he sensed it. He never understood how anybody ever effectively gave a talk or lecture without a live audience in front of them to gauge reaction.

"I see you don't like this," he teased them. "I see that, when the chips are down, you really don't believe it all, do you? When they said 'faith' in the early church, it meant marching out into the arena with no defense to face deliberately starved and mistreated lions. It meant being put against a wall and stoned, or thrown off the side of a wall or cliff. For all this time since, for all those centuries, people have paid lip service but when it came to putting their own bodies there they balked. Very well. *I* am going to the Three Kings. God wants me to, He's handed them to me, and I'm not about to second-guess Him. Some of my closest friends have agreed and are coming with me. Whether we come back or not is also up to God. We may not even have to. But we have to go. *You* do not. I hereby throw you the lifeboat to damnation. We will have to manage a full systems check and transfer those who can not consciously make this choice because they are still in suspension having had *their* bodies already in harm's way and not broken. I'll take no one who does not volunteer. When we reach our transfer point, I will *cheerfully* allow anyone, even if it's most of you, to disembark. Go. Leave. Go anywhere you want. Do whatever you want. You'd better make the most of it, because the only rewards you'll have are what you grab now. I don't *want* you. I don't want excuses. Just go. The rest—we will go together to the Three Kings or to Glory or to the Gates of Hell if need be!"

Critics had always called *The Mountain* a cult, a crazy offshoot of old evangelical Protestantism like so many others that were there before and flourished even more after the Great Silence. But Woodward was no cult leader and these people were not brainwashed or programmed in any conventional sense. To do so, as the medtech had said to John Robey, would have been to deny the free choice he so valued.

They would not follow him blindly, and he knew it. He would have it no other way.

"Now you have the information. The only thing you will not take with you is the route to the Three Kings. *That* we reserve. All else, go and good riddance. Don't come to me with excuses, either! Don't cry about spouses and children and all that. I want you all, but if you're a parent your job is to choose wisely for the family. Just make sure it's the right choice. When the time comes, just—*leave*. Wash your hands of all this because I will consider you dead and damned at that moment! That is all!"

Usually when the Doctor left the stage he got applause or shouts or some sort of audience appreciation, but not this time. There was almost dead silence in the hall and in the chapels and ward rooms. And, after a minute or two, a few began to whisper, then the whispers became talking, and the places erupted in a roar of conversation and debate.

When the duty rosters came out the next day, they showed eleven days until planetfall. It was too long, much too long. It would split families and eat at their souls.

"It's just not fair," Mike, one of Robey's long-time roommates, complained for the umpteenth time. "I mean, we don't have all the data, all the facts *he's* got. He won't even show us what these planets or moons or whatever they are look like, or why they're supposed to be so special! It's like making a test of faith of Russian roulette!"

Robey thought about the analogy. "Well, Russian roulette *is* a test of faith," he noted. "If you really think you're going to get the live round, you wouldn't play. But this *is* the toughest test the old man's ever come up with."

"Have you decided yet? Brother Timothy Supulveda is organizing a group to continue the key parts of the teaching under a new banner, you know. He thinks the old man's gone nuts."

Robey in fact knew about Brother Timothy. He'd been with *The Mountain* for a very long time, maybe since the Doctor had taken over, but he always seemed to be on the periphery of any controversy, never at its center. Now he seemed to feel that things had gone too far, that this comfortable mission life had been thrown into jeopardy by this most risky of decisions. Timothy, in fact, had never felt comfortable going to search for lost colonies along the frontier. No good will come of it, there aren't many out there, the real mission work is in the anarchic but established colonial groups with technology and political systems, all that. Now he was attracting many, particularly men and women with families.

"Do *you* think the old man's gone nuts?" Robey asked his old friend.

"I don't honestly know. Maybe I *don't* have enough faith. Maybe I *am* damned and like the faithless servant should get all I can. I keep wondering about that. I keep praying and I keep coming to 'the way is hard' and I keep wondering if the way isn't impossible for mortal men. And I'm not sure of the way anymore, either. You know how many distinct religious groups are out there, just on our side of the Great Silence?"

"No, never bothered to look. A bunch, I'd guess."

"Over seventy thousand, from a thousand variations of Christianity, several flavors of Judaism, several of Buddhism, three or four of Islam, plus

Hindu, Zoroastrianism, Baha'i, forty or fifty variations of naturism complete with shamans, black
witches, white witches, and that's not counting the
folks who think we're all property of some alien
entity that's using us for entertainment or food or
whatever and all sorts of other stuff. When you start
diagramming these belief systems they all sound
remarkably profound and also remarkably stupid and
primitive. There are even more than a dozen churches
that deny that there is any supernatural at all! I
mean, why bother with a church? A guild hall or
even a decent bar would do, I'd think."

"So you're a true believer but you haven't figured
out what you believe in?" Robey pressed. "That
sounds about as confused as the First Church of
Atheism."

"Yeah, well, why go unless you are totally convinced
that he's one hundred percent, and I mean *one hundred percent* right? Otherwise, like Brother Timothy,
you think of him not as some infallible Pope but as
a guy who got most of it, maybe more of it than others, but he's not infallible and he's not the only agent
of God in the universe."

"Oh, I can think of a good reason for going even
if I were in the First Church of Atheism," Robey
replied.

"Yeah?"

"Greed. You don't think Captain Sapenza wasn't
going?"

"Yeah, but the guys he stole that from didn't go."

"Maybe they didn't have a ship that could take it.
Maybe they were looking to steal only the very best.
Maybe the timing was close and they never had the
chance. But, I think if this location and all this data
were known there'd be a rush to it like the rushes to

riches past. I saw that jewel, that wondrous, weird jewel. It seemed to be able to reach inside the mind, to give each looker a unique vision for good or ill. What kind of natural force could create such a thing? Chance? What other wonders are there that we don't know about, that are maybe too hidden or too big to have been brought back? Even in the old days, when they could make almost anything you could imagine, I don't think they could have made that thing. That's why it's so valuable."

"So you're risking your life for treasure?"

Robey sighed. "I don't know. I doubt if I'm high enough on anybody's list to share in any treasure, or even how the money might be spent. I'd be better on Sapenza's crew for that, providing he had the ship and directions and not us. But, let's face it, I've got no family I know of here. Like you, I was more or less bred in the labs and raised by a group. Lots of friends, yes, but in a sense the only thing I have ties to is the congregation as a whole. That being the case, I keep wondering if I could live my life without going. If I wouldn't always be wandering around and saying to myself, 'What did I miss? What wonders did I give up for boring security? Did I *really* kick God in the ass by refusing?' I'm not sure I can live with that."

Mike stared at him for a moment, as if hearing his own inner thoughts echoed. Finally, he asked, "What *do* you think is there, at the Three Kings? This hasn't been the best trip in the ship's records. We've lost over a hundred lives on three planets that could be described as unfriendly, hostile, and murderous. How many new souls were saved? Any?"

"Some, perhaps," Robey assured him. "We had twenty couples stay behind on that pest hole we just left after all that they did to us. Forty people, stuck there, forever missionaries on a forgotten speck in the middle of nowhere. All volunteers, because they believed that the church could grow there. Now *that's* faith."

On the seventh day he got to see Eve.

She was out of that horrible tank and out of her coma, but still weak and pretty well immobile. Machines now were giving her gentle but regular exercise, getting her brain used to using the newly implanted neural connections to transfer instructions. In a sense, it was like having to learn to crawl, then walk, then do increasingly sophisticated and coordinated things, all over again, but on an accelerated timetable.

Even talking was still a problem, and she was occasionally hard to understand, but the medtechs insisted that she was light years ahead of where she'd been just a day or two earlier.

She looked weak and drawn and haggard, with only traces of the old Eve flashing from time to time. Even her long hair had been shaved and she had only a fraction of a centimeter grown back out. It gave her a curiously androgenous look.

"Hey, how you doin'?" he greeted her, smiling.

She managed something of a smile back, although the medtechs had warned that most of what she put on was a brave front. She was masking nightmares.

"Twying to recite Shakespeah," she managed. "Got a lipsp."

"Yeah, that is a lisp," he agreed. "I'm still working on new eardrums. Got my old ones busted playing hero in the wrong place."

She looked at him for a long time without saying anything, then she managed, "I—wemembah. I wemembah evvything . . . . You *thot* me!"

He chuckled. "Yeah, I shot you, but only to save you. I'd do it again, too, so watch it!"

She shifted, as if trying to use her lower extremities to push off, but she was still too weak for that. "Thoulda used a throngah beam."

He frowned. "A stronger beam? What do you mean?"

"You thoulda used a throngah beam. Then I'd be dead."

His expression grew deadly serious. "I don't want you dead. Why do you? I know it must have been a horrible experience, and you'll never completely push it from your mind, but you have to learn to get past it."

"No! You don't *know*. . . . Can't move, can see, can think, but can't act. Yoah body woaks and you have nothin' t'do with it. Make you do—*evil* sthings."

He couldn't know what she'd gone through, true, but he also couldn't see how she could blame herself for any of it. "But they *made* you. You couldn't not do it. If you don't have a choice, then the evil's entirely on *them*, not you!"

He realized, though, that ministers, maybe even the Doctor himself, had already been down here and were probably better at this than he was.

"Ah you going or sthaying?" she asked him.

For a moment he thought she was asking if he was leaving her bedroom, but suddenly he realized that she was asking about the Doctor's new direction. "Truthfully, I don't know. I'm inclined to stay. How many people get to see mythical places that most folks don't even believe in? Still, I haven't completely made up my mind yet. What about you? Have they made arrangements to get you to a rehab facility?"

She shook her head. "I'm not goin'. I'm sthayin' wight here."

"You shouldn't! You need a lot more than they can give you here!"

"I don't need what sthey can't gimme heah. Moth of uth ah gonna sthay. The captives, that ith."

"Why?"

"Dunno. Maybe justh becauth what sthey did t'us hath gotta mean thumething. . . ."

He stayed a bit longer, but they finally ordered him out. Her therapy was constant and computer controlled and monitored and couldn't be interrupted. He accepted that, and, walking back towards his quarters, he had to think about her and the others.

He was surprised that the medtechs and the psych computers agreed with them that they should not be transferred. *The Mountain* was their home; they were, in effect, natives. This ship represented the only safety and security they could possibly imagine. To throw them out against their will might make psychological rehabilitation impossible. Then you were into mindwipes, and that was something everybody tried to avoid at all costs.

And, in point of fact, most of them didn't care if they lived or died anyway.

Robey was beginning to think that he'd already made his own decision, too.

XI:
SHADOWS AND DOUBT

Although few of the large crew/congregation suspected it, the most nervous man aboard *The Mountain* when it made orbit at Marchellus, a well-developed old colonial world with no dry dock but a great many maintenance facilities and all the services and connections to elsewhere in the colonial region, was Doctor Karl Woodward himself. For all his bluster, he was still half convinced that, when access to the planet below was allowed, he'd find himself almost alone aboard his big vessel.

Well, he thought nervously. *At least we won't have much overhead.*

In the end, some did go. More than he would have liked, far fewer than he feared. Out of a ship's company of well over a thousand, barely ten percent left, and a few of those, around that son of a bitch Timothy, he didn't allow to choose. If they wanted that after all he'd taught them, then they should go after it.

Timothy actually tried to say goodbye and justify himself even though he should have known better. Woodward had refused to see him, and when the man persisted he had sent him a handwritten note that read, simply, "In the name of God, just go now!" Old Timothy and his band would do all right with their "Just believe" campaign, but they wouldn't get anybody to God that way, only create another movement of people feeling good showing off their godliness to each other.

During the refitting, he also received word from some of his old colleagues outside of religion, and those messages he accepted. At least one, Doctor McGraw, whom he'd have wagered a bundle that the old boy had been dead of old age for a decade, was actually on Marchellus and wanted to see him. McGraw was a theoretical physicist, one of the smartest men around, and they'd worked together on a number of complex problems before Woodward's decision to change careers, as he sometimes referred to it.

McGraw had been very young and very handsome in the old days, and it was a shock to see this little, bent old man come aboard instead. Still, Woodward knew that he didn't look much like the young firebrand of physics who'd gotten his first doctorate at seventeen and was going to solve all the remaining mysteries of the cosmos by the time he was thirty.

Yeah, sure, he thought. *That was when I was so arrogant I didn't realize that every time you solved one you got three more puzzles that were worse.* And with computers smarter than the lot of them working nonstop on those problems, few had been solved since.

"I can not believe you are still going around with this God business," McGraw told him over a good meal and good wine. "Karl, I can not understand this. What a waste."

"So you've solved the mystery of the Great Silence, and why all the gates inward and all the wild holes inward no longer work?" Woodward teased, knowing the answer.

"No, of course not, but it is a solvable problem. Nothing supernatural. No voodoo and priestly mumbo jumbo."

Woodward didn't take offense. He long ago realized that there were those who were called and could hear and those for whom the Word would always be blocked off. That was the way humanity was set up. He never set out to convert everybody; he was looking for the few amongst the many.

"So, Oscar, I see at least that medical technology has kept you going as it has me for longer than either of us expected."

"I always expected an exception to be made in my case," McGraw chuckled. "Me, I only fear that one day they are going to say, 'Celebrate! We've discovered the key to immortality and total regeneration of mind and body! But you can't be more than fifty years old or it doesn't work.'"

They laughed over that, but McGraw kept returning to Woodward's sudden decision to chuck a hard science career and pursue a religious vocation he'd never shown any interest in up to that point. "We never could understand it," he told his old friend.

"Oscar, I will wager that in all your intense study

of physics and mathematics you've spent incredible time in deep analytical work, learning all you could, testing what you could," Woodward said. "How much time, almost since you could read, have you ever spent studying religion? *Any* religion? A few years? A few months? Weeks? Days?"

"I gave up those childish beliefs when I discovered the wonders of science. You know that," the little man replied. "You need not waste time on what is a remnant of our primitive past, any more than it would profit me to spend any time studying gnomes and fairies. There are too many *real* miracles in the rational universe for me to go chasing after fantasies."

"Politics and religion are the two areas where every single person is an expert and nobody has to study anything," Woodward responded. "Well, it hasn't been a waste. It's been rewarding and enriching, even though you'll probably hear different from the dissidents I just threw off the ship."

"On the contrary, most of them say you are the smartest and wisest man they ever met, but they just can't live up to your demands."

Woodward's eyebrows rose. "Indeed? They *would* say that. I'd much prefer they said the opposite, or that they took your pragmatic and utilitarian view of the cosmos, Oscar. They're just going to take their misunderstanding of my teaching and pervert a new group as it is. I guess I can't stop them, though. Did any of them say what caused them to walk?"

Oscar McGraw stared into his old friend's face. "They say you've found the Three Kings. Is this true?"

Woodward smiled. "Come, come, Oscar! The Three Kings? Fairy stories! El Dorado, the Mines of King Solomon, the Golden Moon of Perseus. Surely you don't believe in those pie-in-the-sky legends!"

"You are mocking me. You *have* found them, then! I can tell, even after all this time."

"You've done the math. You know that a system like the Three Kings is bordering on unlikely to impossible."

"Karl—there are good reasons why scouts become cybernetic hybrids, fused with their small and highly maneuverable ships. Taking a ship through a natural wormhole into a situation where the forces of gravity alone must create bizarre conditions—this is not what you do with lots of young people and a ship like this."

Karl Woodward looked into the eyes of his former colleague and said, quite simply, "Yes, it is."

Eve had progressed rather well, much faster than anyone had expected. She was now in a maglev chair, able to glide around with minimal effort using a direct neural connection. Her voice, while lower and raspier than before, was back, and she had reasonable control of her mouth, tongue, and vocal chords so the lisping was now quite mild. She had feeling to one degree or another through most of her body, but operations were still difficult and the muscles were still in need of retraining. Still, she was beginning to look, sound, and feel human.

John Robey had tried to visit with her as much as possible every day since the first, and the medtechs had incorporated him into her rehabilitation routine. Machines could do a lot of the basic work on her body, but they were nearly helpless in healing the mental scars.

The old Eve would have been irrepressible and flying all around the big ship in her levitating chair, but *this* Eve, the new one, would not leave the medical facility or even go from one part of it to another without someone else along. Strangers, and there were many aboard during the orbital docking and retrofitting, caused her to freeze and then go back and hide in her room. Anybody she didn't know, even from the ship's company, caused her deep anxiety, even when with somebody like Robey.

"You can't keep torturing yourself like this," he warned her. "You'll go crazy."

"I know it's insane, that there's nothing to it, but saying that and feeling that, deep down, are two different things," she replied. "I keep thinking that somebody's gonna just put something on me or near me and it's gonna go into me and I'll be a puppet again, only this time nobody'll know but me. The feeling of total helplessness is just indescribable. I'd rather be dead than have anything like *that* happen again."

"What are you going to do when we get to the Three Kings? Sit in your room here and watch on the screen?" he asked her. "You know the Doctor hasn't made up his mind about the former hostages yet."

She looked panicked. "What do you mean?"

"He doesn't want anybody to go unless they are demonstrating total faith. If you're hiding out from life the way you and some of the others are, well, he says that's a total *lack* of faith and he won't be a part of it. The work here will be done in a few more days. At that point he'll pick the final company. We're just about broke, you know, as it is. That last mission was all give and no take, and this thing takes some work to keep in shape. I think the only reason he's getting some work at cut rate prices here is that folks know we're off for the Three Kings and they either want to horn in on a share of the riches that might be there or they want to take it from us. He says he wants a committed, determined group."

"He can't! He *wouldn't*!"

"He can and he will. You know the old man."

"But *you're* going, and you yourself said your faith was a little cracked!"

He sighed. "Yeah, maybe it was, maybe it still is. But, well, if I don't have it then what do I have? If I can't live up to my own standards, what good am I? This is the best test I've ever faced or can hope to face. Besides, I want to see what the Three Kings really are. Just more colonial-type planets in an unusual setting? Remnants of ancient alien civilizations? Heaven and Hell? It's almost a part of me, I guess. I looked out at the Brother Timothy kind of life and I couldn't be that kind of hypocrite in a minute. What else would I do? No money, no resumé, everything I've done has been here, and as a part of the Church. I'm not about to join another one, and yet the only marketable skill I've got is bodyguard or event organizer. I don't know about a lot of things, but I know that this is where I'm supposed to be. This is what I do. I think it's where *you* belong, too, but not if you're no good to God or man. I'm not supposed to tell you this, but I think fairly soon you're going to get a test from the old man."

"A test? What kind of test?"

"I don't know. But pass it. If not for God's sake, or your sake, then for *my* sake."

She looked surprised. "Your sake?"

He leaned over and kissed her lightly on the cheek, then straightened up and winked. "I think we made a pretty good team. I think we still can."

And, with that, he left her to her deeply disturbed and thoroughly confused thoughts.

For the first time, the next day he didn't come to see her, and she felt nervous and abandoned. Why had he kissed her and winked? Had he left for good? Was he saying goodbye?

She worked extra hard and long on her therapy, and managed to grasp a stylus with her right hand and even draw a crude sketch, kind of like one a small child might make but it was a great advance considering all the coordination that had to be brought into play just to do it.

Just after dinner, she received a message. It wasn't in the form of an intercom call, but rather as a note hand-delivered by one of the cleanup robots. It looked quite imposing, and she struggled, managed to open it, and pulled it out.

It said, in a classical cursive script that seemed out of a different time and place, "My dear Sister Eve: Please join me in the executive office off the *Olivet* ward room at eighteen hundred hours so that we may discuss your continuing role with our new mission." That was it, nothing more. And it was signed, "Karl Woodward, Ph.D."

She started to tremble, and fought to keep herself together. The office off the *Olivet* ward room! That was virtually the length of the entire ship and several levels up after that! From all the way aft to just about the bow of the entire hybrid vessel. She looked at the small clock in her room. It read "17:20." *Forty minutes! Oh God, I'll never make it!*

She was bright enough to at least suspect that this was either the test John warned her about or a prelude to it.

If she didn't go, they'd pump her with feel-good

drugs and ship her off to a local rehab center and she would be cut off from the body of the congregation, probably forever. But how could she? That far? With all these *strangers* checking over things and lurking around?

She looked around for a hairbrush before remembering that she no longer had hair long enough to brush and in any event it would be more than she'd managed with her arms to that point. She looked at her clock. "17:25." Where was it going so fast? Why was there nobody around? She'd need a half hour just to make it there in the chair!

She called the medtech, and after an interminable wait she appeared. "Yes, Eve?"

"I have to go to the *Olivet* ward room by eighteen hundred," she told the tech.

"Well, then, go ahead. There are no restrictions on you if you've taken your physical therapy and timed medication."

"But—but I can't—wait! Will you come with me?"

"Sorry, I'm on duty. Everybody here is. What about that nice fellow who comes around all the time?"

Yes, yes! That was it! John would come! She turned to the intercom. "Robey, seven one two six six, Arm."

"Buzzing." Pause. "I am sorry. There appears to be no one in that room at the moment. Would you like to leave a message?"

"Yes. No! Page him!"

"Ship's page is not available without security or bridge clearance."

She started to curse the intercom, even though it was a computer and she almost never had said as much as a "damn" or "hell" in her whole life. Suddenly she stopped, realizing that no help would be forthcoming, not from medical, not from the Arm, nor from anywhere. It was arranged that way.

She either would make her way on her own through the ship or she would not, and she now had exactly thirty minutes to do it.

With no one else to help her, she began to pray, silently, but fervently, as she'd never prayed before. *Be with me, Lord. Do not forget or forsake me, and give me the strength to do Thy will.*

The chair glided forward, rather steadily at first, until it reached the first hallway and she looked down the dimly lit and seemingly endless corridor forward and could only think of those miserable, damnable caves under the surface of that cursed planet.

I will fear no evil, for Thou art with me, she prayed, and started on down the hall.

More than once people would suddenly walk into the hallway and look at her or come towards her. In every case she felt her heart jump to her throat and she came to a sudden halt, but each time she prayed a bit more and continued on.

She kept going, straight down the corridor, feeling like she was about to throw up, seeing Sapenza in every shadow or darkened hallway.

She had been born aboard this ship; she'd spent most of her life inside it. This very corridor, like just about every other main corridor, she'd traversed time and time again, knew by heart. She kept telling herself that even as her heart kept pounding, pounding in her chest feeling almost like it was going to burst. She heard herself breathing, breathing hard, and she was tasting bile and having trouble catching one of those breaths.

How could a place so intimately familiar suddenly seem so alien?

On, on down the corridor, past rows of offices and crew's quarters, past rec rooms and classrooms and training areas. From Suite 1200, the main ship's hospital, down now to the five hundreds, the four hundreds, the three hundreds . . .

And then she reached the bulkhead and the stairs and lift to higher levels. She looked at the lifts, which she'd ridden thousands of times, and decided that the time wasn't yet right for them. Increasing power, she managed to levitate the chair up, parallel to the stairs, carefully avoiding any obstacles like the center handrails or reinforcing molding.

On the second level she passed through a vaultlike hatchway into *Olivet*, now docked and parked inside the greater ship. Only the emergency hall lights were on; everything else was dark, shut down, terrifying.

The more she looked down the hall the more she was convinced she could see shapes moving in the darkness, hear whispers and hushed laughter. She hovered there, staring, the terror starting to overtake her, unsure that she could go on, resisting the urge to flee back into *Sinai*'s safety. But it wouldn't be to *Sinai* that she would go if she did; she knew that. It would be somewhere on Marchellus, a planet she didn't know and full of nothing but strangers and dark places.

She went slowly forward down the corridor. To her right was the large cathedral-like main hall where the Doctor lectured whether aboard ship and en route or as part of the camp meeting and revival he set up on the ground at his colonial destinations. Beyond it would be a stair/ramp combination to one more level up, then back along the complex of offices, quarters, cafeteria, and so forth needed when *Olivet* was down on the surface and on her own. At the very end of

it would be the ward room, with exits to the *Olivet*
bridge and the meeting rooms and quarters of the
Doctor and other important high elders.

She was just about to the darkened stairs when she
was startled almost out of her wits by a ghostly, supernatural laughter coming from the meeting hall. She
struck the bulkhead and almost pitched out of the
chair, being saved only by the safety straps. Even so,
if she tipped on her side the magnetic resistance
would be lost and she would be stuck lying on her
side there on the deck until somebody found her.

The sounds came again, and she repressed her
panic and realized that it was just the sound of somebody, maybe a couple of people, somewhere inside,
probably checking out the layout for the next teaching
service once they were under way.

Feeling increasing panic, she nonetheless made her
way up the second stairs using the ramp and came
in sight of her goal. Again, she kept telling herself
that these were places she'd been all her life, that
she'd played hide and seek in the darkened mode up
here when she was a little girl. It didn't help as much
as it should have. Instead, it made her feel even worse
for being more frightened now than she'd been at the
age of seven or eight.

I know more now than I did then, she told herself.

Finally she turned and glided into the ward room.
The door was open, but the lights were on emergency
only, and the place looked locked up tight. The clock
on the wall, synchronized to the ship's master clock
like all the others, read "18:22." So she was already
too late. Had it been over fifty minutes to come this
way? Had she truly been that slow? It seemed barely
five or ten minutes since she'd set out.

And as late as she was, was anybody still there?
Would she have to slink back, a failure, because she
hadn't made it in time?

She glided over to the meeting room door and
pushed the sensor for entry. It hadn't had any illu-
mination, but suddenly it turned green and the door
slid open.

Inside, Doctor Karl Woodward sat in a big fake
leather chair at the end of a long table. To his right
sat John Robey, who looked quite pleased.

"Ah, Sister Toloway!" the Doctor greeted her, half
standing. "Please! Come in! Your young man here has
been telling me all about you and your experiences
back on the colony! You must be really something!
It seems he wants to quit the Arm and marry you!"

The Doctor did not minimize anything in his final
talk before they left orbit. After pretty much select-
ing certain people who'd elected to remain and
throwing them off anyway, primarily because of attitudes and comments made, in a few cases because
they had been traumatized former hostages who had
not been as willful nor as successful as Eve in breaking out of their shells and were therefore going for
the wrong reasons, he tried to talk any wavering
minds out of it.

"I don't want anyone with us who doesn't believe
that this is God's will and that we are *bound* to succeed based upon our faith in Him," he warned. "Anybody else would be a fool to come. Nor will this be
an easy or comfortable task in any event. We've
stripped the old *Mountain* as bare as we could; this
is no missionary or teaching expedition. We've sold
everything of value to insure that we have the most
state-of-the-art navigational computing system

available, and I think we do. I've been told that taking something this large into a wild hole is tantamount to suicide. Well, I don't believe in committing suicide and I think we can do it. There's no choice, anyway. If you all stay, we have to have something big enough to transport you!"

That brought something of a tension-breaking chuckle from the congregation.

"This is going to be it," he continued. "At zero nine twenty tomorrow all the umbilicals and work platforms will be gone, all the hatches sealed. We will power up, and we will move out. You have until about zero eight forty-five to take the last exit, the central hatchway Fourteen A. If you aren't gone by then, you're stuck. Also, be prepared for a lot of bizarre flying even before we do what we intend to do. The word is out: we're headed for the Three Kings and its fabled treasures. In addition to all the tracking devices various groups have bribed workers to implant into the *Mountain*, there will undoubtedly be a small navy shadowing us, ready to pounce right in behind us when we show them where the entrance lies. It's not going to happen, but keeping them from doing so will take some fancy flying and some chicanery. And, when we *do* jump into that hole, the fun *really* begins. It will probably be the longest, roughest, nastiest, most sickening trip any of us have ever taken. Sensors to the new computers will require millions, perhaps billions of minute corrections in all planes every second just to keep us centered. Just remember that, even inside there, God is there, too."

As they left to return to their quarters, John and Eve saw Cromwell standing rather casually at the rear. Although most feared the enigmatic security chief and kept their distance, Robey felt like he had a certain link with the man. He didn't understand him; nobody did, nor probably could who didn't know the details of the rumored dark past. Still, he did not fear him, either.

"Brother Cromwell," Robey greeted the big man as they reached the exit. "I should have thought that you and your people would be busily digging out all those tracking devices."

Cromwell gave a slight smile. "No use in doing that until we're under way. They'd just put them back again somewhere else. At least we think we know where they all are. I understand congratulations are in order."

Robey grinned and looked over at Eve, still in her levitating chair but looking much stronger by the day. "As soon as Eve can stand on her own we plan to have the Doctor marry us," he said.

"Very well. Let me know the time, if you'll allow me to come."

Robey was surprised. "I'd be honored, sir. Thank you."

After they'd gone a ways outside, Robey said, "I'd love to know what drives that man. I'd trust him with just about anything and yet there's something very scary deep inside him, something dark and dangerous."

"I know," she replied. "I wonder if he's still walking a darkened hall, or, maybe, keeping in the ghosts of all those who died by his hand before he found faith. I keep thinking of what happened to me and the others."

"You shouldn't."

"Yes, I should! Too often we take things like faith for granted, and we pay lip service to our beliefs. Maybe we have to get slapped or kicked in the rear and then scared silly in order to fully understand and appreciate it all. We all know that man was a soldier. We just don't know how many people he killed, or caused to be killed. This, all this, may be the only thing that keeps the darkness from consuming him."

The sudden onset of the Great Silence had jolted those left on this side of that now unreachable area of humanity's birth from a solid technological and near totally secular existence back into the arms of religion, which always offered a refuge during times that people could not understand and from things which they feared.

Even with his own emotional involvement, he was certain, as had been the medtechs, that Eve had been headed towards self-destruction. That same sense of faith and religious belief had kept her from going all the way over, and now was the rock against which she pushed to get back to normalcy.

Woodward had always preached that those who had no sense of or feel for religion had simply never been tested. Only those who had really were required to make the most basic of choices.

Robey didn't know if he'd been tested, really, or was simply the product of his upbringing. He wondered what kind of a test had forced Cromwell's choice, or, for that matter, Doc Woodward's.

One thing was for sure: from the time they would shove off tomorrow morning, and ever after, the very nature of *The Mountain* and its mission would be changed forever, and those who were within it would be dragged along.

Absolutely nobody slept well that night, and few slept at all, knowing the truth of that. Most spent at least some of the time in prayer and conversation with God, in private, as was consistent with their beliefs.

Forward, in his luxurious cabin, stripped as it was of many of the valuables he'd collected over the years, Doctor Karl Woodward tried to sleep, and dozed in fits and starts.

After so many decades of bringing the gospel to so many isolated worlds, to have scored so badly and been so wounded this last time out had to mean something. It had to mean that the time for spreading the Word was over, that God was giving him the stewardship He had promised in that first dream, so long ago.

No hallucinogens, no drunkenness, it hadn't been like that. Most of his old friends and colleagues, Oscar among them, thought it was a small stroke caused by overwork and stress. Even he had wondered, but it was impossible to explain it fully to himself or put it aside, even though he could never have explained it to his old colleagues.

You just had to be there, he thought.

Like Ebenezer Scrooge waiting for the Ghosts of Christmas, he had lain there in his bedroom, comfortable and fat, but, like tonight, having trouble sleeping for some reason, and into the bedroom had come an angel.

The creature had been beautiful, radiant, grandiose, an unbelievably wonderful creature, yet as real as anybody he'd ever known. He sensed immediately that he was seeing the creature as something deep down from his childhood told him angels should look like, but it didn't matter. It had been a conscious entity of great power and intellect and a sense of goodness and purity that came through any physical manifestation.

"If you run the next series of simulations, you will get a byproduct, a single series of equations, that will

cause the human race to annihilate itself," the angel had warned him. *"That which has always been feared will come true by your hands, and very quickly. The first practical field test of the equations will do it. Alter the simulation even slightly and these byproduct equations will not come forth. Then study God's word as you have studied God's work. You will find that its logic is sound and that the truth is not what you or most religions think. Your choice."*

And, with that, the angel had vanished.

The next day he slightly altered the simulation and things went rather smoothly. Later, when he'd worked out the method, he was able to privately run a subset of the original under a routine that essentially erased itself as it ran. The byproducts showed up, and, to him, they were obvious in their implications.

Had the angel been a figment of his imagination, a psychological construct to deliver what his mind had already suspected, or was it divine intervention and warning? He'd been brought up in a totally secular environment with just about no religious background at all. What he knew of religion of any sort at that point was what he'd seen and dismissed as childish superstition for the ignorant masses when he'd seen services on broadcasts or passed churches, mosques, synagogues, whatever.

It was the fact that he'd barely given it any thought at all his whole life up to that point that convinced him that the experience hadn't been entirely in his own mind. He began his studies, and the more he studied religion the more he discovered that most of the others seemed to have been based on old traditions, long histories, but nobody appeared to have read the books. And then he found this ministry that seemed to say what he was coming up with, and after the death of its leader he'd assumed the leadership. It seemed so natural and so true.

But he'd not gotten a single divine message after that one. Everything else was either subtle, with things just falling in his way, or realized through hard work. His old colleagues who thought him stressed out and dropping out of serious work to flee from its pressures didn't understand just how tough a job *this* was. Working with computers so smart he could not even comprehend their internal musings, and simulations, and budget committees seemed almost a vacation compared to running a show like this one.

If Oscar only knew . . .

And if the congregation, too, only knew. Knew that he doubted as often as they, and had long periods when his old rational self wondered if he *hadn't* been delusional. It was easy when things were going well; it was exciting, exhilarating, to go out to the colonies and plant new seed. But three worlds now, in a row . . . Three worlds that had been vicious, nasty, had cost a huge percentage of the ship's company, mostly its youth, just to get out in one piece. All those kids . . . Abused, raped, tortured, murdered . . .

This really wasn't to renew their faith. Not really. It was to renew his.

And as he lay there, tossing and turning, wondering if what he was doing was right, wondering if much of his life had been based on truth or delusion, he heard a voice. A familiar voice, one he'd not heard in a very, very long time. There was no physical manifestation, and it might have been in a dream in one of those fitful brief sleeps, but there it was.

"The Three Kings each bear gifts to the Christ child. One of those gifts He gives to you. Choose wisely, but only one."

Gold or spices. He wondered if it would be that obvious.

There was a sudden, persistent, and irritating buzzing noise. He tried to shut it out, to hear if the Voice had anything more to tell him, but he finally couldn't and opened his eyes.

"Yes?"

"Sir, we're about to leave orbit," Captain Lime's voice informed him. "You said you wanted to be notified."

"Huh? Oh, yes, yes! Proceed, Captain!"

He needed a good cup of coffee. No, he needed a good *pot* of coffee. This was going to be a long day. Sure, he could have popped a pill and been wide awake and energized in a minute, but where was the pleasure in *that*?

By the time he reached the bridge, he saw the large carafe in the anchor just to the right of his judge's seat overlooking the whole complex and knew that they had done their jobs and anticipated him.

The bridge of a starship was unlike the bridge of anything else. Even *Olivet* had its bridge forward and actually had both screens and areas of hull that could be made transparent if asked. A starship's bridge was amidships of the engine module, dead center, with the protection of the ship all around it. There were screens to show good representations of what was outside if you wanted to see it or, rather, if there was anything much to see, but they were all taken from the sensors built into the entire vessel.

For the most part, computers flew the ship without human intervention, and in some areas, such as when passing through any sort of wormhole, artificial and stable or wild and extreme as this one was, the computers could not be overridden by human hands or commands. The human brain simply couldn't think fast enough to make any difference in that sort of environment.

Still, it was the computer's job to interpret the wishes of the captain and carry them out, while always maintaining the safety and integrity of the ship and its passengers and crew if at all possible. That wasn't necessarily possible in a wild hole; the kind of chaos-based mathematics that could be used to predict the safety and success levels of such a trip could only be initiated after you entered the hole and had at least some sense of the demands placed upon the ship. That was why you had to have real faith or be crazy, or maybe both, to go through a wild hole like this one.

But first the captain and crew would be doing some decision-making inside the more normal constraints of space and genholes. That was because ships trailing other ships had computers of about equal abilities, so shaking a tail wasn't all that easy. You needed to put in some random, and often illogical, moves just to throw them off.

As soon as they entered the first genhole, Cromwell's people went to work disabling or jamming all the devices that had been planted for tracking purposes. These would be of little use within the wormhole, but would leave signatures when they emerged if left to do their jobs. The way you shook tails in space was to go through increasing genhole gates leading to multiple-choice exits and entrances and, frankly, picking each one at random until you wound up certain that you'd shaken everybody off.

Some of the chasers were good, but Woodward was convinced that his crew was better. Still, it took almost three days before they slowed and then came to a dead stop near one particularly complex junction of gates to get their bearings and also to wait.

The occasional ship would emerge from one and go into another, but none of them seemed to pause or even slow down. They had finally shaken the last of the tails.

Now it would take them another three days just to get to the jumping off spot. If anybody out there was clever enough to have guessed *that*, well, maybe they deserved to come along and see if *they* could ride the serpent.

XII:
THE THREE KINGS

They all stared at the forward screen which showed
a fairly dim and distant starfield and not much else.

"Show spacial abnormalities," the captain instructed.

Suddenly a good three dozen objects of varying size
and intensity flared to life, all in constant motion,
none a consistent shape, and all radiating enormous
energy. It really wasn't an unusual number of such
things for this sort of area, but it was unnerving
nonetheless to think of putting the ship, and themselves, into and perhaps through one of them.

"That's the one in the data, second from the far
left," the captain told Woodward and the others
sitting there at the monitoring and communications
stations.

Invisible to the naked eye, the wormhole seemed to shimmer and twist, elongate and then snap back to nearly round, only to go off in what might be called a twisted frown, and so on. Woodward had to stare at the thing and felt some trepidation in spite of all his comments. *How can you center something this size in* that? he wondered to himself. For that matter, what made them be there at all? A natural wormhole was a transitory affair; it formed for fractions of a second, then was gone unless forced open and locked that way until a ship went through. It was within the capabilities of all modern interstellar craft to do that; this had been the key to the stars in the first place. Once through, the equations said that the trip would be near instantaneous, but for reasons still not fully understood it was not. Still, the hole to the Three Kings, never stabilized and locked down, simply should not be there. It should not be reappearing over a three parsec region in a varying but not quite random order. Something *very* big and *very* powerful was powering that thing.

He suddenly thought of that key simulation, the one that would have given the key to erasing whole areas of space-time, that had forced him out of his old work and into this, and he wondered. *Sapenza, did you give me the right one? Or did you cook the books for revenge?*

It was too late for that now, he told himself. They *had* to trust the figures. They *seemed* to hold up, anyway. It was either that or slink back into port and disband. He wasn't going to do *that*, so there was really little choice.

"Proceed, Captain. Take us in," he told the ship's commander.

Lining up would be slow, careful, precise, with the

computers checking and double checking and awaiting a final command that could only be given by the
human captain. Once that command was given, though,
it was entirely out of his or Woodward's or anybody
else's hands but God's. The commitment would be
total, and at a speed as fast as the old *Mountain* could
give them.

"Put forward screen throughout the ship," the captain ordered, allowing those in their quarters, in the
ward room, and on duty stations to see what was
going on. What was most important wasn't the visual
but the small figure down in the lower right that
began "OPT" and then gave a percentage. The navigational computers were trying out every single
approach while calculating and trying to predict the
shape and size of the wormhole from moment to
moment. When they got it as close to "optimal," or
one hundred percent, as they thought they could, then
they would commit. From that point, no human
would have any control until they emerged at the
other end.

If they emerged at the other end.

"Riding the serpent," they called it, after going
through the long, writhing, snakelike tunnel through
space-time. Woodward thought about that for a moment.
The serpent, the source of evil, of original sin, expelled
from Eden. It was somewhat ironic.

The optimization rate had reached as high as
eighty-one percent twice, but never above that. It
wasn't comforting to think about the odds, even if in
their favor, since you had no room for error, no
allowance for mistakes. Eighty-one percent you live,
nineteen percent you die. With a controlled genhole
the percentage was always just a hundred thousandth
of a point below one hundred.

The captain shook his head. "I've seen and been through about this bad, but it's going to be hairy, sir!"

"Well, we knew that."

And now the captain gave his last order to the computers. He sat down in the command chair, leaned back, and said, "Commit at best possible point."

There was a pregnant pause when it seemed as if all was silent and the only sound throughout the whole ship was the collective heartbeats of the almost nine hundred still aboard, and then the screen said, "OPT 83."

People were suddenly slammed back into their seats or found things rolling away or crashing against bulkheads. The increasing roar of the great engines made the whole ship shake.

Before anybody could react further, the writhing, gyrating oval suddenly grew to immense proportions and then vanished.

There was a massive *bang!* as if something very large and vital had exploded all around them, but they were still there, and the vibration, if anything, was getting worse. Woodward felt his left pant leg get wet. Startled, he looked down and saw that the half a cup of coffee he'd left in his mug had vibrated up and out and all over him.

On the screen was nothing particularly intelligible. It looked gray and black and white and lumpy and irregular and it went on and on. What was unnerving about it was its apparent undulation; genholes were round and very stiff.

"Damage control, report," the captain said, still looking at the screen and the readouts.

"Minor breakage, and a few bruises and possible broken bones from people who don't listen to the briefings, nothing more," a woman's voice responded over the ship's intercom. "Recommend lifelines with clips for the duration, belts when seated or sleeping, and covered food and beverages. Full tie-down."

"Agreed. What was that bang?"

"Unknown. Doesn't show up on any of our status boards, sir. It may be that it was a last second correction just as we entered."

Or it could have been us striking the hole wall, thought not only the captain but just about everybody who knew how these things worked. So far power and shields were holding up at close to perfect, but even a slight tap could take a toll later on as they would have to put out at near maximum power for days.

"Captain? Nav desk," another woman, this one on the bridge, called over to him.

"Yes?"

"I have another object following us keeping regular distance. It might be another ship."

"Put it on my screen."

The data from inside a wild hole wasn't reliable enough to tell much, but there definitely did seem to be an object there, matching them move for move. Either another, smaller ship, or . . .

Or debris knocked off our engines, the captain thought nervously. Still, it *felt* like a ship. Maybe they hadn't *quite* shaken off everybody.

"I wouldn't be all that upset right now, Captain," Woodward told him. "Even if one of the leeches did manage to fool us and come along, they've got a pretty miserable ride, and there's nothing much we can do about them until we all get to the other side anyway, is there?"

"No, sir, that's true," the captain admitted.

It was rough getting used to the ship's motions, too,

particularly as time passed and people needed to move from one part of the ship to the other for various purposes. Some of the old-timers, including both Woodward and Cromwell, likened it to experiences on larger ships on big and rough bodies of water, where the whole environment was going up and down and side to side at one and the same time. Some people could never get used to it; some got violently ill. Most learned to compensate as time went on.

Still, by three days in, everybody was royally sick of the sensations and the vibrations and all the trouble they were going through just to do the most normal of things. That included Woodward, who, nonetheless, used the intercom systems and screens to keep morale up, speak on faith and the future, and also incidentally remind them that this uncomfortable ride was much better than the alternative, which was striking the wall and shattering into a million tiny pieces.

The countdown timer was on every screen, but it was based upon the Three Kings data fed into the navigational computers. It had worked out up to now, but there was simply no way to tell if Sapenza had given them the goods, or perhaps not all of the goods, or if it was going to work out.

With three days to go, Eve tried on a smart body suit that was kind of embarrassing in how it clung to every curve but which allowed her to move, use her arms and legs fully, and also give them the kind of stimulus and energy they needed to keep building. It allowed her to actually move much like everyone else, and with confidence, although with the ship's yawing motions and severe vibration she wasn't about to practice much in the way of long-distance walking, not yet.

As the last day clicked over and they were counting down hours, time seemed to suspend, even drag. It had been so long that it seemed as if this trip would never end, that they would be passing through this nightmare umbilical forever.

And then, almost on the nose of when the count-down timer finally reached all zeroes, there was a massive bang and thump, the entire ship shuddered, and they were in normal space.

Almost at once every single alarm on the bridge went off, and the computers struggled for control of the ship. It took several minutes before there was anything approaching normalcy, but even when the data streams stabilized there was a terrible rumble all around and sounds like metal twisting and breaking.

Captain Lime and the engineering officers brought down small headband units and did a mindlink with the computers so that they could instantly go to where the problem was and have an understanding of it.

What they saw wasn't good.

"Four of the six main tubes are cracked, one crack going for forty-two meters," Lime reported to the Doctor and others who'd gathered on the bridge. "There's also one whole huge section of engine thirty degrees on the port side that's simply, well, *missing*. I'll put it on the screen."

The damage was obvious to anybody who looked, and the nearest place for any repairs was . . . ?

"Sir, computers report *zero* reference point matches," the captain told him. "Either we're on the other side of the galaxy or, well—there's nothing to reference. We might as well be in another galaxy, and maybe we are."

Woodward let out a breath. "You're saying that we're here to stay?"

"Sir, take a look at what we just came out of—or, more properly, got ejected from."

The wormhole signature was gyrating so fast that it was nearly impossible to get any sort of shape for it before it changed. It was a whirling dervish of a signature, and it didn't stay in one spot. As the navigational data had warned, it was a spurting high pressure hose, moving over half the sky.

"We've got about thirty percent power, at least temporarily," the captain told him, "and I'm using that to put some distance between us and that—*thing*. I would suggest, though, that we begin an evacuation of *Sinai* immediately except for essential personnel, bringing everybody into *Olivet*. At the moment, now that we've stabilized, I'm going to allow us to continue to use the full *Mountain* to bring us in-system, but we may have to hop out fast at any moment."

"Do you have enough power to get us in-system to be able to use *Olivet* exclusively?" the Doctor asked.

"Oh, sir, once I've managed this acceleration maneuver we'll have no problems getting in. The real question is going to be whether or not we can stop. At a guess, I'd say we're going to have a very quick exit."

The screens changed, and everyone throughout the ship, from the Doctor on the bridge to Eve and John back in medical gasped at the same moment.

It was one *heck* of a solar system.

The G-class star was slightly larger than average but not outside the range of such suns in the database of known systems; what was spectacular was the fact that there was a series of debris rings where solid planets might be expected, and, beyond, well out from its star, was a single gas giant so massive that had it ignited there would probably be nothing else around at all. At a diameter of almost three hundred thousand kilometers it dominated *everything*, and it had not one spectacular ring but two, eerily paralleling one another above and below its equator.

"That thing is *impossible!*" the navigator exclaimed. "There is simply no logical explanation why gravity hasn't torn this whole system to pieces. Something we can't see or measure as yet has to be balancing this. Either that or we're in a parallel universe where things just don't work the way physics says they must!"

Woodward shook his head. In other circumstances, the physicist in him would have truly loved this sort of mystery, but he didn't have the luxury. He had a crippled ship that, with what acceleration it could muster, would almost certainly be pulled towards that giant planet without sufficient force by then to break away.

"Most likely we have some sort of odd balance involving some sort of dark massive object," the Doctor told them, "and somehow all this has come together just so to keep it remarkably stable. Still, some of the forces generated explain the nature of that wild hole and the lack of obvious smaller solid planets. What a great laboratory for research! It's places like this that throw what you know into a cocked hat and make science fun. Too bad we can't take the time to do it."

"Sir, it's weirder than you think," the navigator reported. "There's a constant heat coming off that thing, although it's pretty stable. The gas mixture is giving off a kind of weak starlike corona even though there's no obvious source for it. It's not going to become a star, but it's acting like, well, not a failed sun, but a sun that was frozen in the instant before it blew. Very, very weird. There's nothing like this in all our data. It's as unlikely as, well . . . "

"The emergence of humanity on ancient Earth," Woodward finished. "Yes, I can see that. If anything, we might be more probable than *this*. How wonderful that for all our knowledge God continually surprises us." He paused for a moment, thinking on that, then asked, "Satellites?"

"*That* thing? Yes, sir! Hundreds. Every shape and size, and that's not counting the double rings. Most follow the rings' angle at about fifteen degrees off the elliptical, but a few actually go through the rings and probably look it, and a number seem to be in their own orbits, a couple running counter to the rest. Captured, most likely."

"Give me large ones in any theoretical life zone that maintain relatively stable orbits," the Doctor ordered.

"There's one right here, and a second over there," the navigator noted, highlighting them on the screens. "Either would be a respectable planet in its own right. This thing is big enough it has its own system and it's amazingly stable. The largest, on the left there, is almost sixty thousand kilometers in diameter, solid, and shows evidence of heavy volcanism. Much of the cloudy atmosphere is actually water, though. My bet is that the place is very hot and very wet all at once. Whether the atmosphere is breathable or the surface temperature bearable, unlikely but impossible to tell without probes and a much closer look."

"The second one, on the right-hand side, is about thirty-eight thousand kilometers in diameter, quite average, a bit farther out and on the chilly side. The large white areas are ice, probably pretty deep, and those are heavy polar caps. Still, atmospheric analysis shows a breathable if slightly weak atmosphere, and those large snow fields could very easily be the frozen tops of oceans. Equatorial region seems to be a cold desert, mostly. Conditions there would be livable, but not pleasant. I don't—"

She suddenly paused and gave a slight gasp as a third planet-sized satellite suddenly came into view. Smaller than the other two at under thirty thousand kilometers in diameter, it was nonetheless a gem, a jewel, and it shouted beauty and life, a blue and white haven in the distance.

"That's water all right, sir," the navigator reported. "Oceans, continental land masses, an atmospheric balance with a very slightly rich oxygen content that's compensated by the humidity. No really cold regions, but it appears to be a bit scorched in spots near the equator. Subtropical over most of the latitudes north and south of there, though. The kind of readings I'm getting, sir, say it's a greenhouse, but one that is optimum for plants and maybe people."

"Correlation?"

"Well, sir, it's hard to say for sure, but I'd say that, checking against the Three Kings data and legends, the pretty blue one is Balshazzar, the cold one is Kaspar, and the large cloud-obscured hot one is Melchior. Not as romantic to look at as the legends, but otherwise things *do* match up. Those are the only planet-sized moons capable of supporting life, and they are in remarkably stable orbits considering that monster of a planet and the chaos it causes all around. Those just about *have* to be the Three Kings."

They also fit the old scout's alternate names according to the legends. A little paradise of a world, a world cold and inhospitable but livable where one might work things off in a kind of Purgatory, and a hot and cloudy place that was Inferno.

"One and one only. Choose wisely."

It would be pretty easy from this early data to choose, and there would be popular sentiment only for the garden, but the Doctor wondered about the other part of that scout legend, where the monk warned to look beyond the obvious. Why hadn't he used his original Dante-inspired names? Why had he thought they would be misleading?

"How long can we maintain ourselves in *Olivet* alone?" he asked the captain.

"Well, sir, we've fewer people than before, but *Olivet* was never designed to take the whole company anywhere. The food generators and waste cycling, water demands, all that will put an enormous strain on it. We can *fly*, although it's going to be a bit tricky with all those gravitational forces and with all the debris bound to be in between those rings—"

"Just cut to the chase!" the Doctor snapped.

"Well, sir, I think I don't want to maintain it in that space for very long in any event, particularly not under these conditions. With so much power to the shields, I'd recommend putting down on one of them and using the small scouts to take a look at the others. If a piece of rock penetrates the shields, then instead of having just one ship we'll have no ship. I know how you hate this sort of thing, and no more than I do, but we're going to have to pretty well choose where we want to go in the next few days, and we're going to have to head there as straightaway as possible in *Olivet* after we do. And that's assuming that *Sinai* can hold together enough to get us reasonably close. You've really got a choice on *Olivet* between shields on the one hand and food, heat, and toilets on the other. You see what I mean, sir?"

Woodward did. This should be a matter of careful exploration and good science, but in this case faith would have to be enough.

The obvious choice to everyone else was not the obvious choice to him, though. The pretty blue and white world with the subtropical climate and spectrographic analysis that it would accept the seeds of key fruits, vegetables, and the like allowing for a stable food supply from the *Mountain*'s supplies seemed obvious, but it also seemed too easy. There would be little to challenge or test the people; it looked like an invitation to grow soft and fat.

Three Kings ... Gold, frankincense, myrrh ... The blue world was certainly one of the spices, the cold world represented gold and might well be where the curious gems and other artifacts from the Three Kings had been found. The clouded, volcanic world had to be another spice or scent; he wished he could see below and know if it really was a place where they could survive. Was the atmosphere toxic, or did the clouds cause some sort of greenhouse effect? Most of his experts doubted the latter; if it had been a planet in orbit around the star, certainly, but the composition and the position around the gas giant would allow for sufficient cooling. As to the toxicity, though, they couldn't guess without probes.

All three were supposedly places where humans could live, but that was legend. Two at least bore this out; if so, there was some reason to believe that the harsh and violent surface of Melchior was livable as well.

But what about the water quality, the soil, the other essentials that would make *sustaining* life possible?

Did he dare commit all of them to that level of unknown?

Please, Lord! Show me what to do!

"Ship!" somebody shouted. "There's another ship just shot out of the wormhole and if looks are any indication, it's worse beat-up than us!"

It looked to be a small Talcan raider, a fast and heavily armed single unit vessel related to the much larger class of ships Sapenza had commanded. These had been built as local warships that could also be used for official business by the more prosperous colonial worlds, and to give them some autonomy from the interstellar naval forces that might not have their best interests at heart nor be under their command.

Many had gone pirate or mercenary, or been turned to it, over the years since the Great Silence. This had to be one such, probably from some colonial trace in the neighborhood of Marchellus who'd picked up the rumor. The captain had to be pretty good; it seemed to be the only one they hadn't shaken.

That, however, appeared to have been a decidedly mixed blessing to the ship, which was desperately trying to right itself, stop its merciless spin, and which was, rather clearly, trailing parts of spacecraft.

The small ship managed a measure of stability and turned itself in-system, but it still seemed to have little control, and even its energy shields were intermittently changing strength or cutting out and then coming back in again.

"What do you think, Captain?" Woodward asked.

"I think that fellow's in far worse shape than we are, that he'd better get himself and his people into lifeboats if he's got them and get the hell down someplace.

He's going about as fast as he can go without breaking apart, and he's going to pass *us* in a matter of hours. That ship just can't take it for very long, and when it gets within the gravitational field of that big planet it's going to be pulled every which way from Sunday."

"Can you talk to them?"

"We're trying, but there's no reply. Either their equipment is damaged or out, or they just don't want to talk right now. They'd better. If they time it right we could snag their lifeboats, but we could never slow or stop their ship."

Over those hours, repeated attempts to communicate with them continued to fail, and the *Mountain* was reduced to simply giving them instructions on crossing over via lifeboat if they were so inclined. Even as *Mountain* continued the monumental task of moving everything and everyone they wanted to save into *Olivet*, they all kept one eye and ear open to see if the mysterious stranger was going to do anything.

"Maybe they're all dead," someone suggested. "It's pretty beat-up. Maybe it's just the ship's computers flying it."

"No, they've still got sensor control and they've used them," the captain told them. "*Somebody's* still alive on that thing."

But when they reached the point of no return, after which they could not launch boats and reach the *Mountain*, they went right on past without any communication.

"They'll be there well before us," the captain noted. "If, of course, they don't wind up as the hundred and first or whatever moon of that thing, crash into its gaseous surface, or skip around and go off into deep space."

From that point, it was simply a matter of tracking them inbound; the people of the *Mountain* had much more important things to do for their own future survival.

Within three days, the gas giant began to fill their vision. It was a very dangerous object, but it was also impressive, even awe-inspiring.

"You know, in ancient times if people had gazed out and seen something like that they would have mistaken it for a god and worshipped it," Karl Woodward noted. "We must make certain that our descendants don't fall into that kind of error and make a mockery of all that we've stood for over the years."

Thomas Cromwell stared at it and nodded. "Curious that it's described in the data from both the original legendary discoverer of this place, Father Ishmael Hand, and Mother Tymm, but neither attempted to name it. It's simply a gas giant."

"Well, then, I suppose *we* can name it, for all the good it will do for the future considering nobody will know it but our people. Nothing divine, though. Nothing that can be perverted later. Maybe that was their problem. The ones here before us couldn't come up with a name that was both adequate for that thing and at the same time didn't run the risk of potential blasphemy." He changed the subject. "And what of our silent friends?"

"I'm astonished their ship held as much together as it has, but it's about at its end now," Captain Lime reported. "They've been doing much what we did, using remote sensors to probe what they can, and they've centered on the Kings. I've seen evidence they're putting all the power they have left into deflecting towards the blue one, Balshazzar. At a guess, they are going to try and get as close as they can and then use the lifeboats to make it to the surface."

Woodward thought about it. "As suckered by it as most of us, I suppose," he commented, sounding disappointed. Still, he had asked for some divine guidance. Was this it? Could he in good conscience lead them to a landing on Melchior knowing that other human beings had landed on Balshazzar?

The near magnetic pull to his own people of Balshazzar seemed to be underlined; his fervent and near constant prayers gave him only this guidance, yet nothing else had emerged to support his instinct to head for Melchior.

He hated having his hand forced like this, but if Lime was right and a lifeboat from the other vessel did get away and settle on the surface of Balshazzar, they'd have to follow. And he was quite insistent, even to himself, that God had given him the choice of only one.

Balshazzar, then, it almost certainly would be, even though everything in his core being shouted against it and, most of all, he hated doing the popular and expected thing.

Halfway into the fourth day inbound all the indicators and full ship's computers began to sound their warnings that the *Mountain* was about to give up the ghost. The crack in the main engines had continued to expand, and if it reached an edge then some of the great power plant modules would rupture and they would cease to exist, making all choices moot.

With enormous sadness and great reluctance, Karl Woodward ordered all personnel off *Sinai*, sealed *Olivet*, and detached the smaller interplanetary capable vessel from the wounded and dying interstellar beast.

They were now headed in towards the double-ringed giant with shields at maximum and power full. All around them they could see evidence that they were going through a relatively dense debris field of mercifully very tiny particles that were hitting the energy shields and burning up. Having committed to a Three Kings approach vector, however, they could not maintain these power levels for long and required much of the power from ship's functions to support it as it was.

As expected, a single lifeboat detached from the mysterious ship ahead of them and headed for Balshazzar. The rest of *that* ship continued on, on a trajectory to strike and bury itself deep into the great gas giant, a rather minor splinter in Moby Dick's backside.

"Did they get down okay?" Woodward asked, feeling guilty that he almost hoped that the answer would be no.

"Yes, sir. At least, no explosion, no major impact in the area they would have gone down. Every bit of evidence says that if anybody was in that lifeboat they're on the surface."

He sighed. "Then the choice for us is the same, I suppose. Balshazzar, Captain."

Now let's see what's so mysterious and special about these three damned moons!

XIII:
EAST OF EDEN

"You know," Eve said to John, "when we were living in that farm village I tried to imagine what it would be like to be truly a native there. Now we're going to be not much different from them. It's kind of ironic."

Robey shrugged. "I dunno. The view's spectacular, but I sure can't see why this is otherwise any different from where we were, that's for sure. All those people, all those legends, and it's just three big moons."

"Maybe. But it doesn't have Captain Sapenza and his band underground like the last one," she noted. "Heaven on top, Hell below."

"I'm not so sure," he said worriedly, looking at the view of the blue and white ball on the screen as they approached. "Seems like the more a place looks like Eden, the more snakes it winds up having."

"That's why Saint Patrick is going down first," Karl Woodward told them, overhearing their conversation. "Cromwell's not a name the Irish ever liked, but Patrick was an Englishman no matter what they claim and *our* Cromwell is very good at dealing with snakes."

Cromwell wore his combat suit, complete with knightly Saint George crosses, but the rest of those he took with him were planetary scientists rather than combat personnel. He didn't expect serious trouble down there; he *did* need to be able to tell *Olivet*, and *before* it landed, that it was safe and proper to do so.

They centered in on a broad mid-latitude continent and specifically an area not far from the eastern seacoast where the other ship's lifeboat was still giving off homing signals. It was the logical landing site, but it was also why Cromwell was going down loaded for bear. No telling if these people were simply unlucky or waiting to pull a fast one.

Close up, Balshazzar looked even more like the old classical versions of Paradise than they'd imagined. Four main continents sitting on well-developed continental plates with quite a number of islands of all sizes in the oceanic realm. In fact, only one ocean area seemed to have no land mass at all, and it was well south and towards the polar regions.

There was a lot of active weather; lightning was quite abundant, but not in quantities any more dangerous than the average colonial world, and there was some continental weather. There were, however, no ice caps, which explained why the islands were plentiful and the continents relatively small.

Temperatures in the mid latitudes seemed to vary little, north or south, averaging about thirty-two degrees Celsius. The equatorial zones were considerably hotter and probably would not be great for any long-term settlement; temperatures there easily reached forty-five or greater, particularly during the period when the planet was on the sunward side of the great giant, but dropped only about five degrees when facing the big planet, no more than ten during the short night.

It was a hot world. Even the poles reached fifteen to eighteen degrees.

That was an oddity they hadn't thought of with light. With the moon's rotation, they had a relatively normal day/night cycle even though, being fairly small, a full day was closer to nineteen hours than the human standard twenty-four. But when it was on the sunward side of the gas giant, night was not very dark; even though you could follow the planetary shadow on the surface of the big planet, the thing was so huge and so dominating that it illuminated the dark side facing it to about fifty percent of daylight levels. This was a very bright world overall.

And plants seemed to have evolved on it just for that. Big plants, small plants, jungle plants, grasses, it didn't matter. Every square centimeter of land was covered with growth, all verdant and abundant. There didn't seem to be much sign of animal life, but they'd have to get down there to find out for sure.

It was certainly carbon-based life, too, which held out the possibility that, as alien as it should be, there might well be plants down there that human beings might eat and take nourishment from.

Cromwell homed in on the lifeboat beacon and brought one of the four scout ships Olivet had left down to the surface about a kilometer from the signal, in a storybook meadow complete with placid freshwater lake.

They already knew that the oxygen-nitrogen mix was breathable, but they checked out all of the elements of the air before opening the hatches. Some slightly heavier than normal concentrations of inert gases might well explain why the slightly elevated oxygen level didn't result in more intense fires, but the overall mix had nothing new or unusual, and nothing they hadn't seen before on other worlds.

"Too good," one of the environmental engineers commented. "Ten to one the place smells like rotten garbage."

"There is only one way to find that out," Cromwell noted, and gave the security code to open the hatch.

Stepping through the airlock felt like someone had soaked a wool blanket in water and thrown it on them. The air was incredibly humid, heavy, thick, and also all-around hot. Still, it didn't smell particularly bad.

"Kind of smells like cinnamon," one of the techs commented. "And several other spices, too."

"More like incense," said another. "Several flavors mixed together. A little sweet for me, but not really bad, I don't think. Beats rotten garbage, anyway."

"Frankincense," Cromwell muttered.

"Sir?"

"The Three Kings, also known as the Three Maji or the Three Wise Men who brought gifts to the baby Jesus. You know that. The gifts were gold, frankincense, and myrrh. The first is self-explanatory. The other two are exotic spices used in ancient times in perfumes and incense. In those days they were all incredibly valuable. What we're smelling here is close to frankincense. That worries me."

"Sir?"

"I do not believe that the atmosphere of this world smells uniformly like frankincense. So why does it smell of it just here, where we land?"

They stood there for a few moments, saying nothing, although a couple of the techs were checking samples.

"Curious," Cromwell noted, not really talking to them.

"Sir?" one of the techs responded.

"Listen. Just everyone stop what they're doing and listen."

There was the sound of wind blowing through the tops of trees, the sound of small ripples from the lake hitting the shore, and the sound of a gurgling brook coming from the lake and heading off towards the sea many kilometers away, but not much else that they could hear, and one of the engineers said so.

"That's exactly the point," the security chief replied. "There's no real sounds at all. No birds, no insects, no animal sounds. Just wind and water. Life sensors?"

"Nothing really, sir. Just plant matter. If the plants here cross pollinate, they sure don't do it in the usual manner."

"Microorganisms?"

"*Those* we got," the engineer responded. "I'd say there's enough new species here to keep an exobiologist happy for three lifetimes just in this pond scum. Nothing extraordinary, though. They don't look like ones in our databases, but why should they? They *do* look like normal evolutionary variants. I expect we're going to find them everywhere, and everywhere a new set of species."

It was impossible at the moment to know if any

were harmful to humans, but it was not only unlikely—only a few dozen organisms had ever crossed the interstellar species barriers—it was also moot. They would have to face them or similar groupings no matter where they settled. It wasn't like they had a wide range of choices.

"Now, here's something interesting," one of the techs commented, examining a fruit picked off a low tree. "Very bananalike, would you say?"

Everyone looked. "Yes? So? It's a common form," another tech said dismissively.

"Yeah, well, it's not a bananalike fruit at all. In fact, the analysis here says that the *only* thing it can possibly be is a real, live banana, ancient Brazilian strain, no significant genetic differences nor abnormalities."

"What! That's impossible!" Cromwell roared. "Are you certain?"

"Yes, sir. Just like *those* are common coconut palms imported and raised on countless planets—I'd need to run the genetics to tell you which variety—and I'll bet most anything that those are mangoes, those are papayas, and so on." She stopped and shook her head, looking incredibly puzzled. "If we find a grove with a bunch of apple trees off by themselves, I'm out of there," she added, muttering.

Cromwell was suspicious. "If there are no noticeable insects here, how are they pollinated? Who brought them? They seem to be growing wild, but there's not a lot exotic here. They don't look like they aggressively displaced anything."

"Sir, there were large areas of the planet having no correlatable growths to anything we know," the other tech noted. "In fact, this region here showed to be far smaller and more mixed from above, but it has definite boundaries. Kind of like a self-maintaining greenhouse for somebody's exotic fruit and vegetable collection."

Cromwell looked around suspiciously. "I wouldn't be the least bit surprised, considering the legends about this area. Who knows who or what is here, or has been here before, or in fact was trapped just like we are? Keep at it, people. I'm going to take a look at that crashed lifeboat."

The lifeboat was about a kilometer or so from them, but fairly easy to locate using the orbital positioning system relayed down to his suit. As he walked, slowly, carefully, deliberately, but without any sense of real danger to himself, he heard an odd sound. At first it seemed like the rustling of wind in the higher trees, but there was no wind to speak of here and now, and the more he listened the more it sounded close, on the ground, not up in the forest heights.

It was kind of like, well, sand, or very smooth pebbles, rippling along on glass. That was the best way he could think of it. It certainly didn't seem to be closing on him, but it *did* appear to be following, perhaps watching. It was possible that the local botanist was indeed in residence.

A true highly advanced alien intellect would in and of itself be something of a breakthrough here. The few sentient creatures discovered in humanity's expansion had been quite primitive, really. *This* one, if it indeed was living and not some sort of computer on automatic, would be something else entirely. Something that could grab plant DNA and duplicate, raise, and vary it without compromising it. That would be quite impressive.

The lifeboat sat inert on a meadow floor, looking a bit banged up but hardly crashed. It was a fairly standard unit, which could hold as many as four people in a pinch, and if its cryo units were operable could sustain those four almost indefinitely. Little wonder they chose to land here instead of being frozen, though; this place was almost a golden Christmas tree amongst the terror and gloom of interstellar isolation.

The airlock hatch had been left open; whoever had come down in it had crossed his or her Rubicon when landing here and there was no particular purpose to sealing it off once they'd committed and landed. He looked around for signs of where the inhabitants might have gone, but saw no traces.

"Archangel, any human life signs that aren't our people?" he called up to the mother ship.

"Affirmative, but it is very difficult to keep them on scope and tracked. There's an energy field down there that is just unbelievable. Got a fairly good lock on you, though."

"How many unknowns?"

"We count two. One about a hundred meters northwest of your position, the other less than half that and to the east of you. They fade in and out, almost like ghost images. There is also an indistinct anomalous blob at your back, perhaps thirty meters. We have no correlation for what it is, but it does seem to be able to move."

Cromwell turned and looked back in that direction but saw nothing. He didn't expect to. Still, that meant that the unknown crackling sound had corporeal form.

"Entering the lifeboat," he told them.

The inside wasn't much, and he spent little time with it. There was probably a log someplace, though, and he tried all the switches and controls to see if he could locate information that would tell him who and what this one had come from. The ship, however, was dead, no power at all. It was as if all the energy cells had been totally depleted, something not normally found outside a service dock. Still, all this thing was now was a lump of metal and synthetics. With no power, the energy-to-matter converter wouldn't produce food and water, nor much else that was needed. Whoever had come down in this thing was at the mercy of the planet, which was probably why they were out scouting around. Odd, though, that they hadn't headed for the *Olivet* scout when it landed. This close, they *had* to have seen it come in, or at least heard it.

He emerged from the lifeboat, puzzled but confident that the answers weren't too far away nor terribly exotic. The familiar fruits and such here could easily have been drawn from computer files or an older landing where they might have had samples that could have been copied. These two might well think that they'd be targets of the *Olivet* crew, since people tended to think that anybody on the other side thought and did just what *they* thought and did, or they might just be terrified of being trapped for life on a world with hundreds and hundreds of Bible thumpers. *Serve 'em right*, he thought.

If it wasn't for that clicking, rustling blob he might not be that concerned about this place at all.

"Is the anomalous life sign still in the same position?" he asked Archangel.

"Affirmative, sir. It came in a bit while you were inside, but backed off to its old spot rather quickly. We should have been able to see it, but all we got was a kind of glassy, reflective distortion. We don't know what it is, but it is masked in a way that we can't compensate for. What do you think it is?"

"I think it's the manager," he replied, looking out at where it should be but was not. *Was* there a kind of shimmering distortion there?

"Hello!" he called out, palms out. "Will you speak with me, or communicate with me in some fashion? I mean no harm to anyone or anything that means no harm to me."

There was that rustling again, only not constant, more like marking a space but unable to keep completely still. This close it reminded him of old-fashioned marbles, only filling and contained in some kind of frame. That was the sound, anyway.

No, you're not going to show yourself, are you? he thought to himself. *You want to wait until we're all down here and you have the advantage.* He couldn't blame it. He would certainly have done the same thing.

Well, if there wasn't going to be any first contact today, then maybe the other two, who were undoubtedly human, would suffice.

"One of the human figures is doubling back your way," Archangel told him. "Watch your back."

"Oh, I think if he wanted to come up on my back and get the drop on me, we should let him," Cromwell responded. "Keep the techs away, though. Just me."

"Affirmative. You're sure?"

"Just keep an eye on me, that's all." He could *feel* the other person there now, feel the eyes on the back of his neck somehow. He'd always been able to do that.

"Would you prefer I kept my back to you or should I turn around?" he called aloud in a nonthreatening tone of voice.

"You can turn around, but no funny stuff," a man's voice responded, the smoothness of his voice masking the fear bordering on terror that Cromwell sensed in him.

The security chief turned and found himself looking at a young bearded man, somewhat Oriental in features but a big man, perhaps physically larger than Cromwell, and aiming a very nasty needler right at the security chief's head. The body armor was obvious, although there was little to indicate its capabilities, but Cromwell's head was exposed, at least apparently, to anyone who hadn't seen a suit in action.

"My name is Thomas Cromwell, son, security team chief of the starship *Mountain*, or what's left of it. I believe in self-defense, but I'm not in the business of harming anyone."

"You have the big ship up there?" the young man asked, sounding increasingly nervous.

"More or less. The interstellar one is shot, bad as yours. We have a fairly large secondary ship in orbit, but it's strictly interplanetary."

"You got to get us off of here," the young man said firmly, the pistol still aimed at Cromwell's head. "You got to get everybody off this world. I don't care what happens after that."

"Well, nobody invited you along. You chose to follow us," Cromwell replied. "Now we're all in the same boat. The difference is, wherever we are, we are home."

"You gotta get us off this place," the young man repeated, almost as if he were in shock.

"To *where*, son? Only three places in this system we can live on indefinitely. This one, one that's cold and barren, and one that's got far too much lava for my liking and probably stinks to high heaven. And that gun's no way to welcome the only possible friends and allies you got. What *is* the matter with you, son? You had the guts to follow us through a wild hole. What's got you so petrified now?"

The young man's eyes were wild. "You haven't seen it, felt it. This may look like Eden but it's Eden with the snake as boss. We ain't gonna be no slaves to no *thing*. It sucked our lifeboat engines dry, and it'll do the same to you sooner or later. It's just waiting for you to land the rest of your party and your big ship, that's all."

He nodded. "It came up to us just as we all cleared the hatch. We were just breathing our first fresh air and checking for wounds when it come right out of the woods there and straight for Captain Terashkova. She drew and fired, but it didn't make any difference. Point-blank range. It—it kinda just *smothered* her. And then that was it. Nadya and me, we just took to the woods. It moved in, drained all the power from the lifeboat, and it's been kinda loafing around, like it's waiting. Waiting for us, or you, or everybody!"

Cromwell doubted it. It sounded like the thing had simply defended itself, something he'd have done in similar circumstances. "What happened to your captain, boy? Where's the remains?"

The young man pointed briefly with the pistol. "Over there. See what it's done?"

Cromwell looked to the right of the open hatch. There was nothing there but a small bushy tree. "You don't mean *that* is your former captain?"

"Yeah, you got it. Thing turned her into a fuckin' *bush*. That's us, too, mister. That's everybody up above, too, if they come down here. Now, you turn and lead me back to your shuttle."

"Oh, we'll go back over there," Cromwell promised him. "However, what makes you think it'll let *us* go?"

"It smells all them people of yours up there. It's waiting. It's smart, it is."

"Come on, then. Let's get back to my ship and my people," Cromwell told him, trying to soothe him. He was less concerned with what the kid might do than he was with a panicky set of shots at whatever it was out there which might cause all sorts of problems. If it could drain the energy out of a lifeboat, then it was probable that the combat suit was no more use than a medieval suit of armor, if that.

"Why in God's name did you take the risk to follow us here, boy?" Cromwell asked, hoping to keep the boy talking. There was a companion someplace, too, probably as panicked and as well armed as the kid was.

"Riches. The Three Kings—*jeez!*—*everybody* knows about the Three Kings. A tiny number of soul gems alone would set us up for life."

"Yeah, well, your captain picked the wrong place, son," Cromwell told him. "No soul gems or weird alien artifacts or anything else on *this* one. And, all things considered, we could be hip deep in them for all it would matter. We're not going anywhere."

The crackling, rolling noise began off to their left. He could feel the kid stiffen, but, if anything, it only increased his resolve. "Keep going!"

"What's your name, son? Mine's Brother Thomas."

"I ain't your son and you ain't no brother of mine, neither!" the boy snapped. "The name's Alan Chu. I'm from Quen Cong."

Quen Cong was a world just barely outside the barrier of the Silence. Cromwell remembered it as hustling, bustling, energetic, but with a premium on the old ways and values.

"Yes, I am familiar with Quai Son City," he responded. "Kind of primitive, rugged, but great food."

The rustling had now gone in front of them, and seemed poised to cut them off just short of Cromwell's landing.

"Well, Mister Chu, I'd say whatever that is has a problem with guns and such. Did your captain fire at it? Or try to?"

"Of course! It attacked, didn't it?"

Didn't it? "I think if you put that gun down, or just in your belt, it won't attack. It might try and communicate, but it's not going to attack. But if you keep it out, if you make it ready to shoot, then we can both be dead men."

"Like *hell* I'm gonna put this thing away! You just keep going!"

"There are people," Cromwell muttered sadly, "who simply refuse to be saved."

"What's that?"

In one motion the combat suit snapped on full and Cromwell whirled, hit the man a knockout blow on the chin, and grabbed the pistol as the poor guy crumpled to the ground. The suit snapped off just as quickly, leaving a sad-faced Cromwell holding the gun.

He looked at the pistol for a moment, sighed, and then tossed it well into the woods. He then reached down to pick up the limp but still very much alive Mister Chu and take him along.

There was something there in front of him. He put Chu down once more and stared at it.

An energy field, that was for certain. Some kind of distortion behind which something could hide, but it wasn't clear what. It was pretty transparent, although it gave a major distortion of whatever was behind it, and it seemed to be just standing there.

"Hello," Cromwell said as pleasantly as possible. "And what can we do for you?"

The thing did not respond, moving only slightly back and forth and producing that loud snapping marble crackling sound. They sure didn't work by sneaking up on things, that was for sure. Not unless all on their world were deaf.

Cromwell tapped out a code on a small wristband and the combat suit peeled off and collapsed at his feet. He reached down, picked it up, and with two more presses of controls it was nothing more than a meter-cubed metallic object with a handle.

He let go of it, turned back to whatever it was, and spread his hands. "All right, I doubt if that was worth much anyway, so here I am. Now what do we do?"

The thing seemed to be just about to resolve itself into something intelligible as Cromwell and those above via his small body camera watched breathlessly when suddenly there was a bloodcurdling scream from the left and sharp beams went off all over the place. One of them struck Cromwell directly in the back between the shoulder blades and went right on through; others focused on the alien distortion.

"Thomas! No!" Woodward's shocked voice sounded in his ear. *"Oh, my God! No!"*

The alien suddenly lunged for the area from which the shots had been fired with a speed that was startling. Cromwell, in shock, feeling that he was dying, tried to shout, "No!" but it would not come. He dropped to his knees, unable to see the commotion behind him and to his left, and then keeled over onto the ground.

Within seconds the alien crackling presence was back, barely giving any attention to the slight moan of the

young man, who was just now coming to, concentrating
entirely on the fallen and still figure of Thomas
Cromwell.

Something, some of the distortion, reached out and
turned him over. His eyes were half open, there was
blood at the corner of his mouth, and the wound was
surgical but effective. There was no question either
to the creature on the ground or to the monitors
above that Thomas Cromwell was dead.

And then the distortion, flowing, rolling almost like
a blanket, completely covered Cromwell's body. It
remained there for a couple of minutes, masking out
the dead man from the overhead surveillance camera, although you could see a human-sized rippling
form beneath.

"What the devil is it doing?" Woodward muttered
to himself, watching transfixed from on high, as were
they all.

Chu, his senses mostly restored, also saw what
seemed to be happening. He'd been knocked out when
the action had taken place, and from his vantage point
it appeared that the thing was attacking, perhaps eating, Thomas Cromwell. He tried very hard to slowly
and deliberately move back and away from the scene
and into the forest. He'd just about made it to cover
when the thing rolled off of Cromwell's body.

For a moment, it appeared that nothing had happened, and the observers all thought that the thing
must have simply made a thorough examination.
Maybe death didn't come that way, or that easily, to
its own kind.

Suddenly Cromwell's body began to move. It
underwent a series of increasingly severe convulsions,
then his eyes opened wide and his mouth gasped and
he drew in big, heaving breaths.

The convulsions stopped, although he continued to breathe hard. He managed after a moment to sit up, and he looked confused, then puzzled.

Karl Woodward watched it, and leaned forward. "Thomas? Can you hear me, Thomas?"

Somebody behind him said, "It's a miracle! Lazarus risen once more!"

Woodward turned to them and frowned. "Don't count your chickens before they're hatched. It could be technology, or it could be the Opposition."

Cromwell had not responded to their calls; still, they watched him get unsteadily to his feet, look around, then shake his head in wonder, turn, and head back towards the shuttle. He left the suit where it was.

The technicians on the ground had heard but not seen the action. Still, they were unsure how to react when Cromwell returned to them.

"Brother Cromwell? Are you all right?" the botanist called to him.

The question seemed to throw him for a moment. "I—I'm not sure. I would swear upon a stack of Bibles that I've just died, but aside from a real burning in my gut someplace like a badly upset stomach, I feel okay. Damndest thing. Up until now I thought I'd already gone through everything. Now maybe I have." He shook his head as if to clear it. "My implants are dead. You still in contact above?"

"Yes, sir. They want you back up there and fast. The Doctor in particular."

He looked around. "Yeah, I think so, too. Any sign of the boy?"

"Boy?"

"Yes. I was with one of the survivors from the lifeboat. He wasn't there when I—came to."

"Not here."

"Well, without his gun he's no threat to whatever that is. I think we'll find him, sooner or later. Let's get back up there."

"Are you sure you're all right, sir?" one of the techs asked.

He nodded. "Once you die, everything else is an anticlimax," he responded.

XIV:
THE SOUL COLLECTORS

It had not been an easy final decision to make, but Karl Woodward decided that he had no choice. For better or for worse, Balshazzar had sufficient ready food and water and a nearly ideal climate to support over eight hundred people right out of the box; no dependence on flaky technology when you had nowhere else to go.

Cromwell's recovery from what appeared to be certain death was another factor. The thing down there might be evil, good, or simply an alien, singly or collectively, as stuck as they were, but in any case it had no percentage in doing away with them.

A medical scan on Cromwell had shown traces of a clean and absolutely lethal wound; it was also clear that the damage had been repaired with a minimum of internal scar tissue in a way no surgical computers could match, and that the damage left seemed to be slowly but methodically cleaning itself up. Cromwell had no memory of that last death strike, only of being knocked out by something and awakening gasping for air. When he watched the recording of it, though, he was somber, silent, and he never once asked about it nor spoke about it again.

In Woodward's case, he felt that he'd made the commitment the moment he'd sent the shuttle down the first time. He still had doubts, though, not so much about sharing with an alien presence but rather whether or not there was a sufficient challenge there to keep the people's faith renewed.

They found the remains of the woman who'd shot Cromwell and shot at the creature; it was as if the life force had been sucked right out of her, and she was rapidly decaying into the ground, just so much fresh fertilizer. They did decide to give her a proper Christian burial, although she probably wasn't a Christian nor much of a believer in anything, but it was all they could do.

Olivet was a monstrous hillside presence, but it wasn't good for an awful lot other than shelter against the frequent gentle rains. Something here tended to drain any standby power sources, so that within weeks they were left with only those devices that could use backup solar power. Even that wasn't great; the gas giant that gave such a spectacular sky half the time wasn't nearly as efficient for solar-powered devices and in fact blocked some useful solar wind.

Of Alan Chu they hadn't seen or heard a trace. If he was still alive, if he hadn't also been a victim of the creature or gone mad and perhaps done away with himself, he certainly kept away from the colony. When fear replaced faith, you made your own Hell.

John and Eve, along with a huge number of other couples, were married in a natural grove of trees festooned with colorful flowers.

For a while they set up guards and perimeters and security patrols, but it didn't last. There just didn't seem to be any threat, not to them, anyway.

Woodward presided as much as he could, and held regular teaching sessions, but he knew that there was trouble down the road and it worried him. Already many of the new colonists had taken to nudity or at least nothing more than a symbolic type of fig leaf. Why bother, when the temperature rarely varied from twenty-four to thirty-one degrees Celsius? Besides, it wasn't like any of them in this day and age could make clothing using only needles and thread, even if they'd had a lot of thread.

The truth was, that worried him less than the fact that they didn't really have to work any more. It was all just *there*. A balanced, vitamin-enriched diet of fruits and veggies whenever you wanted, and in whatever quantities you wanted. Nothing much to sustain a fire, so little or no baking, but that was okay. Freshwater streams, juice-filled fruits—you had all the basics, and in something of a tropical paradise.

One day Woodward, wearing only his old broad-brimmed straw hat, walked up to where *Olivet* remained, like some ancient, abandoned temple to the Greek gods of yore. He kept his book collection there still, and it was pleasant to read and sometimes to just look out and think.

This time, relaxed on the grass just beyond the "tent" assembly, he thought of Captain Sapenza and his curse and wondered if the Captain had been right.

The ultimate revenge against the Bible thumper. Send him to an ersatz Eden and watch all that faith just dissipate.

It wasn't going to happen, at least not on *his* watch. After, God would anoint someone else to lead them, teach them, give them their choices.

There was a crackling sound nearby. The creature had not bothered them nor attempted much communication with them, either, after that first encounter, but they always knew it was there. It no longer bothered or frightened them. You can be afraid of the unknown only so long when it doesn't bite.

Woodward sensed that, today, the thing was much, *much* closer to him than ever before, yet there was nobody else around to see and hear. They were all down there, in the meadows and forests.

"Come on up," the Doctor called loudly. "I'm not doing anything much that can't be disturbed. It may be about time that we talked, don't you think?"

He was conscious that the rustling was *very* close now, perhaps only a few meters to his right.

The distortion effect was always fascinating. *Viewing through a glass, darkly*, he thought, but that really wasn't it. More like viewing through a misshapen but transparent glass container that rippled and distorted whatever was behind, kind of like a trick mirror.

He turned back and looked down on his people below. "I have to thank you for Thomas. He is the closest friend I have in this life, and I would have missed him a great deal."

There was no response. He didn't expect one; even Cromwell hadn't been able to get the thing to really communicate, yet both of them had the feeling that the thing understood them.

"You are losing them, you know," came a voice.

It was a strange, nonhuman voice, whispered, throaty, rasping, yet clear.

He was startled. "So you *can* speak!"

"It was time," said the creature.

Woodward nodded. "Are you native to here, or, like us, a stranded traveler?"

"Native . . . No. Something of a . . . caretaker. There is no other way to explain in your language. *Any* of your languages."

"A caretaker. For whom?"

"Someone you think you know."

Woodward smiled. "I doubt that. I think you got here, by accident, by scouting, by curiosity, and then you got stuck here just like us. These worlds—they're traps, I think. Traps that lure all sorts of people here from all over the galaxy, maybe beyond."

"Possibly. I never made it to the others. Have you?"

"You know we didn't. Just surveyed them."

"Mostly I have been surveying you," the creature responded. "It is nice to have company, but the mental processes of your species totally bewilder me. You can reach the stars, yet your entire organization is based upon the worship of a God that never replies and a Son of God who was tortured and murdered in your primitive past."

"Your people have no religious beliefs?"

"We—outgrew them."

"Ah, just as you grew into honesty but out of tact, I see. Still, I should be delighted to discuss your people's history and belief system sometime, and mine as well. I assume, though, that what you can't pick up mentally you have picked up from hearing my talks."

"Essentially. Your entire belief system appears based upon resurrection. Why is this so unusual? I was able to use the genetic code of your friend to reconstruct the damage inside him and bring him back."

"And again I thank you for it, but it's not the same thing. You got to him before brain function had ceased. He was dead, but he was still at home, as it were. We speak of someone tortured to death, pronounced dead, put in a hillside cave and sealed, who walked out hale and hearty and better than before three full days later. Can your skills do that?"

"No more than yours can. Still, within a generation of your people, your own beliefs will be mostly irrelevant to them. You must know that intellectually."

"I concede nothing of the sort."

"Look at them. Naked, soft, pretty much reverting to children who don't have to obey their parents. The way this soil and this system is set up, when you die, you are absorbed, recycled. No traces are left in very short order. They will be innocents, ignorant of good and evil, but also incapable of growth of any sort. The Eden of your myth is set up as an ideal, but it is static, boring, a kind of forever childhood with no goal or purpose of any kind. No wonder those two rebelled."

"You misunderstand faith."

"And you misunderstand your own people's nature," the creature responded. "Or, more accurately, you are in denial about it. A wager, then, for two old intellectuals who can not go romp in the fields with abandon."

Woodward frowned. "A what?"

"A wager. Your faith in them and your god against my belief in the least common denominator. Why not? It's going to be a very long time, if experience is any guide, before the next ship shows up. Faithful worshipers versus brainless children. Faith in God and

God's nature in you all versus my faith that the least common denominator always wins in the end."

Woodward turned to the crackling distortion, and out of that distortion arose a figure. It, too, was transparent, with what was on the other side twisted and distorted, but it was a clear figure.

And the serpent was the most beautiful of all God's creatures . . .

"You're on," Woodward told it. "Until the next group shows up."

"Done. Although I can not imagine them being in any way as interesting as you."

"Perhaps they will arrive in sufficient shape to get back. A few things have from here."

"Perhaps. And perhaps, if they do, they won't find anyone here worth taking back."

Karl Woodward sighed and relaxed. He'd thought he'd chosen wrongly, but now he understood that God's hand had been behind this all along.

Head to head, faith against unfaith, for a generation's souls.

What could be better?

DAVID WEBER

<u>**The Honor Harrington series:**</u> *(cont.)*

Flag in Exile

Hounded into retirement and disgrace by political enemies, Honor Harrington has retreated to planet Grayson, where powerful men plot to reverse the changes she has brought to their world. And for their plans to succeed, Honor Harrington must die!

Honor Among Enemies

Offered a chance to end her exile and again command a ship, Honor Harrington must use a crew drawn from the dregs of the service to stop pirates who are plundering commerce. Her enemies have chosen the mission carefully, thinking that either she will stop the raiders or they will kill her . . . and either way, her enemies will win. . . .

In Enemy Hands

After being ambushed, Honor finds herself aboard an enemy cruiser, bound for her scheduled execution. But one lesson Honor has never learned is how to give up!

Echoes of Honor

"Brilliant! Brilliant! Brilliant!" —*Anne McCaffrey*

Ashes of Victory

Honor has escaped from the prison planet called Hell and returned to the Manticoran Alliance, to the heart of a furnace of new weapons, new strategies, new tactics, spies, diplomacy, and assassination.

continued ☞